LEXI'S PROTECTOR

MEN WITHOUT A CAUSE

LANA LYNN

Cover Art by Lila Dubois

Edited by Kyla Bailey

eBook ISBN: 978-1-937249-40-3

*For my daughter Lisa,
who is also a best friend.*

*Someone I can always
depend on.*

ACKNOWLEDGMENTS

Special thanks to my son, Lee Swift, who helped me through this process from beginning to end. Also a shout out to Lila Dubois, who did a fantastic job on the cover. I want to say thanks to Lexi Blake, who has always encouraged me, hence the name of the heroine in this book. And last but not least, a big thanks to Kyla Bailey who edited my grammar and *typis*... I mean typos.

_____

D*allas, Texas – 24 months ago*

LEXI BLY STARED through the peephole of the front door to her 1-bedroom apartment expecting her Chinese food delivery, but instead found two men—a uniformed police officer and a man in a suit. Both wore grim faces, which sent a sliver of unease through her.

Opening the door but leaving on the chain lock as a precaution, she asked, "May I help you?"

The man in the suit appeared to be in his fifties. He was a very distinguished Latino with salt and pepper hair.

The one in the uniform looked to be a couple decades younger, and quite thin. Both seemed professional and serious, which added to Lexi's concern.

"I'm Detective Steve Torres and this is Officer Ted

Sims. We're with the Dallas Police Department," Mr. Suit said, showing his badge with one hand and slipping his card with the other through the open gap of the door. "Are you Lexi Bly?"

"Yes. That's me." She took the card with his contact information.

Everything seemed on the up and up and Detective Torres had a kind face, so she took off the chain and opened the door wider, though just a little.

"Is there a problem?"

"Unfortunately, there is," Detective Torres said. "This is about your boyfriend, Matthew Hill."

Her stomach clenched.

Oh my God, why do I keep falling for the wrong kind of guy? I thought Matt was so nice. Are my instincts that off?

"I'm not sure I'd call Matt my boyfriend quite yet, but we have been on a few dates. How did you get my name and address?"

"It was on Mr. Hill's phone record," Detective Torres told her.

A big ball of concern rolled through her. "Is Matt in some kind of trouble?"

Officer Sims leaned forward. "No, Ms. Bly. Matthew Hill is dead."

Lexi's entire body went numb and her mind couldn't process what she was hearing.

Detective Torres shot a disapproving glance at the young officer and then said, "Sims, being in DPD's Homicide-SIU requires officers to be more sensitive and less abrupt."

"Yes, sir." Sims took a single step back. "Sorry, sir."

Barely registering the exchange between the two men, Lexi tried to pull her focus back to what Sims had said.

"Matthew Hill is dead?" The shock caused her knees to weaken.

Even though things between Matt and her were quite new, she still had feelings for him. *He's gone.*

She held onto the door to steady herself. "I can't believe this."

"I'm sorry," Detective Torres said, turning his attention away from Officer Sims and back to her. "May we come in?"

"Of course." Finding it hard to breathe, she opened the door wide and the two officers entered her sparsely furnished apartment.

She quickly gathered up some loose files and folders and moved her laptop and phone from the futon to the kitchen table. "Excuse my place, gentlemen...uh...officers. I was working on a project for my new job. I moved here a couple of months ago, but I haven't had time to get it set up. I have some friends that plan on coming next month for a girl's weekend to help me with the rest...uh...the apartment...my apartment, I mean."

When she saw the two police officers staring at her, Lexi stopped her rambling. Rambling had always been her weakness whenever she faced difficult situations. And right now, she was facing a difficult situation, and was also utterly traumatized.

"Please, have a seat?" She pointed to the memory foam futon, which doubled as her guest bed, not that there had been any out-of-town guests since moving to Dallas.

"May I get you something to drink?" she asked. Part of

her wanted to delay hearing more, while another part wanted to know every detail.

When she noticed Torres glancing at her hands, she realized they were shaking and shoved them into her jean's pockets.

"That's very nice of you to offer, but I think *you* should sit down," he said. "You look somewhat pale after hearing such news, as anyone would."

"Thank you. Yes. You're right." Feeling tiny trembles all over her body, she pulled over one of the chairs from the kitchen table. "Let's all sit."

After she took her seat, Torres and Sims sat on the futon, facing her.

Her gaze locked onto the framed photo on the shelf behind the officers. It was a selfie she had taken of her and Liz in Cancun last summer, looking tanned, smiling, and carefree—pretty much the opposite of what she looked now. She wished Liz were here to help her through this nightmare.

New city. New job. New possible boyfriend. Lexi had been so happy with her life in Dallas, leaving behind all the craziness she'd endured during grad school. She *had been happy* until this very moment.

Still trying to hide her nervousness, Lexi clasped her hands in her lap.

Her mind spun with several possibilities of how Matt had died. Had it been some kind of accident?

She remembered how much fun her second date with Matt had been riding in his black Corvette Stingray Convertible. He'd put down the top and they'd flown down Interstate 20. Now, all she could picture was the car mangled with his lifeless body inside.

Or had it been a health issue that had taken him?

Matt had seemed the epitome of health to her. In fact, she'd received several texts when he'd been working out at the gym.

Suicide?

She couldn't imagine that from Matt. He'd been upbeat and fun during all their time together.

Drug overdose?

Unlikely. She wasn't an expert on the subject of drug use, but she did have a few friends and relatives that struggled with addiction. There had been no signs Matt was using.

Centering herself, she cleared her throat. "Please. Tell me what happened to Matt?"

Detective Torres answered in a fatherly way, "Last night, Mr. Hill was murdered."

The entire room seemed to lose all oxygen and the only thing Lexi could choke out was, "Murdered?"

A massive void seemed to swallow her whole, leaving an overwhelming horror inside her.

"I don't... What...? He was murdered...?"

Unable to hold back the tears of disbelief, a couple escaped down her cheeks. She wiped them away, staring at the two men who had brought the devastating news.

"I know it's a shock, but we want to get to the bottom of this as fast as we can," Detective Torres stated.

"You said it happened last night." Lexi closed her eyes and took a deep breath, as some things began to clear up for her. "Now I know why he didn't text or call me today."

"So you were concerned?" Officer Sims asked.

"I guess so. Yes. Definitely. I was concerned. Since our first date we've texted or called each other several times every day. When I didn't hear from Matt at all I started to get worried."

"When was the last time you were with Mr. Hill?" Detective Torres asked.

Sims flipped open a notepad.

"Last Saturday night," she answered.

"How old are you?" Sims asked.

"Twenty-seven."

"Uh huh." He wrote in his notepad. "Green eyes. Long dark, brown hair. How tall are you?"

"That's enough, Sims." Detective Torres snapped, then turned back to her. "Ms. Bly, when did you last communicate with Mr. Hill?"

"I got a text from him yesterday. We are going... I mean, we *were* going..."

She and Matt had been on five dates. Five great dates. Five dates, which meant tomorrow night, would have been their sixth. And six dates had always been her personal benchmark to be open for things to move to a more intimate level.

"Ms. Bly, you and Mr. Hill were going to do what?" Officer Sims asked in a stern tone, which pulled her back from her own thoughts.

Lexi would answer him, though still keeping back the more personal details. "Matt and I were supposed to have dinner tomorrow night."

Even though she'd only known Matt for a short time, she still couldn't hold back the liquid welling in her eyes from the jolt of it all. Since her breakup a year ago with her horrible ex, Matt was the first man she'd felt safe enough to trust.

"Where were you supposed to go for dinner?"

Officer Sims asked, looking at her like she'd kicked his cat.

Or like I just killed someone?

"I don't know. Matt told me it was a surprise."

"Mm, got it," Officer Sims muttered, jotting something in his notepad.

She was startled when her doorbell rang. "Oh. That's my dinner."

"Please," Detective Torres said, motioning to the door.

She didn't give a damn about her order of Kung Pao chicken with brown rice from her favorite Chinese restaurant, though before Torres and Sims had arrived she had been famished.

"Thank you," Lexi somehow was able to tell the delivery girl despite the storm of emotions inside her.

She took the sack of food, closed the door, and returned to face the two men who had turned her world upside down and sideways.

"Smells good," Officer Sims said, earning him another glare from Detective Torres.

"It is, but it can wait." Her appetite had fled and wouldn't be back tonight. She placed the food on the kitchen table and returned to the chair.

"Just a few more questions," Detective Torres said.

"Yes. Please. Go ahead."

For several more minutes, she continued providing answers, until she couldn't hold back any longer.

"Please. Tell me what happened to Matt."

"Are you sure you don't know, Ms. Bly?" Officer Sims said flatly.

"That's enough," Detective Torres's tone was even firmer than before.

Officer Sims shrugged slightly. "Just trying to get to the facts, sir."

Lexi felt like Sims had charged, tried and sentenced her to prison already, while Detective Torres seemed more open.

"Here's one fact for you," Detective Torres said, "If you want to work on this case and also be considered for a permanent position in Homicide you need to follow my lead, understand?"

Officer Sims closed his notepad. "Yes, sir. Sorry, sir."

Detective Torres turned his attention back to Lexi. "His body had been found outside of his apartment on the sidewalk with a single gunshot to his head. Even though he lived in a very trendy and busy part of Dallas, no one heard or saw anything."

"How is that possible that no one heard?" she asked. "Guns are loud when they're fired."

"We're not sure yet, but when the ballistics report comes in we'll know more," Detective Torres said.

"If it's okay with you, sir, can we circle back to what Ms. Bly did last night?" Officer Sims said in a less accusatory tone.

Detective Torres nodded his agreement.

Lexi took a deep breath before answering. "Again, I was home working on a project for my job."

"So there isn't anyone who can corroborate your whereabouts last night between 9 p.m. and midnight?" Detective Torres asked.

"No. I was alone," she answered truthfully.

He can't believe I have anything to do with this. But why shouldn't he? He doesn't know me.

"Does Mr. Hill have any enemies you're aware of?"

Detective Torres continued. "Anyone who might have wanted to harm him?"

"Like I said before, we've been on a few dates. He didn't seem like the kind of person who would have enemies."

The truth was that Matt had always been sweet and thoughtful. She couldn't imagine why anyone would want to kill him. "Do you think it might have been a robbery gone bad?"

"Not likely," Officer Sims answered. "He was shot in the back of the head and his wallet was still in his jacket."

"In the back of the head...?" She had a sudden onset of queasiness. "Oh my God. That sounds more like an assassination."

Officer Sims nodded slightly. "May I see the text messages between you and Mr. Hill?"

"Sure, but don't you already have them on his phone?" she asked, leaving her chair and standing.

"We do have Mr. Hill's phone, but we need to be thorough," Officer Sims said.

Thorough, my ass. He wants to check all my messages.

"I have nothing to hide."

At that very moment she heard the familiar ding that a new message had arrived.

Probably it's from Liz. God, I need her right now.

When Lexi opened up the messenger app, she saw the text was from a number she didn't recognize.

As she read the name in the text, dread cut through her entire body.

Hi sweetheart. Roman here.
I see you have company.

Miss you, in town on business.
Hope to see you soon.
#urmine

"Something wrong?" Detective Torres asked. "Your face turned white as a sheet."

"Yes. Something is very wrong." Time froze in place as a feeling of cold pumped through her veins. "This can't be a coincidence."

"What coincidence?" Officer Sims asked, sounding very far away.

He can't be back. I can't go through it again.

"Ms. Bly? Ms. Bly, are you okay?" Detective Torres asked, touching her lightly on the back of her hand.

She looked away from the terrible words on her screen, and said, "Matt dying and Roman reappearing after all this time can't be a coincidence."

Oh God no. He is back.

"What do you mean?" Officer Sims asked.

Trembling, she handed her phone to Detective Torres. "That message is from my ex-boyfriend, and he knows you're here. He must be close."

"Officer, go check," Detective Torres ordered.

Sims left the futon and went out the door.

"We're here with you, Ms. Bly. Nothing to worry about," Detective Torres reassured her.

"I appreciate that so much." She let out a shaky sigh. "All of this is a lot to process."

Did Roman know about Matt and me? I know he's crazy but is he that crazy?

Deep inside, she already knew the answer about Roman's psychotic behavior.

"Don't be hard on yourself, Ms. Bly," said Detective Torres. "You're right. It is a lot to deal with."

Officer Sims returned and in a condescending tone said, "There's no one out there."

"You don't know Roman like I do," she said. "He could be hiding in plain sight."

"I assure you, no one is there." Officer Sims returned to his seat and opened up his notepad again. "What's your ex's full name?"

"Roman Koslova. We met in grad school. He's from Belgium." She attempted to compose herself and keep her voice steady, though she didn't quite succeed.

"Hashtag *urmine*?" Detective Torres seemed confused. "Oh. I get it. *You are mine.*"

"I have never been Roman's, and I never will be his," she stated emphatically. "I haven't heard from him in over a year. We ended things badly. Roman is..."

After several silent seconds ticked by, Officer Sims asked. "He's what?"

"He's scary." She hated feeling helpless, but what could she do?

Detective Torres leaned forward on the futon. "And you think he's involved in Mr. Hill's murder?"

"I don't know for sure, but Roman's the only one I know who might be capable of something this horrific. One of the reasons I broke it off with him was because of his obsessive jealousy." As her all too familiar regret for having ever dated that monster took hold, she replayed Roman's last words to her on the day she'd ended their relationship.

. . .

He kissed the top of her head. "You need time alone, my dear? Okay. But know this. You are mine," he growled, squeezing her arms until she winced. "No one else's. You'll see. Goodbye, Lexi."

Lexi rubbed her arms in the places that had taken a very long time to heal. The bruises were gone but not the damage he had done to her.

She slumped down into the chair, knowing her worst nightmare was back.

2

M*insk, Belarus – 23 months ago*

CLINT RICHARDS OPENED the panel to the biometric lock on the door, while the other two CIA officers, Atkins and Richards, kept watch using the latest night vision tech to scan the darkened alley.

The lock was on the door of the back service entrance of the large warehouse.

This was a *black ops* extraction of a deep cover officer —an officer Clint knew well from his pre-CIA days.

After two years in deep cover with a cabal that laundered money across Europe and Asia, Gary had sent an encrypted message through secure channels for an emergency extraction.

Continuing to work the lock, Clint prayed that his friend was still alive, though deep down he had doubts.

Two days earlier, when the team had gone to the agreed upon location to rendezvous with Gary, his old buddy was nowhere to be seen. After they checked the two alternate locales, the outcome had been the same. No Gary.

The Agency's urgency to find Gary was high given how much valuable intel he'd gathered over the past two years. If he wasn't located soon, all of that work would be lost and the Agency would remain in the dark about one of the most powerful and dangerous organizations in the world.

That's when Clint had been brought in for his uncanny ability to track down both missing officers and high-level targets alike. It was a skill that the leaders of sensitive ops, similar to this one, had called on him to use again and again. No surprise Clint's nickname became "*The Bloodhound.*"

It hadn't taken Clint long to identify the best odds for Gary's location. This warehouse was next to a casino, where it was suspected that the criminal organization laundered colossal amounts of dirty money.

At lightning speed, Clint clipped a sequence of multi-colored wires to get past the biometric alarms. After eight seconds, the device's display went from red to green and he and the rest of the team heard the click of the lock disengaging.

"We're in," Edwards said in a hushed tone, informing Command at Langley, which was monitoring them through their comms and body cams.

"Acknowledged," a voice came back. "Proceed."

Heavily armed, Clint and the other two officers rushed into the darkened building.

Having memorized the warehouse's layout, Clint took the left hallway, while Edwards headed to the right one and Atkins went straight ahead.

The plan was to meet up in the expansive area at the other end of the warehouse that Clint expected Gary would be held.

Smelling cigarette smoke, Clint crouched low and close to the wall. As he approached the next intersection, Clint could hear footsteps in the hallway to his right. Luckily, he could tell the echoing steps were heading away from him.

Even with a silencer on his gun, he didn't want to fire. The mission's success required as little interaction with the hostiles as possible.

In and out. Quick and easy. No mistakes. That was the plan.

If something happened to him, Atkins or Edwards, there would be no rescue, nor any acknowledgement from the Agency that they ever existed. They were on their own.

As Clint continued forward to his destination, he kept his thoughts on the task at hand, though parallel thoughts of his friend Gary also itched at the back of his mind.

He and Gary had attended a small, private university together. When the two of them had met at a party, they'd hit it off because of their common interests and became close friends right away. Clint had dreams of joining the Marines when he got out, while Gary had his sights on the Army. They were both shocked when the Agency recruited them after graduation. He remembered his conversation with Gary about how dreams could change.

They'd been two of the youngest recruits in their class, as most of the others had been selected after several years in special ops military careers, which tightened the bond between them. They were like brothers in every way but blood. Actually, in a strange way their bond was also in blood, having once worked together on a deadly mission. After Gary got selected for undercover jobs, their career paths had drifted apart but that didn't impact their friendship in any way. No matter how long it had been since they'd seen each other, they would always pick up right where they'd left off.

"Richards. Behind you," a voice at Langley warned.

Clint twisted around and fired his gun at the guard, who was pulling out his weapon from the holster. The pop from his muzzle was muted, thanks to the silencer.

The dead man fell to the floor with a thud, creating a sound louder than the shot.

Using all his senses to identify any sign of approaching hostiles, Clint detected nothing.

Even though he was grateful for the assist that had saved him from getting a bullet in the back, there was no time or need to thank Command.

He bent down to the guard's body to check his radio. It was in the *off* position. The dead guy hadn't warned his buddies before drawing his weapon.

Placing the earpiece of the radio in his free ear, Gary clicked the button to *on*. Nothing was coming through, so it seemed his and the rest of the team's presence was still unknown.

Clint raced up the stairs to the higher levels as noiselessly as possible until he reached his target.

Entering the expansive space from a catwalk above,

Clint saw Gary below tied to a chair surrounded by four men.

Not terrible odds, since they were oblivious to his team's presence.

Gary's swollen eyes, labored breathing and bloody mouth made it crystal clear that he'd taken quite a beating. But he was still alive.

"Eyes on the package," Command came through his comm. "We are still a go. I repeat. We are still a go."

Clint raised his weapon, setting his sights on the guy closest to his friend.

Edwards came through a door opposite the one Clint had entered. He kneeled down next to Clint, aiming his gun at one of the other men.

Atkins was positioned opposite them on the catwalk with a rifle locked and loaded.

Clint watched as two more men came into view below and walked over to Gary. The one in the suit had jet-black hair and was tall, at least 6 foot 4. The other wore a uniform.

The Intel Langley had provided them was proving to be total crap. Six hostiles, not three.

Damn.

Not good odds but Clint still believed they could succeed. They must.

"Command, you getting this?" Edwards said in a very quiet tone.

"Hold," the order came. "We're checking on the two new arrivals."

Clint didn't like the changing odds. They needed to act now to save his friend, not wait until Langley got IDs on the two new hostiles.

He aimed his weapon, whispering, "Got the suit in my crosshairs and can get the guard next to our guy right after."

"The two to the South are mine," Atkin's voice came through his earpiece.

"Hold," the voice from Langley instructed. "I repeat. Hold."

"Command, standing by," Edwards sent back.

Clint suspected the Langley team was calculating the risks and possible fallout. They'd expected three guards. One thing was for certain when it came to the top brass, they erred on the side of caution when things could go sideways.

He looked at Edwards. "We've got this. Tell them."

Edwards nodded. "Langley, on your order we are a go."

Clint watched as the guy in the suit stepped right in front of Gary.

"Hello, Gary," the man said in perfect English. "That is your real name, isn't it? We haven't been properly introduced. I'm Roman Koslova."

The creep punched Gary in the gut. Gary let out a groan.

"Pleased to meet you," Koslova said with a laugh.

Clint was ready to drop the bastard once the order came through.

The name Roman Koslova didn't mean anything to Clint, not that it made a difference either way. He was getting his friend out of this mess no matter what, so he kept his aim set on the man in charge of the rest.

"Seems like you've been doing a lot more than

accounting for us," Koslova said, pulling out a gun from his jacket. "We can't have that."

"Stand down," came the directive from Langley. "Again, stand down."

"No." Clint stared down the sights of his gun. "I can't. I won't."

Edwards placed his hand on Clint's shoulder. "Langley, come again. Please repeat."

Another voice came through their comms. "This is Deputy Director Brown of the Counter Intelligence Center. Your order is to stand down. I repeat. Stand down. Koslova works for the Vice Chairman of the Belarus Security Committee and is one of our assets."

Clint had a good idea what that meant. Assets came to the Agency in a variety of ways. Some didn't support their governments, wanting to work as confidential informants to bring change to their homeland. Others were blackmailed into working for the Agency. Another group were those "*useful idiots*" who unwittingly funneled information.

But Clint could tell that Roman Koslova was part of the last category, the least trustworthy of the lot—assets working for monetary gain alone.

The *Roman-Koslova-type* of asset could flip to another organization willing to pay a higher price.

"I do admire you, Gary," Koslova said with the wickedest grin Clint had ever seen.

Following orders had been drilled into Clint from his very first day at the Agency. And he'd never failed to comply. Until now. He wasn't about to let Gary die because of some Belarus bureaucrat who was as dirty as they came.

"Stand down. That is an order," the Deputy Director's voice came through louder. "Exit now."

"Richards?" Edwards said, squeezing Clint's shoulder. "No. I can't."

Edwards glared at him. "We have our orders. Let's go."

Clint turned away for a second to try to convince Edwards there was still a chance if they stayed out of view and waited for another opportunity to save his friend.

"Fuck the orders." As the words left his mouth, Clint heard a gunshot.

Edwards collapsed to the catwalk's floor.

The unexpected guard had gotten the drop on them coming through the door that Edwards had entered. He continued to fire at the team while shouting a warning in Belarusian to the others.

And then all hell broke loose as shouts and bullets zinged through the air in every direction

Clint fired off a round at the guard on the catwalk. The man tumbled over the guardrail, falling to the warehouse floor two stories below.

As more guards flooded into the space and fired up at him and his team, a single tone came through his comms which was the signal Langley was pulling the plug on the ops. Clint and his two buddies were on their own, and the shit show just kept on coming.

While communications had been cut, he knew Langley would keep the video feed live until the very last moment.

"Go," Edwards choked out. "I'm toast."

"Not on my watch." Clint fired at their attackers. "Atkins? You still with us?"

No answer.

"Atkins?" he shouted as the barrage continued. "Do you copy?"

Still nothing.

Scanning the other end of the catwalk, Clint spotted Atkins's lifeless body hanging over the railing. "Come on, Edwards. I gotta get you out of here so I can come back for Gary."

Before he could sling Edwards over his shoulder and make a beeline for an exit, Edwards took another hit. Clint watched as his eyes fixed and his body slackened.

He checked for Edwards's pulse but found none.

Fuck!

Clint's training and common sense demanded he find an exit and get the hell out of there. But if there were even the slimmest chance that he could save Gary, he wouldn't leave without trying.

Clint rose up enough to get a better view of what was happening below him. Roman and a guard were dragging Gary away.

He's still alive.

Hope sprung to life inside Clint. Recalling the layout of the warehouse he'd memorized for the mission, he took Edwards' weapons and ammo and raced for the door to the mechanical room through a hail of bullets. That room led to a fire escape.

He shut and locked the door behind him, hoping it would give him even a split-second of extra time.

The narrow room wasn't meant for humans. Mechanical and electrical equipment hummed and buzzed like crazy around him.

Racing to the solitary window on the opposite side of

the room, he tried to open it. No luck. The thing hadn't been opened in decades.

Improvising, Clint grabbed a trash bin and smashed the window's glass to bits. In a flash, he crawled through and rushed down the stairs.

The cool night air slapped him in the face, as he remained focused on the difficult task of staying alive and also saving his friend.

With a gun in each hand, Clint rounded the corner of the warehouse, coming face to face with impossible odds —twenty more hostiles.

Despite the zero probability of survival, Clint would have fired on them had he not seen Koslova holding a gun to Gary's head.

"Hold your fire, gentlemen," Koslova said. "I believe our new guest doesn't want to see his comrade hurt. Isn't that right?"

Clint didn't answer.

What can I do to save Gary and myself at twenty to one odds?

"That's it. Think long and hard," Koslova said, keeping the barrel of his gun pressed at Gary's temple. "No more blood needs to spill. Let's make a deal."

"What kind of deal?" Clint asked, stalling, trying to keep all options open.

"Drop your weapons and raise your hands over your head," Koslova said in a sickening, sweet tone. "Then we'll talk."

Clint shook his head. "No. I don't trust you, and you don't trust me. But you and I have mutual friends, don't we?"

"Enough pointless negotiating." Koslova smiled. He barked out an order in Belarusian.

Several guards charged Clint from behind before he could get off a shot and slammed him to the ground.

"Excellent," Koslova said. "Let me finish my business with his comrade and then I'll decide what to do with him."

Struggling but failing to get free of the guards, Clint watched Koslova kiss Gary's cheek.

"Goodbye, my friend," he said and then pulled the trigger.

As Gary crumbled to the pavement, Clint felt a primal scream blast out of his throat.

Somehow, he was able to break free of the guards holding him down, as the solitary urge inside him propelled him forward to rip Koslova's black heart out of his chest.

"You'll pay for this, motherfucker!" he yelled, charging through Koslova's men. "You will pay."

For a fraction of a second, Koslova looked concerned.

But there were too many guards between Clint and the bastard. His helmet was ripped off, ending the video feed to Langley. Command had witnessed Koslova murder Gary. Whatever deal the murderer had with the CIA, that was over now and he would be hunted and brought to justice.

"Foolish Americans. Why can't they realize when they are beaten?" Koslova motioned to one of his men.

A bag was placed over Clint's head and manacles were clamped on his ankles and wrists.

Rage and grief swamped every cell in his body, as he head butted one of the guards holding him.

"Let's make this quick, gentlemen," Koslova said.

Clint felt a large object slam against his head.

This is the end.

Knowing Koslova would get a bullet for what he'd done to his friend did make dying a little easier.

3

As Clint gained consciousness all he could feel was the pounding pain in his head. Whatever Koslova's man had slammed against the side of his face had likely given him a concussion.

He blinked several times while realizing the bag over his head had been removed.

Focusing on his surroundings, he curled his hands into fists. Both his ankles and wrists were bound and he was tied to a metal chair.

Does Koslova intend to torture me before he puts a bullet in my head like he did Gary?

He looked around the room, which was much smaller than the space at the warehouse. Where had they taken him? Why was he still alive? Did Koslova believe he could extract information before he killed him? If so, the asshole was about to be disappointed. He might take a beating before he died, but the joke would be on Koslova. Clint wasn't about to divulge even the smallest intel he had.

There were two armed standing on either side of the door men but no Koslova.

Where the hell is he? I'd just as soon get this over with.

As if on cue, Koslova came into the room, ordering his men to leave.

After the two men exited the room, Koslova lit a cigarette. "It's your lucky day, Officer Richards."

How the hell does he know my name? "You're wasting your time. I won't give you anything."

Koslova chuckled. "You already have. Like you said earlier, we have mutual friends. They wired a large sum to my account for your useless ass."

"What?" Clint felt betrayed. "Didn't the feed show them what you did to Gary?"

"Oh yes. Langley saw everything, but I'm afraid I'm too important for them to end our business relationship."

"You murdering asshole. You'll pay for what you did. I swear it."

"If you ever get tired of working for the CIA, look me up. I might have a job for you."

"Fuck you!"

"Goodbye, Richards." Koslova left without another word.

In the two hours that passed between Koslova's exit and the arrival of the operatives that came to release him, Clint made the decision to leave the Agency.

Their betrayal was seared into his bones. He vowed to deliver Koslova's head on a platter at the doorstep of the CIA.

DALLAS, Texas – 23 months ago

CARRYING a bag of groceries from her car, Lexi was surprised to see Detective Torres at her door wearing khakis and a Polo shirt.

"Hello, Detective. Do you have new information for me?" She tried to juggle the grocery sacks in order to bring out her keys.

"No. Not exactly. Let me help you with that."

"Thanks." She passed one of the bags to him, and fished out her keys, then invited him in.

She placed the groceries on her counter, putting away the items that needed to go in the freezer and fridge, and left the rest for later.

"Can I get you something to drink, detective?"

"Yes. Tea. Water. Anything you have. But I'd prefer you calling me Steve, since I'm no longer with DPD."

"Seriously?" She got out two Diet Cokes from her fridge, handing him one and keeping the other for herself.

They sat down at the table.

"It's only been a month since you and Officer Sims knocked on my door. What happened?"

He grinned. "Thirty years happened, Ms. Bly. I'm fifty-seven and divorced. My kids are all grown. In fact my daughter is about your age. I'm ready to retire."

"Please. If I'm calling you 'Steve' then you have to call me 'Lexi.' Congrats on your retirement. Is that why you're not in a suit?"

"Trying out a more casual look," he said, taking a sip

of his drink. "Though to tell you the truth, Lexi, I think I'm going to go back to the suit."

"Steve, you can pull off either look just fine."

"I'm sure you're curious why I'm here," he said in that fatherly tone that he'd used the first night they'd met. "I've opened up a private investigation firm. I'm the lone PI at present, but I hope to grow the business."

"So not fully retired yet?"

He smiled. "I'm not the kick-back-and-relax kind of guy. Helping people has always been the core of who I am. And you, young lady, could use some help."

"What do you mean?"

"You are a person of interest in Matthew's murder investigation."

"I know I am. I wish I had an alibi for the night of his murder, but I don't."

"I wish you did, too, but I believe the answer to clearing your name is finding this Roman Koslova character."

"Me, too. I've called everyone who might know where he is, but it's like he's a ghost. I thought after he contacted me that night he would try again, but so far nothing."

"That's one of the reasons I believe he's Matthew's killer. His message showing up on your phone wasn't some fluke. I did a little digging on him, and he's no Mr. Clean. But he's smart. Though he's been implicated in some high level crimes, nothing has ever been proven."

"What kind of crimes?"

"Extortion. Manslaughter. Arson. The good news is Koslova isn't in the country. The bad news, Lexi, is Sims has been promoted to Detective and is doing everything he can to prove your guilt."

"I knew it. I could tell that very first night he thought I'd killed Matthew."

"You're right. I've seen Sims' type before. He's hell-bent on making a name for himself in the department."

"What does that mean for me or for Matthew's case?"

"Unfortunately, it means Sims will make your life miserable until the real killer is found. That's why I'm here. Together, you and I will find Roman Koslova, the real killer, and bring him to justice. But in the meantime, you need to protect yourself in case Koslova returns."

"How do I do that?"

"We're getting you a gun. Then you and I are going to the gun range."

"You're brave, Steve. I suggest you get yourself a suit of armor if you're planning on teaching me."

4

B *aracoa, Cuba – 48 hours ago*

WHEN CLINT SAW the heavyset man in the white straw fedora shove the young woman in the colorful floral dress to the floor, he didn't hesitate. He immediately leapt over the bar, knocking down several drinks and two empty chairs.

The local patrons of the off-the-beaten-track *Cantina de Enrique* stepped back as Clint charged the man, who was cocking his fist back to punch the terrified woman.

"Maldita perra, tú—"

Before the prick could lay another finger on the girl, Clint bulldozed him to the ground. In a flash, he leapt to his feet, side kicking one of the man's two stampeding bodyguards in the gut while smacking the other body-guard over the head with an empty chair.

During the commotion, the young woman darted to the other side of the smoky room, as several other women encircled her.

Clint had recognized the bastard the moment he'd walked into the bar with his two thugs.

Diego Martinez, the son of Santiago Martinez.

The elder Martinez had both local politicians and gangs in his pocket, which allowed him to lead a criminal syndicate that reached all over the island as well as much of the Caribbean. Santiago was also an asset he'd tapped from time to time in his previous life with the Agency. He doubted that would happen again after this encounter.

As Diego's two bodyguards got back on their feet, Clint shouted, "¡Alto ahí!"

He found it odd that they both complied, not moving a single inch closer. The two bruisers seemed intimidated.

It was crystal clear to Clint that all eyes were fixed on him, the muscle-bound, white bartender strong-arming Diego and his two buddies. He didn't like the attention, much preferring to be under the radar as he had been for the past few months—until now. Though he should have stayed out of the situation, he couldn't let a man hurt a woman.

Diego rose and reached into his jacket for a gun, but Clint slammed him back to the floor, retrieving the weapon.

As the two bodyguards started to move his way, he aimed the gun at them, while keeping his knee on Diego's chest, "No."

They once again stopped in their tracks.

Still keeping a close eye on the duo, he turned to Diego. "Get the hell out and never come back."

"Let me go, *bastardo!*"

"Not until I'm sure you'll leave without causing more of a scene. *¿Comprendes?*"

Diego tried to twist free of him but to no avail.

Not only was Clint much stronger, but he also had years of training to his advantage. Diego wasn't going anywhere without his consent.

He glanced at the bar's entrance, a rickety wooden door. The crowd parted, creating a clear path between him and the exit, which one customer was holding open.

"*¡Mata a este pendejo!*" Diego shouted to his bodyguards.

As he'd expected, they tried to rush him, both bringing out guns. But he was too fast, kicking one in the throat and jabbing the other in the groin. The two *wind-milled* backwards, choking and groaning before landing on their backs and writhing in pain.

Tucking the gun into his pants, he lifted Diego to his feet and marched him through the bar's front door and into a crystal clear Cuban night. He shoved the bastard hard out into the street, where he landed on his ass.

Holding their drinks and smoking cigars, several curious patrons filed out of the bar transfixed on the exchange between him and Diego like fans at a sporting event.

Blood dripped from Diego's nose onto his starched white shirt. He struggled to his feet and dusted off his fedora before slamming it back on his head.

He yelled, "Do you know who I am, gringo?"

Answering in his Midwestern American accent, Clint

came back in a deep, quiet tone, "Yeah, I know who you are and who your papa is. But I don't give a fuck about any man who abuses women, asshole."

Diego's father was the man who Clint had paid to secure his off-the-grid spot in Cuba. After the Agency turned a blind eye to what Koslova had done in Belarus to Gary, Clint had left and not looked back.

Clint wasn't a traitor, but he still didn't want to be found. He just wanted to find Koslova.

That was why he had come to Cuba to work the one lead he had—rumors that Koslova liked to vacation in Havana.

Clint had made inroads into Koslova's favorite hangouts when he came to the island. Once the bastard showed, he would have him. But now all of that work was in jeopardy.

When Clint took a single step forward, Diego took three steps backwards toward a blue 1958 Chevy Impala.

He watched closely as Diego opened the car door.

"Now, you'll see who you're up against, motherfucker." Diego reached into the Impala and came out with a gun in his hand.

Instantly, Clint jumped into the air, landing a flying kick at Diego's shoulder, causing him to drop the gun and once again land on his ass.

"Yeah, I see who I'm up against—a coward who goes after innocent, young women."

Keeping his foot on Diego's throat, Clint retrieved the second gun he had drawn on him. He slipped it next to its twin in the back of his jeans. "Now, let me make this crystal clear again. Get the fuck out and never come back."

"You don't—"

He pressed his foot harder on Diego's throat. "Nod if you understand."

Gasping, Diego nodded.

He lifted his foot and stepped back, when he heard the footfalls of the two bodyguards. This time he was too slow, and they were able to slam him into the side of the Impala.

As each of the bodyguards went in for a punch, he brought out the two guns he'd taken from their boss and shot them both in the kneecap, downing them immediately.

Diego stood unsteadily. Without another word, he stumbled back to his car, got inside, slammed the door, and started the engine.

With tires screeching, Diego rolled down his window and choked out, "You will be sorry."

As the Impala sped away leaving the two thugs on the ground behind, Clint knew he'd crapped in his own bird's nest.

This wasn't the first time he found himself in a mess of his own making, nor would it be the last. What had the deputy director called him his last day at the Agency? *Hot-headed and reckless.*

After this shit storm he wasn't sure how he could remain in Cuba. It would be difficult if not impossible since he'd used all his funds for this personal operation.

Slapping his hands together to dust them off, he turned back to the cantina and the smiling patrons passing money back and forth. Apparently, they'd been taking bets on him and Diego. From the exchanges he saw, it seemed he was a favorite over Diego. He wished he had gotten in on the action because he needed the cash now.

He rushed back into the bar, as several of the customers slapped his back in approval. He guessed they were the ones who had won money on him. Still others were leaving the bar while whispering their concerns about what would be coming next from the police and Santiago Martinez.

Clint walked up to the young woman. "Are you okay, *señorita*?"

"*Sí. Sí. Gracias. Gracias,*" she said, wrapping her arms around his neck.

"*De nada.*"

She released him, and said in English, "Diego does not believe me when I say I am not interested in him. I have a boyfriend, though I would never let him know that."

"That's a good idea," Clint said, remembering the young, thin guy who had sat with her at the cantina once or twice.

Lifting the fallen barstools off the floor, Clint announced to the remaining customers, "Next round is on me."

As the crowd cheered, a man with gray hair and trimmed beard walked up to him.

Shocked, Clint stared at the man who had trained him to be a spy. "Sir?"

Blake Atlas offered his hand. "Since we're both no longer on the inside, call me *Blake.*"

"That might be difficult for me given our history as trainer and trainee," he said, shaking hands with one of the Agency's former legends.

At 40, Blake was only ten years older than him. His resume was exceptional. He had eliminated some of the most dangerous men in the world. Who knew the countless lives Blake had saved in service to the country?

Along with Gary and six others, Clint had been in the last class of new recruits that Blake had trained.

Clint remembered the shock that had rocked Langley after his unexpected departure.

There had been tons of speculation as to why Blake had left.

One theory had been that he'd flipped to the other side.

Another was that he'd never gotten over the loss of his twin brother, who had also been with the Agency before getting killed in a mission gone sideways.

And still another was that Blake had lost his fire for the job after one of his ops went awry.

But to everyone's surprise the top brass had given a reluctant stamp of approval for Blake's departure.

"So what brings you to Cuba?" Clint asked, knowing it must have something to do with him.

"I've got a lead on the man who killed Gary, and I need you, Bloodhound."

"Roman Koslova?" Clint asked. "That's why I'm here. Koslova is known to vacation in Havana. I've been in Cuba two months waiting for him to show."

"Koslova's never coming back to Cuba, Clint. He's burned here with Santiago and the authorities. Speaking of..." he trailed off as the distant wail of police sirens filtered into the bar. "But I still have a few tricks up my sleeve you can learn," Blake said with a slight grin. "Clint, the Agency thinks you and I are men without a cause. They're wrong. You and I can never stop or forget."

"So you know what happened in Belarus?"

"I do."

"You're right. I'll never forget." The memory of Gary's death replayed in Clint's mind.

"That's what I'm counting on, buddy."

"So am I. Tell me about your lead on Koslova."

"I need your help locating his ex-girlfriend."

"I didn't know he had a girlfriend."

"I'll tell you everything I know," Blake said as the sirens grew louder. "But right now we better get going before the PNR arrives and we both land in jail, don't you think?"

Without waiting for his answer, Blake exited out the back.

Clint ran after him, realizing this was the only choice he had and his best hope to find Koslova.

5

Paris, France – present

LYING on the bed in her hotel room, Lexi glanced at the clock on the nightstand. The green numbers showed 4:33 am. Five hours before the meeting with Pavel at his hotel.

Despite just coming off a grueling one-stop flight from Dallas to Paris, she couldn't sleep.

Unfortunately, all the direct flights had been sold out. With a single day to get to the meeting with Pavel, she'd taken the last two seats available for her and Steve.

Steve had been working on her case for ages with every lead ending in a dead end. Lexi's optimism about their chance of finding Roman was dwindling. But then two days ago, Steve had tracked down a man living in Paris. The guy, Pavel Koslova, was Roman's cousin, who claimed to have information on his involvement on Matthew's murder.

As a precaution, Steve had insisted they stay at a different hotel than Pavel's. At first she'd thought he was being too cautious, but since they were trying to track a possible killer, she realized he was right. Steve's room was across the hall from hers, which did make her feel a little safer since she wasn't allowed to bring her gun to France.

She heard the familiar sound on her phone that a text had come in.

Knowing sleep was impossible, she swung her legs off the comfy bed and retrieved her phone.

The text came from Liz.

Wanted to make sure you're okay.
Anything else I can do?

She typed back:

I'm fine. In the hotel room.
You've already done so much.
Thanks for everything.
I promise to pay you back.

Pavel had demanded ten thousand US dollars, which was at the bottom of Lexi's purse. Four thousand of the stash came from the monies she'd cashed out of her 401k. The other six, Liz had provided through a wire transfer.

Stop. We've already discussed
this. I want you to be past this
nightmare with Roman.

*Me too. What time is
it there?*

There? I'm in New York.

*New York? What are you
doing in New York
and not Florida?*

*On standby for a flight
to Paris so I can be with you.*

*Liz! You shouldn't
have.*

*Flights are booked solid,
but I will pull strings to get
a seat. Won't make it to the
meeting but will text when
I arrive. I want to help all
I can.*

*I'm glad you're coming.
I hope we get answers to
find him so I can clear
my name.*

We will get answers.

She hoped Liz was right, though she felt like she was waiting for the blade to fall while her head rested in the wooden crook of a guillotine.

Rested? Wrong word.

She hadn't had a good night's sleep since Steve and Sims had come to her apartment to deliver the horrific news about Matt.

Text after the appointment.

Okay. I will. Bye.

Lexi placed her phone back on the charger and walked to the window. Knowing Liz was on her way made her feel better. She needed the moral support.

Lexi wanted to enjoy the view of the city she'd dreamed of visiting for as long as she could remember, but she couldn't. The case of Matt's murder remained unsolved, though in her gut she knew the identity of the killer.

Her ex, Roman.

She'd known he was responsible for the horror since receiving his text less than 24 hours after Matt's death.

Hi sweetheart. Roman here. I see you have company. Miss you, in town on business. Hope to see you soon. #urmine

That had been the last communication she'd received from Roman.

Two years had passed. *Two years?*

God, it seemed like a lifetime ago.

Would Pavel have real answers for her? Would he know how to find Roman?

Lexi glanced at her purse once again. Carrying that much money made her nervous. She remembered how concerned she'd felt as the teller counted out one hundred bills with Benjamin Franklin's face. But she had to keep moving forward. There was no other choice.

Several hours later, Lexi exited her hotel onto the sidewalk and felt the cool morning air. She spotted Steve in a gray suit and tie sitting at a table where they'd agreed to meet, because of its close proximity to their hotel.

The café had a quintessential Parisian flair with its red awning, tiny chairs and tables, and customers enjoying their meals outside on the bustling sidewalk.

"*Bonjour*," Steve said, as she sat across from him.

"Bonjour," she answered. That and being able to count to twenty was about all she had retained from her high school French classes.

"I need an espresso after that long journey, how about you?" he asked.

"*Oui, monsieur,*" she answered with a grin.

"Anything to eat?" He motioned to a waiter, who was nearby wearing a crisp white shirt, black vest and slacks, and an apron that wrapped around his waist and fell to his knees.

"Maybe some toast and fruit," she answered, feeling nervous about the meeting. "I'm not hungry but I need something I suppose."

"Yes. You do."

The waiter stepped over to their table. "*Avez-vous choisi?*"

Steve gave their order in perfect French. Once again his language skills impressed her as they had since their arrival last night at Charles de Gaulle. With ease, he'd gotten help to navigate getting their bags, finding a taxi to the hotel, and making sure their rooms were next to each other. Without him on this trip she wasn't sure how she would have managed.

After the waiter left, she turned to him, "I'm so grateful you were able to come on this trip."

He grinned. "All in the job, Ms. Bly. All in the job."

"Like you let me pay you."

"Well, you were my first client, after all."

"It's more than that with you and I know it." She reached across the table and squeezed his hand.

"Of course you're right. Until your name is cleared, you're stuck with me, young lady."

Having lost both her parents, she liked having him as a friend. She'd even gotten close to his daughter and son. He treated her like a father, and Sara and Brad treated her like a sister.

The waiter returned with their espressos. With her limited French, she wasn't able to follow the quick exchange between him and Steve.

She took a sip from her cup, enjoying the warmth and richness. Feeling the fuzziness around her thoughts, she needed the caffeine to stave off the jet lag for a little longer. Once their task was done and the documents were in her hand, she planned on crashing back in her room at the hotel.

After the waiter walked away, she asked Steve, "What did you say to him?"

"I asked him how far it was to the Eiffel Tower."

"Were you thinking about a detour before our meeting?"

He nodded. "It's so beautiful here. It's a short walk to the tower. We have plenty of time."

"Maybe afterwards, but I'm too keyed up for any

sight-seeing." She patted her purse and in a low tone said, "Plus, carrying this amount of money makes me very nervous."

"Let's fix that, but in a way prying eyes won't see." He took off his jacket and placed it on the table. "Slip the envelope with the cash under this. I'll carry it for you."

She considered his offer for a moment, but decided against it. "I know you don't think we should pay this much—"

"No. I still don't think you should pay anything for the information. Let me go to the meeting. I'll get what we need one way or another."

"Once a cop, always a cop, right?"

He shrugged.

"Thank you, but no. You're not talking me out of this. Until now, we've only hit dead ends. This guy is the first break we've had. But I promise I won't turn over a single dime until he gives us everything he has on Roman."

"Now who's acting like a cop?" He slipped his jacket back on. "I know I've said it a million times, but it's true. You have the instinct of a cop. Plus I've never seen anyone shoot better than you. You're a natural."

They had a standing date every Saturday morning at the gun range.

"Like you've told me. It takes a lot more than being able to fire a gun to make a great cop."

"Yes it does, and I swear you have that and everything else, young lady, to become one of the best."

"Once we find where my ex is hiding, then we can talk about possible career changes. Okay?"

"You got a deal." He took a long sip from his cup. "Damn. That's good stuff."

"Yes, it is. And it's magic zing seems to be working," she said, feeling her fatigue lessen.

Was it the caffeine in the espresso or the anticipation of their appointment that made her heart flutter?

"Are you ready?"

One last sip and she left her chair. "You bet I am."

The extraordinary panorama of the city of Paris surrounded Lexi and Steve. Located in the touristy 7th arrondissement, the area was packed with both tourists and locals. They headed to the agreed upon meeting place, via a stroll near the Eiffel Tower.

To their right and above the century-old trees she could see the top of the iconic landmark. Though the weather was cool, people were lounging on far-reaching, manicured lawns.

Under different circumstances, she would have been thrilled to enjoy every sight and sound.

"Look." Steve pointed to a sign as they passed. "One of the museums has a temporary exhibition of urban and contemporary French artists next to the tower."

Seeing his genuine excitement surprised her. "So you're into French art?"

"*Oui*," he answered with a grin and a wink, as they continued on the sidewalk past the tourists filing out of the bus. "What do you say? Shall we come back and check it out after our meeting? Get our culture on in *La Ville Lumière*—the City of Light. Afterwards, we could grab a bite."

"Why not?" She guessed his banter about the exhibition had more to do with trying to calm her nerves than it had to do with the art. But her mind continued to spin like a dryer full of wet clothes.

Would she find some proof to clear her name? Would Pavel have info on how to locate Roman? And why was he willing to betray his cousin? All she could go on was the dossier that Steve had put together on Pavel.

Roman's cousin didn't have a criminal record. In fact, the guy was squeaky clean. According to the dossier, Pavel and Roman had grown up separately—Pavel in Paris and Roman in Minsk. Steve had put together that Pavel and Roman had only seen each other at family gatherings once or twice when they were still kids. The possibility of them being close was next to nil. So what was Pavel's motivation to help Lexi? He'd lost his job and had endured a nasty divorce, hence the need for money. That thought had her keeping a tighter hold of her purse than normal due to the massive amount of cash inside.

With the trained eyes of a former police detective, Steve stayed very close to her, scanning the street ahead. Having him with her did help ease her anxiety, though as they walked across Pont de l'Alma, one of the bridges over the Seine, her heart rate still increased.

As they turned down the narrow street with Parisian 5-story buildings on each side, Lexi noticed that the primary color of the setting was cream. The secondary colors that tempered the display were red and black. A handful of shops and boutiques sported red awnings over their doors, while the tiny balconies attached to the edifices were adorned with black rod iron. Finishing out the romantic area was the sliver of blue sky and puffy white clouds above. But the whole scene didn't make her feel romantic at all. Instead it felt like she was walking into a canyon about to be ambushed.

"There it is," Steve said, pointing to the sign of Pavel's hotel.

She nodded, as they stepped up to the entrance—a single, wooden door.

The hotel was much more understated than what she'd expected for a place in the center of Paris.

"By the looks of this, I guess our guy is down on his luck," she said.

"Looks can be deceiving, especially in Europe." Steve opened the door, and they walked in.

He was right. The lobby was luxurious with its marble floors, expensive artwork, and plush furnishings. Even the curved hotel desk with its inlaid wood screamed opulence.

"If Pavel can afford to stay here, why does he need my money?" she asked in a hushed tone.

"Maybe his room is a broom closet," he answered.

She realized that Steve was once again trying to lighten her mood, which did have a slight impact on making her feel a little better. "Maybe so. Let's find out."

They took the elevator to the floor of Pavel's room. There were eight rooms off the hallway. The last door on the left was their destination. Room 208.

When they got close, they could see the door was ajar and there was no light coming through from the interior of the room.

Steve stepped in front of her. "Hold on. Let me check it out first."

She nodded. "Be careful."

"You bet I will."

A voice from inside called out, "*Bonjour*. Is that you,

Ms. Bly? I left the door open for you. Come in and make yourself at home. I'll be right out."

As Steve pushed the door wider, the back of her neck tingled.

"Wait." She grabbed his arm. "This doesn't seem safe."

"I'll be fine." He took a single step forward.

Bang!

The gunshot echoed in her ears.

Steve crumpled to the floor in front of her.

Before she could react, two men jumped over him, grabbed hold of her arms and jerked her into the room.

She kicked.

She clawed.

She bit. Anything to try to get free, but the men had the advantage of surprise.

The thinner of the two shoved her onto the bed, aiming a gun at her face.

The heavier man was doubled over in pain from her foot jamming into his crotch. "Stan, her asshole friend is blocking the door."

"Shut up, Boris. We'll fucking deal with him in a second."

Stan brought his gun-free hand up to his face to wipe the blood oozing from the deep scratches she'd given him. "Damn you, you little bitch."

Still aiming his gun at her, he pulled out a knife with his bloody hand. He leaned forward and ran the tip of the blade near her cheeks.

"I should slice up your pretty face for this."

Although the thug's words terrified her, there was no time to worry about them. She needed to protect herself.

She needed to help Steve. She needed a way out of this nightmare.

"You better not harm the merchandise. You know she's Koslova's squeeze."

Boris started to drag Steve's body away from the door. "You know how the boss is. She comes back damaged and he'll put a bullet between your eyes and mine, too."

"You're lucky," Stan said to her, putting away his knife.

As she glanced around the room to find a makeshift weapon, she saw another guy on the floor near the bed—a man she assumed was Pavel. He lay in a twisted heap with glassy unblinking eyes. What had happened here before she and Steve had arrived? Why had they killed Pavel?

Boris groaned, as he tugged on Steve's body. "This guy is a monster. I could use some help."

"I'm a little busy," Stan said, turning his head toward his buddy.

That split-second of his attention being diverted gave her an opening to act. She grabbed the lamp on the nightstand and hurled it as hard as she could at Stan.

The base of the light hit him square in the back of the head and he stumbled to his knees.

"Boss or no boss, you're dead!" Stan screamed, swinging around with the gun.

Before he could fire, two more men charged through the open door, gunning him down. He collapsed to the floor on top of Pavel's body.

Boris dropped his weapon and held up his hands, yelling, "Don't shoot."

"On your knees," the younger of the two with dark, piercing eyes commanded.

Boris obeyed him, though his stare remained fixed on the older man as if he recognized him. "Okay. Okay."

"Don't move a muscle." Mr. Piercing Eyes kept his gun aimed at the thug, while retrieving Boris's discarded gun off the floor.

The other man, who appeared older with gray hair, removed his belt and used it to restrain Boris's hands behind his back. "That should hold you. I'll check on the others." He knelt down next to Stan and Pavel and shook his head. "These two are dead, Clint."

So, Mr. Piercing Eyes has a name.

"You okay, Ms. Bly?" Clint asked.

Still shaken, all she could muster was a tiny nod, wondering how he knew her name.

He grabbed her hand and squeezed. "Are you sure?"

Clint's features included dark hair, dimpled chin and a rugged, handsome face. Wearing a black leather jacket, gray T-shirt, and dark Levi's, Clint stood at least six-two and had a muscled frame.

And those eyes of his? There seemed to be something primal and dangerous about them to her.

Suddenly, she began to shake uncontrollably. "My friend."

She slipped off the bed and knelt down next to Steve, who had taken a bullet for her. His eyes were closed and his breathing was ragged. His shirt was soaked with blood from the gunshot to his chest. "Please. He needs medical attention."

"Let me check him," Clint moved next to her. "He's breathing, but barely."

He pressed his fingers to Steve's neck, continuing to

check his vitals. Then he unbuttoned Steve's shirt, as Blake tossed him a towel.

Clint wiped away the blood, exposing the gunshot. He bent down, placing his ear close to the wound. "Sucking chest wound."

"What does that mean?" she asked.

He leaned back up. "The bullet pierced his lung. As your friend tries to breathe, air is trying to come in through the wound. The good news, his lung hasn't collapsed yet. The bad news is it will unless we seal the wound."

"This should do the trick." Blake handed him the plastic liner the hotel provided for the ice bucket.

Clint nodded and placed the liner over the wound. "Perfect, but she's right. He does need medical attention, fast. We have to get to Doc."

Blake produced a phone from his jacket. "I'll stay, but you need to get her out of here before more of her ex-boyfriend's buddies show up."

"So this *is* about Roman? He knows I'm in Paris."

"He does," Clint said. "Come with me, Ms. Bly. I'll make sure you're safe."

"I can't leave Steve. No. I can't. I won't." She took a deep breath, steeling her resolve. "I'm staying with him. I don't have a clue who you are or why you are here. We need to call the police to get an ambulance for him."

"No police," Clint stated firmly.

Is he just another bad guy?

A powerful urge to flee the horrific scene ran through her. But she couldn't. Steve had been shot.

Blake stepped over to the window. "Doc, I've got a male, mid-50s with a gunshot wound to the chest at *Hôtel*

Ciel Bleu, room 208. Hurry." Blake put away his phone. "He'll be here with his team in ten minutes. I've got this."

"Okay," Clint said, turning to her. "We need to go."

"No," she said despite the fact she already knew first-hand that he and Blake were killers. But they didn't seem to want to hurt her. Why? It didn't matter. Steve needed her help. "He is my friend. I'm not going anywhere with you."

6

Clint's gaze remained fixed on Lexi.

Her long, dark brown hair hung past her shoulders, framing her gorgeous face. Her green eyes, delicate nose and soft lips transfixed him. Even though she wore a cropped-jean jacket and purple sweater, he still could get a glimpse of the fullness of her breasts underneath. Her black slacks revealed more of her curves, which he appreciated in every way. The purple high heels accentuated her long legs.

But what undid him the most was her courage and loyalty. What other civilian woman would be so strong and determined in the face of such danger to help her friend?

"Ms. Bly, you are not safe here," he told her. "We need to move fast."

She shook her head. "No."

"You're going one way or the other. You can either walk out with me or I will carry you out. Your choice."

"Time is ticking, Clint," Blake said.

He nodded, and without hesitating, lifted her off the floor and into his arms.

"Put me down," she said, pounding on his chest. "Who the hell are you?"

"The guy trying to keep you out of a French jail." Holding her tight, he walked out of the hotel room into the hallway.

"What are you talking about?" she asked. "If my friend dies, I swear you will pay."

"He's in the best hands with Blake. I promise you, he'll get the best care available." With a nod to Blake, he closed the door with his foot.

"That doesn't answer my question about me getting arrested," she said, still defiant, though no longer beating his chest with her fists.

"Your ex, Roman Koslova has some dirty contacts inside Interpol, which has issued a Red Notice on you."

"Roman did that? And how do you know about him? And what is a Red Notice? And—?"

"How about one question at a time? A Red Notice is a kind of international warrant that will extradite you to Belarus, where Koslova holds a position in the government."

"Wait. What? Roman works for the Belarus government?"

"Yes, as a front. Koslova works for the Vice Chairman of the Belarus Security Committee."

"Security? Roman? That's got to be a joke."

At the elevator doors, he turned sideways so he could tap the call button with the back of his hand while continuing to hold Lexi in his arms.

He'd come into this wondering if she was a criminal like her ex. Now, he wasn't so sure.

Lexi was smart and inquisitive, two more things he liked about her. But what kind of woman could get in a relationship with someone like Roman Koslova?

Still, he couldn't stop thinking about her courage and loyalty for her friend.

There was more to Lexi Bly than the information he'd collected in her dossier. He had scanned the circumstantial evidence in the two-year old murder investigation where she remained as a person of interest. To him, there wasn't enough information to prove her innocence or guilt.

"Put me down now," she commanded.

"I don't trust you not to run to your friend Steve, which will put you back in danger as well as him. If you show up with Steve at any hospital, you'll be arrested and he will be implicated. You don't want to make it worse for him, do you?"

"Of course not."

The doors opened. Thankfully, no one was inside the elevator. He hoped his good luck would continue. It must, if he was going to be able to keep her safe.

With her in his arms, he stepped into the elevator.

If Interpol found and extradited her to Belarus, it would be next to impossible to track her to Roman Koslova. Or if Koslova's men captured her, Lexi would vanish and he would never get his revenge. But there was more to his desire to protect her. Trying to tamp down his emotions, he focused on the immediate task in front of him: *get Lexi Bly to a safe place.*

He attempted to punch the ground floor button with

his elbow, but since it was recessed and his elbow was too big he failed. "Damn it."

As the elevator doors shut, she said, "It might work better if you set me down."

"Like I said before, I don't trust you."

"Feeling's mutual, though apparently, my creepy ex is screwing with my life again and I need help. I still only know your name, but not why you and your friend arrived in time to save the day."

He lowered her to the floor, and hit the button. "Let's just say, we're the good guys."

Her green eyes stared right into him. "Good guys, who don't want to call the police?"

"Red Notice. Remember?"

As the elevator doors opened to the ground floor, she asked, "You don't know me, Clint, but you believe I'm innocent?"

He didn't know how to answer, but he needed her to trust him. "I know enough about you that I want to keep you safe."

"And I don't know a thing about you."

As they walked through the lobby, he was pleased that Lexi remained next to him and didn't run, as she'd promised.

"And you are sure that your friend will call with any news on Steve?"

"Of course he will."

"You promise?"

"I don't make promises, but he will. Trust me."

"Trust you? I don't even know who you are."

"Let's spend a little more time together, and I'll fill you in the best I can. Deal?"

"I don't have any other choice." She shrugged, and then nodded. "Yes. You got a deal."

He needed to figure out why she was so important to Koslova. Was she connected to some plan of his without her knowledge?

When they stepped out of the hotel and onto the street, she asked, "Where now?"

LEXI FELT a warm tremble shoot through her when Clint took her hand in his.

"This way," he said, heading the opposite route she and Steve had arrived from earlier.

"That's a direction, not an answer to my question about where we're going." To keep up with his pace, she had to take two steps to his one, which was a little difficult in her heels.

"It's the best I can give you right now, since I don't know yet." Clint kept scanning their route like a soldier on a mission.

She tried to do the same, glancing towards every shadowy corner that could house an attacker, every nearby rooftop that could hide a shooter, every person that seemed even the slightest out of place. But the more she looked around, the more danger she imagined.

She took out her phone to call Liz and give her an update. Was Liz already on a flight? God, she hoped so.

She was shocked when Clint stopped and grabbed her phone.

"What the hell, Clint?"

"This is how Blake and I got your location in Paris."

"You hacked my phone?"

He nodded. "And I bet your ex-boyfriend has too."

"Damn. So I should turn it off?"

"Not exactly." Clint tossed her phone into a trash bin. "That's not paid off yet."

"Sorry, but keeping it is too big a risk. One of Koslova's hackers would find a way to activate your phone remotely. Then, your ex would be able to find you."

"Got it," she said, realizing she was putting all her trust into Clint, a man who was a complete stranger. "I need to get some things from my hotel room."

"The authorities and Koslova will be expecting you to return there."

"Then where should we go?"

"Still working on that." At the next intersection, Clint stopped.

Her heart skipped several beats. "Something wrong?"

"Not sure." He looked over his shoulder. "Come on."

Since he was still holding her hand tight, she couldn't refuse—not that she would. It was clear he had some kind of military training at the very least, and having him at her side did make her feel a little safer, if only a little.

Clint picked up their pace.

She thought it might be best to slip out of her heels, but by God she wasn't going to toss them. The purple Louboutins that matched her top had been a gift from Liz.

As Clint continued looking over his shoulder, she knew he was concerned they were being followed.

When they got to the next intersection, he rushed her through a door into a small bakery on the corner that was filled with patrons.

"Stand over there." He motioned to a display where several people were eyeing the delicious and beautiful pastries.

"Okay." She wondered what had triggered him to go into the bakery.

When his hand disappeared into his jacket, where he had put his gun away earlier, she felt the tension building inside her. Though he kept his hand inside his jacket, he never brought out his weapon.

What was he looking for on the other side of the shop's windows? Had some of Roman's men spotted them? Or the police? Would this nightmare that Roman had created for her ever end?

She watched as Clint remained near the windows, though still out of view from those outside.

The chef in the classic white hat and apron greeted her in French from behind the counter.

"Nothing yet. *Merci*," she answered frantically. "Still looking."

The chef turned his attention to another, a paying customer.

Not a person on the run from killers who want to kidnap me and take me to Roman. God, my mind is spinning.

She took a deep breath.

I need to get a grip and focus.

The image of Steve lying on the hotel room's floor cut through her like a hot knife.

Please let him be okay.

She held her breath when two thuggish-looking men dressed all in black walked past the bakery's window in a rush and Clint brought out his gun. Since all the customers had their backs to the windows, no one but her seemed to notice.

After what seemed like an eternity but clearly was less than a minute, Clint put his weapon away.

He moved closer, taking her hand again. "It's time to go."

"Were those men following us?"

"Yes."

"We need to get out of here."

"Wait." She removed her heels, tucking them into her purse on top of the cash. "Since we may need to run, better to be barefoot in Paris than a sitting duck."

"I gotta say you're impressive, Ms. Bly."

His compliment made her feel good. "I think after all we've been through today you should call me 'Lexi.'"

He smiled, which pleased her. "Lexi it is."

They exited the bakery, and headed in the opposite direction that the two men had gone.

Two blocks later, Clint stopped at a line of scooters parked near the sidewalk. He hopped on a blue one, motioning for her to get on behind him.

Once in the seat and her purse secured on her shoulder, she asked sarcastically, "This is yours?"

"I'm borrowing it for now." In a flash, he had some wires loosened from the handle. Another second later, the scooter fired to life. "Put your arms around me."

She did, feeling how tight his muscles were.

He sped them through the crowded lanes, zipping in and out of traffic. When they drove around the Arc de Triomphe, Lexi tightened her hold on him.

"I need to get you out of the city center," he said,

raising his voice so she could hear above all the street noise.

An hour later, he stopped in front of a single-story, tiled-roofed house. "We're here."

She got off the scooter. "Where is *here?*"

"Home of a friend, who will help us."

"Okay, but first I want to know how Steve is doing."

"Of course." He brought out his phone and called Blake. "It's me. I've taken her to Camille's place. Right."

"How is he?" She was terrified the answer would be bad.

"She's worried about her friend. Talk to her." Clint handed the phone to her.

"How is Steve doing?" she asked.

"He's doing well. The doctor says he will pull through and should be back on his feet in a week or two."

"Thank God," she said with a sigh. "Is he awake? Has he sat up? Has he asked about me? Can I talk to him?"

"Not yet, but I'll call Clint's phone once he's awake."

Why should I trust him? "Please, send a photo of Steve to this phone."

"You bet I can, Ms. Bly. I promised you I would take care of him, and I have. I swear."

"You better have." She clicked the phone off. "He's sending a photo of Steve to your phone."

Clint nodded. "I don't blame you for verifying anything we say. It's smart."

His phone dinged, and she clicked on the message with the photo.

Seeing the image of Steve lying in a hospital bed hooked up to tubes and wires made her heart sink low.

She handed the phone back to Clint. "I can't stand seeing him in that condition. It's all my fault."

Clint put his arm around her shoulders. "You're not to blame for that. And remember, he's alive. Don't know much about Detective Torres, but he seems like a tough guy to me."

"He is tough." If anyone could pull through, Steve could. "Hold on a second. I never told you he was a detective."

"There is plenty of time to go over everything. For now, we need to get off the street."

Why does he keep deflecting whenever I ask a question? When we get to wherever we're going, he better tell me everything.

Lexi pulled out her shoes from her purse to slip them on, and then used her fingers to try to tame her wind-blown hair. "Let's do this."

His smile calmed her insides a bit. "Yes. Let's go."

They walked up to the front of the house and rang the bell.

The door opened, and a gorgeous blonde woman appeared, wearing a red jumpsuit with a plunging V-line that went all the way down to her navel. Her blue eyes widened when she saw Clint.

"*Mon chéri*," the French woman said with exuberance, wrapping her arms around him. "And who is this, may I ask?"

He can't be into her. She must be at least a decade older than him.

"She's a friend who needs a place to stay," he told her. "Camille, let me introduce you to Lexi Bly. Lexi, this is

Camille Moreau, who has gotten me out of more than a few scrapes in the past."

Maybe the age difference doesn't matter to them.

She extended her hand. "Pleased to meet you, Ms. Moreau."

CLINT WATCHED as Lexi and Camille shook hands. There seemed to be tension between the two.

Maybe it was because Camille was a trained spy, and suspicion often kept spies alive. After all, she was one of the best France had.

Three years ago, due to an error from the Agency, Clint had arrived ten minutes too early for the exchange of fifty million in counterfeit US dollars and a massive shipment of illegal military-grade weapons. Several men had gotten the drop on him, bringing him forward to the counterfeiter and Camille, who was posing as the broker for the deal. The weapons dealer would have arrived shortly, and she would have scored two big fish. But instead she'd fired at the men holding Clint. The counterfeiter escaped during the gunfire exchange, and the weapons dealer never showed. Despite over eighteen months as an undercover operative, Camille had chosen to torpedo the entire operation to save him. Clint would never forget what she'd done for him.

But Lexi had been through so much today and didn't know the history he had with Camille. How could she not be filled with doubt about her?

Or me? She doesn't know either one of us.

"*Bienvenue,*" Camille said. "Come inside."

They walked into her home, which was decorated in a modern minimalistic style. The color of pure white dominated the living room from the leather sectional to the walls and floors and everything in between—everything except for a solitary red abstract sculpture near the floor-to-ceiling window that resembled the letter Q.

The sleekness of the kitchen matched the living room. A mix of steel, glass, high-end appliances with glossy-gray Italian cabinetry, so clean and pristine one could eat off the solid-white, marble floor and not worry.

"Your home is beautiful," Lexi offered.

"Thank you," Camille said. "Would you like something to drink?"

"Actually, may I use your bathroom? I'd like to freshen up. The ride here on Clint's scooter ruined my hair."

"Of course." Camille turned to him and winked. "Let me show her where it is and I'll be right back."

As the two of them walked down the hall, Clint fired off a message to Blake.

We're safe at Camille's.

Good. Stay put for now.
Getting some buzz about
possible movement of target.

Will do. Keep me
informed.

After weeks of being in the wind, Roman Koslova was

coming out of hiding. Why? The only thing that made sense was it must have to do with Lexi.

He'd tracked her down to find Koslova, but how had Koslova known she was at Pavel's hotel? Was Pavel a snitch? Well, if he was it had cost him his life.

Camille returned without Lexi. "She seems nice. What's her story?"

Something about Camille's demeanor seemed off. "Lexi's ex-boyfriend is Roman Koslova. You ever have a run-in with him?"

"No, but of course I know his reputation." She smiled, and ran her finger down his forearm. "So you want to use this woman to flush him out."

"No."

"Seriously? It would be easy to set up a trap for Koslova with her as the bait."

"Not happening, Camille. I wouldn't let her get in the same room with that fucker. She's been through enough already."

Camille stepped back. "I never took you for a softy."

"I'm not. What intel do you have on Koslova?"

"Last I heard he's in Belarus, running his money laundering while still being a gun for hire."

"Gun for hire? That's putting it mildly. Koslova is one of the most prolific assassins in the world. You remember what happened in Romania?"

"That was Koslova?"

"Yes it was."

She opened a cabinet and brought out a bottle of wine and a bottle of Scotch. "Is 15-year-old Macallan still your drink of choice?"

"You remembered."

"Hard to forget after all we've been through together, Clint."

Something seems off with her. Is it my imagination or just my overactive suspicious nature? Probably the latter.

She poured him a glass and handed it to him, before filling two wine glasses.

He took a sip. "Very nice. Thanks. I needed this."

"You're very welcome."

"There are at least ten more assassinations Koslova is responsible for that I know of, including a CEO of a major tech company."

"You mean Franklin Masters?" She sipped from her glass. "That was his work, too?"

"Yes."

Camille motioned to the hallway where she'd taken Lexi. "Poor girl. Hard to shake that kind of man when he's hell-bent on keeping you."

Again, Clint got that strange feeling that something wasn't right with Camille. "How did you put together that Koslova was fixated on Lexi?"

She grinned. "She's beautiful. He's a psychopath. They have history. You're here protecting her. Seems to me that's the most logical reason. Am I mistaken?"

He didn't answer.

Lexi returned from the bathroom looking absolutely gorgeous.

"I poured you a glass of red," Camille said. "I hope you don't mind."

"Thank you." Lexi took the glass.

Camille's phone buzzed and she looked at the screen. "HQ. I need to take this. Please, both of you make your-self at home. I'll be back shortly."

When she walked out of the room, Clint turned to Lexi. "Would you like to sit?"

"Yes, I would." She landed on the sectional. "It's been one helluva day."

With a sudden urge to inhale her intoxicating scent, he took a seat close to her.

"Clint, I need to know who you are and why you are involved in all of this."

"You're not safe. That's why I'm here. Koslova is a danger to you."

"Not that. I know that. I've known I've been in danger since my third date with him."

As she took another sip of wine, Clint wondered how much she knew about Koslova.

"I want to know about you," she said. "Who are you? Military? CIA? Law enforcement?"

"At present, I'm a free agent."

"So you're a mercenary. Who hired you?"

Before answering, Clint took a sip of his drink.

Everything he'd learned about Lexi hadn't prepared him for this. Her pointed questions sounded more like they were coming from a seasoned operative instead of a young woman with a college degree.

"Well?" she said, not letting him off the hook.

"You're a natural interrogator, Lexi."

"Don't deflect, Clint. Who hired you?"

He decided it would be best to tell her *some* of the truth, but not all. "Blake hired me to find you. He's trying to bring Kosolva to the US."

"What for? What has Roman done?"

He took another drink of Scotch, finding her intensity overwhelming. Her forcefulness, passion and green eyes created a perfect combination that he found irresistible, making it hard to concentrate.

"What else do you know about your ex?" he asked, trying to turn the tables on her.

She sighed and sat the wine glass down on the coffee table. "He's insane, and he's ruined everything in my life."

"Matthew Hill's murder? That was Koslova's doing. That's why you and Torres are in Paris to meet with Pavel."

She shook her head. "See. You know everything about me and I don't know anything about you."

"I don't know everything, but I hope to learn more."

"Why? What's in it for you?"

Finding Koslova and putting a bullet in his head. He couldn't tell her that. "My job is to keep you safe, and that's what I'm going to do."

"You're still evading my question."

"Damn, you're a tough one."

"I've had to be."

"Listen Lexi. My job is my life. It's all I have left, and I intend to be good at it."

She leaned in closer. "So you lost someone too?"

Her question shocked him. How had she put all of that together? It felt like she could see through him.

"I did," he confessed. "My best friend. He was like a brother."

She placed her hand over his. "I'm sorry."

Because her touch felt so good, he stood, needing to get some distance. "Thanks."

"Oh. I overstepped."

"No. It's fine. I'm fine." He downed the rest of the Scotch in his glass, and refilled it. "You want more wine?"

"No thanks. I'm good."

He sensed that she was uncomfortable from the awkward situation he'd created.

Damn it. I have to keep my head straight and not let her gorgeous green eyes get to me.

She left the couch, turning her back to him. "What could be taking Camille so long?"

"She's an operative with French Intelligence. Could be anything."

"Oh my God. Really? She's a spy?"

"Camille was in the field, but now she's a desk jockey at DGSE. That's why I brought you here. She's more than capable of helping me keep you safe."

"And you were a spy, too? CIA, right?"

Her unyielding insight kept on coming.

"Ancient history."

"What happened? Was it about losing your friend?"

Thankfully, his phone vibrated before he could answer. "It's Blake."

"Maybe Steve's awake," she said, moving in close enough for him to catch a whiff of her scent.

"Hey. Lexi wants to know if Torres is awake?"

"Not yet," Blake answered.

"Still asleep," Clint told her.

"You're at Camille's?" Blake asked. "Lexi is safe?"

"We are. She is."

"Good. I need you now. I got a hit on one of Roman's aliases. An executive charter company has him listed as a passenger on a flight from Minsk to Orly airport in thirty minutes. This is our chance, Clint. I'll text you the address."

"I know the directions. On my way." He tucked his

phone back in his pocket and turned to Lexi. "I've got to go."

"Where? Why?"

"It's about Koslova. If Blake and I get to him before he finds you, this will all be over for you. No more looking over your shoulder."

"I'm going with you."

"That's not smart. You're not trained. I am. If I bring you along, it will make things more difficult for both of us. I'll be back as fast as I can. Stay put and out of sight. Remember, there is still a Red Alert out on you."

"Okay."

He walked to the door.

"Clint?"

He turned. "Yes?"

Her green eyes locked on him. "Please, be careful."

7

Lexi's world had been shaken, turned upside down, and flattened—all in a single day.

She stood in a French spy's house, wondering how in the hell she'd ended up here. Camille hadn't returned from her call somewhere in the back of the home.

Clint had left on the stolen scooter to try to capture her awful ex. Clint's leaving was hard for her. Even though he was still a stranger like the owner of this house, Lexi felt better with him around than she should have. It wasn't like he'd told her much. When she'd pushed him for answers, he'd been closed and not forthcoming. After all they'd been through, that was unacceptable to her.

Back in college, she'd dealt with another man keeping secrets from her. Roman. Whenever her gut told her something was off with him, she'd let it slide. Somehow he had been able to keep her off-balance. Whenever she started to get her mental footing again, he would find a way to knock her down like the day she'd tried to end things with him.

"PLEASE, ROMAN," Lexi said to the man, who was sitting across the table from her. "You don't understand."

He grabbed her hand, squeezing hard. "My love, I understand perfectly. It's you. You don't understand."

"You're hurting me," she said.

He shrugged, still holding on tight to her. "And you're hurting me, sweetheart."

She'd chosen the coffee shop on campus to tell him she was done because it was so public. In truth, she was scared of him and what he could do. She'd believed he wouldn't make a scene here, though she'd definitely been wrong.

"Let me go, Roman," she said quietly. "I mean it."

He laughed, which irritated her. "You mean what?" He leaned in close, his dark stare stabbing her in the gut. "What exactly will you do to me, Lexi?"

"Please. Let go of my hand."

He released her and leaned back in the chair. "But I won't let go of you. Ever. You're mine. Always."

"Roman, don't be like this. We had fun, but it's over." One more lie. Fun was not what she'd experienced with him.

Another sickening laugh shot out of his mouth. "We did have fun. We will have fun again. You'll see."

"You're not listening to me."

"Why should I? You're confused." He took a sip from his coffee cup. "Should we order some sandwiches? I'm a little hungry."

"Please. Don't dismiss me. I hope we can remain friends," she lied, knowing that would be impossible with a possessive man like him. "We both need to move on. I'm sure there is someone out there who is perfect for you."

His eyes narrowed. "And for you? Are you cheating on me, Lexi?"

"Of course not, I'm saying—"

"Stop talking," he commanded in a razor-edge tone. "You listen to me. You are mine. You will always be mine. And if I learn that any motherfucker takes you on a date..." He opened his jacket, revealing a holstered gun.

"Roman? What are you doing with that on campus?"

He closed his jacket and grinned. "A meatball sandwich sounds perfect to me. You sure you won't have one?"

Terrified, she shook her head.

He stood and came around the table. Then he got behind her, placing his hands on her shoulders. "I get you might be confused right now, babe. That's okay. I'm leaving the country for a job tomorrow. I'd planned on taking you with me, but it seems it might be better if I go alone. I have some friends who will keep an eye on you while I'm gone." He placed a credit card on the table in front of her. "Use this to buy some new clothes. Make them sexy, honey, so I can show you off."

There it was again, one of the reasons she wanted this over. Roman thought of her as a possession. Arm candy. Nothing more. But the main reason she was ending things was the more time she spent with him, the more concerned she became about what he might do if pushed. Murder? But she'd never considered him capable of murder, until now.

"Later, I'll send for you to join me. By then, you should have more clarity about our relationship in this sweet little head of yours."

He placed his big hands on the back of her neck, whis-

*pering in her ear, "So tiny and delicate, like a twig I could snap
in two with my fingers."*

She gasped.

*He kissed the top of her head. "You need time alone, my
dear? Okay. But know this. You are mine," he said wickedly,
squeezing her arms until she winced. "No one else's. You'll see.
Goodbye, Lexi."*

*As he walked away from the table, she felt frozen in place.
She watched him step up to the counter and order a sandwich.*

*After he took his food from the cashier, he turned and
waved at her before leaving the coffee shop.*

*She sat there for what seemed like hours, trying to figure
out what happened.*

THAT HAD BEEN the last time she'd seen her terrible ex.

Roman's word *later* had turned into two years. She'd
thought he'd given up on possessing her until Matt's
murder. She'd come looking for him to try to clear her
name, oblivious that he was already endeavoring to
capture her.

She'd been younger when she'd dated Roman. Naïve.
Blind. Stupid. She'd vowed to never be that foolish again.
Never.

But was she being smart with Clint? Were her eyes
open when it came to him? Her gut told her to trust him.
Was her gut wrong? What did she know about him?

According to Clint, he was working for Blake to find
Roman. That's why they had followed her and Steve to
the hotel. Clint had been with the CIA. What about
Blake? Why did he want Roman back in the US? Was
Blake an international bounty hunter of some kind or

did he work with the government in some other capacity?

The few answers she'd gleaned from Clint led to more questions. When Clint had admitted to losing someone close, she'd touched his hand in an attempt to comfort him. That's when he'd jumped off the sofa away from her like she was some kind of pariah.

"I need to talk to Liz," she said aloud to the empty room, pouring another glass of wine.

She felt alone. So alone. Was Liz already in Paris looking for her? Maybe, though Liz had said the flights had been booked solid. Since Clint had tossed her phone, Liz had no way to reach her. How would that make Liz feel?

Steve was at a God-only-knew-where medical facility that Blake had taken him to. Pavel, the man she'd come to Paris to get info from on Roman, was dead. So was one of Roman's men, the one named Stan. What had Blake done with the other guy, Boris? And what about the other two thugs who had been following her and Clint? Were they still searching for her?

God, it's like I landed in the middle of a thriller movie.

Lexi took a long sip from her glass.

There wasn't much she could do right now to find more answers. Her gorgeous French spy host, Camille, was tucked away somewhere in her deceptively large house. She decided to take another pass at her hair, which she'd made a quick attempt to fix earlier. Doing something normal might help to ground her a little.

She put down the glass and walked to the hallway, hearing Camille's muffled voice coming from another place deeper in the house.

She opened the door to what she thought was the bathroom. It wasn't. That was the next door down. The house was new to her, so she'd been turned around.

This door opened to an expansive bedroom in the same modern style as the rest of the house. Its color palette of stark whites and muted grays seemed cold and unwelcoming to her.

Lexi started to close the door until she spotted the assortment of items on the bed: a pile of cash in multiple currencies, at least ten passports, a set of car keys, three phones, and two open designer suitcases—one filled with beautiful clothes, the other with an assortment of deadly weapons.

This is so crazy.

Clint had told her that Camille worked at a desk at the French spy agency. Seeing the stack of spy gear, Lexi knew that wasn't quite true. Camille was a full-blown, cloak-and-dagger, secret agent.

Lexi guessed Clint had fudged the truth a little to ease her mind, or perhaps he'd fibbed because of some spy-to-spy protocol not to out other agents.

By the looks of the bedroom, it was apparent Camille had been about to run out the door on some mission before she and Clint had arrived.

Unable to hold back her curiosity, Lexi stepped over to the bed to get a better look. She'd never seen so much money in her life. There were stacks of US dollars, euros, pounds, yens, rubles, and more.

Lexi picked up the keys with the Porsche key ring.

Of course Camille drives a Porsche.

Imagining what it would be like to be behind the wheel of such a beautiful car, Lexi tossed the keys back onto the bed next to the passports and phones. The only time she'd even been a passenger in that kind of luxury ride was with Liz, who owned a Maserati.

Like the cash, the passports were from different countries. She opened the Canadian passport and saw Camille's photo, though the name printed on the page was Alison Davis. It was the same with the other passports. With Russia, she was Irina Bykov. With the UK, she was Penelope White. Australia, Fiona Walker. And on and on.

Lexi turned her attention to the weapons, which were stored in foam compartments in the second suitcase. Once closed, no one would be the wiser as to its contents. Having been to the gun range and some gun shows with Steve, she recognized the assault rifle was broken down into two pieces with a variety of state-of-the-art upgrades. There were two pistols, three knives, and other things she couldn't identify. It seemed obvious that Camille had to be a one-woman attack machine.

Feeling bad about snooping and fearing Camille would find her, Lexi left the bedroom, dreaming up all kinds of scenarios about what mission the female spy was going on. She'd always been a sucker for suspense novels, especially if they included a little romance.

What an exciting life Camille must lead.

Lexi shook her head, realizing she'd been through quite an unusual day herself, not that she'd call it exciting. More like terrifying.

When she walked back into the bathroom, she discovered the floor was wet. The toilet was overflowing. Earlier she'd walked out after flushing without looking back. That had been a big mistake. She jiggled the handle to stop the flow of water, but it didn't work. Why was the water coming over the edge? For crying out loud, she'd only peed.

The high-end toilet looked like it came right out of NASA. It even had a control panel on the wall she'd had trouble figuring out earlier. The icons had seemed to indicate the thing was like a luxury spa for your butt. Had she punched the wrong button?

Hoping to stop the flow of water, she removed the tank's lid. Everything inside was foreign to her. Frantically, she bent down trying to find a cut-off valve. Still, no luck. *Damn it!*

Lexi hated to interrupt Camille's call, but if she didn't her entire home might be flooded.

She ran down the hall to where she could hear Camille's voice coming from.

At the end of the hall was a glass patio to a garden, where Camille was taking a video call on a laptop.

Blake's image was on the screen.

Lexi opened the door, temporarily forgetting about the overflowing toilet and just wanting an update about Steve.

Blake said, "Sweetheart, Roman is expecting delivery in two hours."

Oblivious to her arrival, Camille said, "I'll be there with the pretty little package as promised, my love."

Hearing she was *the package* for Roman, Lexi felt like the ground was about to swallow her whole, but grabbed onto her survival instinct to quietly close the door.

She had to get away.

Running back to the bedroom, she grabbed the keys, hoping she could find the car and drive away before

Camille discovered she was on to her. She picked up a phone, and also closed the suitcase with the weapons, unwilling to leave them for Camille to shoot her with.

She ran back into the living room and heard the patio door open and slam.

"Lexi?" Camille's voice called.

She opened the door at the side of the kitchen, praying it was the garage.

It was.

Inside was a Red Porsche convertible. She threw the suitcase in the passenger seat and got behind the wheel. She put the key in the ignition and fired up the engine.

Where is the garage door opener?

She found the clicker, punched the button and anxiously watched the door slowly rise.

Camille ran into the garage with a gun, having at least one more weapon than had been in the suitcase.

Lexi floored the accelerator, the car barely clearing the garage door.

Camille stepped out onto the street behind her, firing the gun.

Lexi didn't let off the gas, squealing the tires as she turned down the closest street to get out of the line of Camille's fire.

She didn't slow down until she was miles away.

Everything she'd gone through today had been one giant lie.

Clint had lied.

He wasn't hired to find Roman. He was hired to find her.

Camille wasn't protecting her like he'd said. She was the delivery person who was meant to take her to Roman.

And Steve? What had happened to Steve? She'd seen the photo Blake had sent. How could Blake have put together a fake photo of Steve in a hospital bed so fast? She prayed he couldn't have and Steve was still alive, but she couldn't be sure. All the books she'd read made it seem like spies and bad guys had unlimited tools and resources. *That's only fiction, Lexi. Only fiction.*

But she felt like she'd dropped down the rabbit's hole and had landed in Alice's world—a world with liars and killers like Clint.

She was afraid to go back to her hotel. Roman and all his cronies might be waiting.

And what about the Red Alert on her that Clint had told her about? Was that a lie, too? Probably, but she couldn't know.

Lexi felt alone. She needed help.

Pulling into a public garage, she drove up to the booth with the attendant.

"*Bonjour, madame,*" the young man said. "*Dix euros.*"

Lexi reached into the bottom of her purse where the cash she'd brought for Pavel sat and brought out a five hundred note.

He shook his head. "*C'est trop.*"

"I'm sorry, but I don't understand. Do you speak English?"

"Yes. I cannot change such a large note."

"I don't think I have anything smaller." She reached back into her purse and found a two hundred euro bill. "Will this work?"

"Okay. Yes." He took the money and gave her the change. "Beautiful car. *Magnifique.*"

"Yes. I love it," she said, turning her lips into a pretend

smile, though her insides were still roiling with worry and fear.

"There are spots on the third level," he said, lifting the security arm.

Once she parked the car, Lexi grabbed the phone she'd taken from Camille's house.

"Please don't be locked." She punched the button, and the home screen lit up. "Thank God."

Why would a spy like Camille not lock her phone? Lexi had no idea, but was glad she didn't.

The next hurdle she had to get past was finding out if she could make an international call on this phone. She needed to contact her friend.

Even though she depended on the contacts list in her phone that Clint had tossed for most people's numbers, she actually knew Liz's by heart.

She punched in the digits and then hit the green button.

Ring. Ring.

The next obstacle? Liz picking up the call even though it was coming from a number she wouldn't recognize.

Ring. Ring.

"Pick up, Liz. Please." What message would she leave if the call went to voicemail? Lexi didn't even know this phone's number.

Ring. Ring.

"Hello?" Liz's questioning voice came through like a beam from a lighthouse in the darkest storm.

∾

TWENTY-FIVE MINUTES after leaving Lexi at Camille's place, Clint parked the scooter at Orly International outside the terminal for private charters and commuter flights.

He fired off a text to Blake.

I'm here in the car park. Where are you?

Inside.

Armed?

Nope. Couldn't figure out a way past security with this quick turnaround.

Any sign of Koslova?

His plane pulled up to the passenger jet bridge. They should be unloading any minute. I'll flush him out to you.

I'll be ready.

Clint found a position that gave him an unobstructed view of the terminal's double doors. After all that had passed since Gary's murder in Minsk, Roman Koslova would finally pay. The second the bastard walked through those doors, Clint would have him. What he would do then remained to be seen.

He wondered how someone so sweet as Lexi ever ended up with someone as evil as Roman Koslova.

What was it about her that made Clint feel so out of kilter? His training seemed to fly out the window when it came to her nascent interrogation skills. He'd told her so much more than he should have. Why? He'd never divulged even a single digit of the practice code after enduring waterboarding, electric shock, sleep deprivation and other proven techniques during his survival training at the Farm. But when he looked into Lexi's green eyes he felt powerless to hold back anything.

He'd fired off a text message to Camille about

having to leave Lexi with her. She'd sent a quick response—*No worries. Let me know when you're headed back.*

He couldn't stop thinking about Lexi. He'd never known a woman as sexy and smart as her. And her sense of loyalty exceeded anything he'd ever experienced from anyone else. He was certain that the first thing she'd ask him once he returned to Camille's would be about her friend Steve.

During his research about Lexi, Clint discovered she and Torres had met as part of the murder investigation of Matthew Hill. As a detective, Torres kept working to find the real killer, though his partner at the time was convinced they'd already found their culprit in Lexi. It was evident from the details Clint had found that Officer Sims, now a detective in his own right, remained determined to build a case against Lexi.

I'm going to prove you wrong, Sims. There's no way she's a murderer.

When three men walked out through the terminal's double doors, Clint's attention returned to the dangerous task at hand—apprehending Koslova.

Shit. None of those men are my target. Where are you, you son of a bitch?

Once in custody, Clint would make Koslova confess to everything, including Matthew Hill's murder, which would exonerate Lexi. Before her, he'd always stayed dispassionate about persons connected to missions.

What the hell is wrong with me?

But he couldn't deny that he cared about what happened to her. If he could make her life a little better, that's exactly what he would do.

As more people exited the terminal, Clint fired off a text to Blake.

Koslova?

No, and the last passenger and the crew are off the plane.

Damn it. Where is he?

Hold on. Getting a call from Max.

Clint didn't know much about the guy, except Max was Blake's main data miner. He and Doc were back at the place they'd set up as their operation central, OC for short, for this mission, the same place Blake had taken Steve and their prisoner Boris.

Clint's frustration exploded inside him like a volcano. They were so close. Had Koslova slipped through the cracks like a rat? Another text from Blake popped onto his screen.

Koslova isn't here. I'm coming out now. Tell you in person the rest of the details.

Hoping to get a message to Lexi, Clint tried to call Camille.

No answer. *Damn it.*

Surely Camille wasn't on another call.

Blake walked through the double doors and headed straight for him.

"So?" he asked, not holding back his agitation.

"Max identified four more hits in the systems on Koslova's known aliases. The airports he could be at besides here are CDG, LBG or BVA, not to mention the Gare du Nord train station."

"Damn it. And who knows what other aliases he's using," Clint said. "Koslova is being extremely cautious, even for him."

"I agree. I think we better get back to our friend Boris

and see what we can get out of him. Max is keeping an eye on him until we get back."

"Max? You're sure he's up for it?"

"I am. He may not have much field experience, but he's more than capable."

"I can't seem to reach Camille by phone or text, so I'm going to head back and check on her and Lexi."

"Don't be too concerned. You know how French spies can be after getting pulled out of the field."

"Once a spook, always a spook," Clint said. "Camille's been like a caged animal ever since her cover was blown on that last mission in Ukraine and DGSE put her on desk duty."

"Right. I'm sure Camille is on the phone with her bosses as we speak trying to get reassigned back to the Action Division."

"She was on a call when I left, so you might be right. But I won't be satisfied until I am sure Lexi is safe."

8

"Thank God, you answered, Liz." Lexi felt like her legs might buckle any second, so she leaned against the red Porsche for support.

"Lexi, I've been so worried. What did Roman's cousin tell you?"

An image of the scene back at Pavel's room burned in the back of her mind. "He's dead. And Steve's been shot."

"Oh my God. Are you okay?" Liz asked.

"I'm not hurt, but I'm far from okay. It was all a trap—Roman's trap for me. Where are you?"

"Germany. Just landed. Unfortunately all the flights to Paris were full due to a soccer championship game. I thought I could get a flight from here to you, but no luck. So, I'm going to the rental car counter now."

"How long a drive is it from Berlin to Paris?"

"GPS says about eleven hours, but you know I love a good road trip. I'm sorry I'm so far away, but I will be there."

"Knowing you're on the way makes me feel better."

Lexi told her what had happened since their last text to each other. About Stan and Boris shooting Steve and pulling her into the room. Also Clint and Blake blasting in seconds later. About what had happened at Camille's after Clint had left.

"And when I got to the patio and saw Clint's boss on Camille's screen calling me 'the package' I had no choice but to run. Clint lied to me, Liz. All of it was a lie. He and Blake must have been hired by Roman to bring me in."

"Oh Lexi, I'm so sorry you had to go through all of that on your own."

"I'm grateful you'll be here soon. So do you understand why I can't go to the police? If I show up at the US embassy with this story, it will make things worse for me on Matt's murder case."

"Do you think Clint was telling the truth about Interpol having a Red Alert on you?"

"Maybe. But he did lie about so much." Her insides tightened thinking about him.

It shouldn't hurt this much that he betrayed me, but it does.

"I can't be sure about anything," she told Liz. "I'm scared. One thing I do know for certain—Roman and his men are out there hunting for me. I don't know what to —" *Hunting?*

She pulled the phone away from her ear and stared at it.

This is Camille's phone.

"Lexi, are you still there?" Liz's panicky tone came through loud and clear.

She placed the phone back to her ear. "I'm here, but I

need to ditch this phone. Clint tossed my phone because someone could track me through it."

"He was probably lying and wanted to make sure you couldn't reach out for help."

"Maybe, but the thing about being able to track someone's movements through their phone *is* possible. I've got to get rid of this. Camille can find me using this phone's internal GPS. Wait. GPS?" She stepped away from Camille's car. "This Porsche. I bet Camille can find me through its navigation system somehow."

"Listen to me, Lexi. I'm going to send a car to take you to *Le Doux Hôtel*. Tell me the address you're at."

"I don't know where I am. I think south of the city center."

"That's too far to walk."

"I've got to get off this phone and away from this car, but I'll find that hotel."

"It's close to where you and Steve were staying." Liz rattled off the hotel's address. "The manager is great. Monsieur Fournier. He's helped me many times when I've stayed there. I'll make sure he has a phone for you."

"Thank you, Liz. I'll get there as fast as I can."

"In the meantime, I'm going to make some calls to get you some help and figure all of this out."

"I love you, Liz, but I have to go."

"I love you, too. Please be careful."

"I will." Lexi clicked off the phone and tossed it as hard as she could, sending it sliding underneath another car.

Grabbing her purse and the suitcase full of weapons, she hurried to the stairs.

When she came out on the ground floor, the attendant waved at her. "Did you find a spot on the third level for that dream car of yours?"

Lexi faked another smile. "Yes. Thank you."

She considered asking him for directions to the hotel, but decided against it. She didn't want to leave any trace of where she was going.

She walked out of the garage and onto the busy sidewalk, fearing that from any direction some criminal might attack her.

It dawned on her that she could be spotted. Wanting to change her look, Lexi ducked into a small clothing shop.

The clerk acknowledged her with a slight nod.

Rushing through the racks, she grabbed a jacket, a T-shirt, a pair of jeans, a floppy hat, running shoes and sunglasses.

"*Bonjour,*" she said to the clerk. "Do you speak English?"

"*Oui, madame,*" the woman answered, smiling when she spotted the designer suitcase. "Yes. How may I help you?"

"Where may I try these on?"

"The fitting rooms are in the rear of the store, through that doorway."

"Thank you." Lexi rushed to the back.

Through the doorway was a long hallway, with racks of clothes and three dressing rooms with blue curtains for privacy.

She went to the farthest one from the doorway. Inside was a typical bench and full-length mirror. She slipped out of her clothes and into the new ones.

After scanning her reflection in the mirror, she

twisted her hair up into the hat and put on the sunglasses.

Satisfied with the change, she opened the suitcase and selected one of the pistols. Thankful for all the time she'd spent with Steve at the gun range increasing her knowledge about weapons, Lexi loaded the magazine into the gun and shoved it into her purse.

She placed the clothes she'd taken off on top of the other weapons and closed the suitcase.

As she started to come out to pay, she heard the bell of the entrance chime.

She heard a male voice saying something in French. She understood enough to know he was asking about her.

She felt trapped. *How am I going to get out of here?*

Tossing a few bills from the bottom of her purse onto the bench and ditching the suitcase, she twitched aside the dressing room curtain and ran down the hallway opposite the doorway.

Please let there be a way out. Please. Please. Please.

At the end of the hallway, she saw a door. Hoping it was the exit she so desperately needed, she wrenched the handle.

The door didn't budge.

She pulled harder.

Still nothing.

As the clerk and unknown man's voices seemed to be getting closer, Lexi tugged again and again on the door, but it didn't give.

She turned and saw the clerk and another man enter the hallway.

Oh my God, he was one of the men who followed Clint and me to the bakery.

With every ounce left inside her, she planted her foot on the door's frame and yanked as hard as she could.

The door opened.

ONCE AGAIN, Camille listened to the audio of Lexi's call to her friend Liz.

The burner phone's spyware had recorded the entire conversation and transmitted it to her laptop.

"I'M GOING to send a car to take you to Le Doux Hôtel. Tell me the address you're at."

"I don't know where I am. I think south of the city center."

"That's too far to walk."

"I've got to get off this phone though and away from Camille's car, but I'll find that hotel."

WHEN HANS CALLED EARLIER after finding her Porsche, he'd informed Camille that Lexi was long gone.

Camille cursed her bad luck. She'd ordered him to continue searching the area while she sent Carl to intercept the bitch at the hotel in case she made it that far.

The last thing Camille wanted to do was tell her lover she'd lost the package. If her men could find, capture and return Lexi, he would never have to know about the screw up.

Anxious to get an update, Camille called Hans.

"I see her, ma'am," he answered, out of breath. "I'm gaining on her."

"What happened?"

"She's ahead of me. Ran out the back of a shop. But I'll get her. She's fast, but I'm faster."

Camille closed her eyes and let out a long sigh of relief.

"Damn it," Hans voiced loudly.

Camille opened her eyes. "What's happening?"

"She got into a taxi. I lost her. I'll follow in another taxi."

"No. Let her go. She can think she's gotten away. We know where she's going, and Carl can intercept her there."

"Yes, ma'am. I'll give her a few minutes before getting a taxi to join him at the hotel."

"Perfect. Contact me when you have her." Camille clicked off the phone, as a video call from her lover popped up on her laptop's screen.

"I understand we have a problem," Drake said.

How does he know?

"I'm on it, baby," she said. "I'll have the package back and ready for delivery within the hour."

He frowned. "What do you mean? Where is Lexi Bly?"

Damn it. He didn't know.

"Gone, but not for long." Camille decided it was best to tell him everything, even though that terrified her. "So you see, I should be getting confirmation from Carl that he has her very soon."

"You better. There's a lot riding on this. I don't want any problems. I want the job done quick and clean. Roman gets what he wants and I get what I want."

"You will. I promise. I'll meet them at the hotel and make sure she doesn't escape again."

"No. Stay put. One of my men spotted Clint Richards and my brother at the airport."

Oh, that must be the problem he was talking about.

"He got close enough to pick up their conversation. Clint is on his way to you, and Blake is heading to beat the truth out of one of my men who he has in custody. I'll handle my twin brother, and you take care of Clint. I want to know everything he knows."

"I understand. Interrogate, then eliminate."

"Exactly."

In the corner of her screen the feed from her front door camera popped up, revealing Clint's arrival. "He's already here."

"Excellent. I trust you to take care of the situation."

"I love you, Drake."

"Of course you do." He grinned and then her screen went dark.

9

The second the door opened, Clint demanded, "Where is Lexi?"

Camille shook her head. "She's gone."

"What do you mean she's gone?"

"She stole my car and left," Camille said in a sugary-sweet tone. "I don't even know why. I came out after my call to HQ and she was gone."

"Don't give me that bullshit, Camille."

He'd sensed something was off with her earlier. He should have taken Lexi with him. Rage and guilt burned his insides raw.

He grabbed hold of Camille's wrists. "Something had to have happened."

She jerked free of his hold and stepped back. "Yes, something happened. You wanted my help but then left, leaving your mess for me."

Clint now knew he'd made a huge mistake bringing Lexi here. "I sent you a text message, which you responded to without any concern."

She shrugged. "I was still on my call. If I'd known she was going to bolt I would have told you."

He didn't believe a word coming out of her mouth. What had happened to the Camille he'd once known— the Camille who had saved him from more than one difficult scrape. He looked into her eyes, realizing *that Camille* was gone.

As much as Clint hated what he saw in his old friend, all he could think about was Lexi. She was in more danger than before because of him. "Lexi doesn't know anyone in Paris. Why would she leave?"

Camille stiffened. "I don't know why she would do anything. You're the one who brought her to my house. Why don't you tell me?"

"You're lying, Camille. Where is she?"

"Fuck off, Clint. She ran and stole my Porsche."

Something about how Camille exploded let him know at least that part of her story was true.

He pushed his way past the door to see if he could find some clue why Lexi had left.

"Is there more to her Roman Koslova connection than you told me earlier?" Camille asked once again in a sugary-sweet tone while following him down the hallway.

"That's none of your business," he said, examining every room.

Camille remained a few steps back from him during the entire inspection.

The passports and cash on her bed supported his doubts. "What's with this shit?"

She grinned. "HQ is putting me back into the field. The call I took was about a new mission."

"Really?"

"Yes, really."

Every word from her seemed like bullshit to him.

"If I find out you have done something to Lexi you'll live to regret it. And trust me, I will find out the truth."

"*Mon chéri*, you know me better than that."

"Shut up, Camille. I have no time for your games."

He hurried into the garage and found it empty. Was his gut wrong about Camille? She would never let anyone take her beloved Porsche, even for a mission.

"How long ago did you notice she was missing?" he asked.

"Oh, maybe fifteen minutes ago or twenty. The conference call briefing on the mission took much longer than expected." Camille smiled through her lies. "Clint, come and sit down, and I'll call HQ for some help. I'm sure they can find her. In the mean time, let's have a drink. We both could use one, don't you agree?"

"You have a drink. I'm going to check your computer. Where is it?"

"Calm down. She means more to you than I think you realize."

He grabbed hold of her wrists again. "Your computer. Now."

Defiant, Camille asked, "Why do you want my computer?"

"Show me where it is."

"Fine." She tilted her head, motioning down the hall to a single glass door. "It's on the patio table in the garden."

Clint released her, heading to the door.

"I'm still going to pour us drinks," she said, ducking into the kitchen.

He walked out onto the patio.

Camille's laptop sat on the table in the middle of the garden. The screen was blank.

Remaining on his feet, he hit the return key and the prompt for a password came up.

He turned to yell for the password, but instead found Camille standing behind him with a gun pointed at his head.

"I'm sorry, my love. This woman has a spell over you and we can't have that. You know how jealous I—"

Without hesitation, Clint charged Camille.

She fired the gun, hitting the laptop and shattering it's screen.

Camille fell to the ground, hitting her head on a stone figurine of a gnome. Blood spilled from the gash at the back of her head.

In a flash, Clint took off his leather jacket and pulled his gray T-shirt over his head.

Leaning down to Camille, he wadded up his shirt and pressed it on her wound. "Camille, what happened to Lexi?"

No answer. She was unconscious.

All the history he shared with Camille seemed insignificant compared to his primal need to find Lexi.

Wanting to secure Camille in case she came to, he retrieved a couple of zip ties from a pocket in his jacket, placing one set on her wrists and the other on her ankles.

Once she stopped bleeding, Clint turned his attention back to her damaged laptop.

Camille had made it quite clear how much she didn't want him to see whatever was on it.

He brought out his phone and called the one guy who

might be able to hack into the laptop despite its current condition.

"Max, I need your help and fast."

Clint got the tech genius up to speed. "Can you help me?"

"I'll try," Max said. "You sure its screen is thrashed?"

"Yes."

"What about the keyboard? You see any light? A power button? Anything?"

"Yes. There's a tiny blue light on the upper right."

"That's good. It's working. What I want you to do is put your phone on speaker and place it next to the keyboard."

"Done," he told him.

"Great. Now type in what I say exactly."

"I understand," he placed his hands on the keyboard. "Go."

Max walked him through several minutes of mysterious steps to hack into Camille's laptop.

"Clint, I'm in. Looking at the video feed now."

"Tell me what you see that can help me find Lexi."

"Camille was telling you the truth about Lexi. Her security feeds show Lexi taking her Porsche. Wait. Camille followed her on foot into the street with a gun. Shit. Camille took shots at Lexi."

Every cell inside Clint tightened.

"Camille's cameras show me that Lexi went left before disappearing from the feed. From how Camille is acting in the video it's clear to me she got away."

Thankful beyond words, Clint pressed on. "Give me something I can work with, Max."

"Looking. Huh? Wait a sec."

Clint's patience was gone as the time kept ticking by. "Well, what do you see?"

"There's an audio file that uploaded to Camille's laptop. Not sure if the laptop's speaker survived, but let's see if you can hear it."

When Lexi's voice came through, Clint leaned in close to hear every syllable.

"Lexi, I've been so worried. What did Roman's cousin tell you?"

"He's dead. And Steve's been shot."

As Lexi laid out all that had happened to her, Clint's focus sharpened when she described what went down after he'd left.

"And when I got to the patio and saw Clint's boss on Camille's screen calling me 'the package' I had no choice but to run. Clint lied to me, Liz. All of it was a lie. He and Blake must have been hired by Roman to bring me in."

Fury detonated inside Clint.

Blake lied!

"Oh shit," Max's voice came through his phone, as he stopped the audio playback.

"Max, was that intel about Koslova's alias being used in Paris true? Or was Blake floating false info just to get me away from Lexi?"

"Not false," Max answered. "I'm the one who discovered the aliases were active here, not Blake. I'm certain that Koslova is in Paris. "

"But based on what Lexi saw, Blake has been lying to me."

"If true, he's been lying to all of us," Max said. "But I can't believe that. I've been working for him for two years. He's always been honest."

"That doesn't explain what Lexi saw," Clint snapped back. "Where is he now?"

"I don't know. He hasn't come back from Orly yet?"

"He had plenty of time to get back to OC to interrogate Boris. He's playing us, Max."

"We can't be sure about that yet. " The doubt in Max's tone was impossible to miss. "Shall I play the rest of the audio?"

"Yes. All of it."

Lexi thinks I'm a liar, but who could blame her? I left her with Camille and now she's in grave danger.

If Blake had anything to do with this and something happened to her, Clint would kill him.

"LISTEN TO ME, *Lexi. I'm going to send a car to take you to Le Doux Hôtel. Tell me the address you're at.*"

"*I don't know where I am. I think south of the city center.*"

"*That's too far to walk.*"

"*I've got to get off this phone though and away from this car, but I'll find that hotel.*"

"SMART WOMAN," Max said. "Looks like she's on foot."

"Text me that hotel's address," Clint grabbed his leather jacket, putting it on as he ran out the door. "And send Doc and the medical team for Camille. I want her alive so we can interrogate her."

"Done and done."

"And none of this gets to Blake, Max."

"Agreed, but I have to believe there's a simple explanation."

"We'll see," he said, racing through the streets to get to Lexi—*before anyone else did.* "Max, I'm at least an hour away from that hotel. Since you're much closer, I need you to go there and find her for me."

"Clint, I'm an analyst, not a field operative."

"Doesn't matter. Lexi needs us both."

"When you put it that way, what other choice do I have."

"Good man. The second you get to the hotel—"

"I'm to contact you. I know and I will. And I will also have Ahmed and Geoff tap into the hotel's feeds."

Clint drove like a madman, fighting the dark dread trying to devour him whole.

NOT WANTING to wait for change, Lexi handed the driver a one hundred euro bill and jumped out of the taxi, looking in every direction for the thug she'd seen at the clothing store. Thankfully, there was no sign of him.

Did I actually get away?

As she walked to *Le Doux Hôtel's* entrance, someone came up behind her pressing the barrel of a gun into her back.

"Hello, Ms. Bly," the guy said in a thick German accent. "Don't turn around."

I guess I didn't get away.

"I'll do whatever you say, but at least, tell me your name," she said, trying to appear calm.

He laughed. "Since I know you won't be talking once you're delivered to Mr. Koslova, telling you my name shouldn't be a problem at all. My name is Carl. My friend Hans saw you at the clothing store and now I'm here."

So he's the other guy who followed Clint and me to the bakery earlier.

"Let's take a little ride," Carl said. "My car is the silver BMW across the street. Now move."

"Carl, there's almost ten thousand dollars in my purse. Let me go and I'll give you all of it."

"Nice offer, but you're worth a lot more than ten thousand. Besides, I have my orders and I'll still take that money."

"Orders from whom?" she asked, hoping to keep him talking until she figured a way to get to the gun in her purse without his knowledge.

"I'm to take you back to Camille."

Lexi's stomach tightened into a knot as she Camille firing a gun at her through the Porsche's rearview mirror. "I can get you more money."

"Enough. Let's move." Carl jabbed her back with his gun.

She took a step into the street, fearing for her life.

"You're a hard one to track down, Ms. Bly. Hans and I told Camille—"

"You're working for Camille. What about Blake? And Clint?"

Before Carl could answer, a man in a suit and tie plowed into him, landing Carl head first onto the concrete with a loud thud.

"Asshole," Carl growled in pain, as he tried to break free from the man in the suit.

As the commotion between the two continued on the ground, Lexi pulled out the gun from her purse. Not able to get a clear shot, she watched as her rescuer held a cloth to Carl's lips.

When Carl's pupils dilated and then his eyes closed, Lexi realized the man in the suit had drugged her attacker.

The man stood, dusted himself off, and then positioned Carl next to his parked BMW. "This is the best I can do to reduce the chance of pedestrians seeing him. Thankfully, there aren't any too close at the moment, which increases our odds for a clean escape."

Taking off the sunglasses she'd gotten at the clothing store earlier, Lexi aimed the gun at him. "Who the hell are you?"

"Please don't shoot me." He lifted both hands into the air.

He was a nice-looking guy with brown hair, trimmed beard, Roman nose, and dark eyes. He wore a stylish black suit and matching tie with a crisp white shirt. He had a swimmer's build and an honest face.

Still holding his hands up, he said, "I'm here to help, Ms. Bly, but might I suggest you conceal that gun before we attract any undue attention. My family is from Montana, so I'm no stranger to guns. But here in Paris guns are very unusual." He motioned to the people heading their way from across the street.

She knew he was right. "Lower your hands, but one wrong move and—"

"I won't. I promise."

Never letting go of the trigger, Lexi placed her hand holding the gun into her purse to keep it out of view from any unwanted onlookers.

"You know my name, like this guy." With a tilt of her head, she motioned to Carl's inert form. "Who are you and who do you work for?"

"My name is Max. Actually its Maximilian though everyone calls me Max. Maximilian Charlemagne Edward Henry Henderson. I know. It's way too long. My dad is a history professor, hence all the names of notable monarchs. Maximilian is for Maximilian the First, Holy Roman Emperor from 1493 to..."

Despite the terrible situation she found herself in, Lexi had to fight back a grin as he continued on with his encyclopedic explanation of how he'd been named. Max had an innocence she liked. And he was smart. *Really smart.* In other circumstances she could imagine being Max's friend.

"My name Charlemagne comes from the—"

"Enough about your name," she said. "Who do you work for?"

"Clint sent me."

She inhaled a deep breath to steady herself. "All the more reason not to trust you."

"I can understand why you feel that way, but t here are facts about Clint you are missing." He rattled off a list of things that had happened at Camille's house after she'd escaped.

"You remind me of myself when I'm nervous."

"You're holding a gun on me, so I believe I have a right to be nervous."

"Yes, you do. I'm a good shot," she said trying to sound tougher than she felt. "So how does Clint feel about Blake now?"

"We aren't sure about his allegiance because of what you saw. When we listened to your call to Liz, Clint knew you were in danger and sent me."

She wanted to believe Max, especially the part about Clint's concern for her safety, but remembering Camille calling her *the package* she couldn't. It seemed like every unsavory person in Paris wanted to deliver her to Roman. She wasn't letting that happen.

"Tell Clint to leave me alone. I can take care of myself." Without another word, she turned and rushed to the hotel's entrance to find the manager Liz had told her about.

Max came up to her side, matching her step for step. "Good idea. Get off the street."

With her hand still on the gun in her purse, she said," Max, I've got this."

"I'm sure you do, but in this case you might need my backup." He chuckled. "Did you see what I did to that guy back there? Maybe I am ready for field work, though I much prefer my laptop to guns."

The grin she'd been holding back broke through her steely resolve. "You mean you're not a spy like Clint?"

"Yes and no," he said, as they walked into the hotel's lobby. "I was an analyst with the Agency a couple of years back. A damn good one, if I do say so myself."

The more she learned about Max, the more questions she had for him. Those questions would have to wait.

Right now, she needed to follow through on the plan Liz had set in motion for her.

"May I please speak to the manager?" she asked the young woman behind the counter.

"Is there a problem, *madame*?"

"No problem. Please tell him that Liz Everton's friend is here."

"Of course."

When the woman exited through a door behind her, she turned to Max. "The guy on the street? Did that drug kill him?"

"Oh no. He'll be asleep for a couple of hours and then he'll wake up with a killer headache."

"Serves him right." Lexi wanted to believe Max was one of the good guys, but how could she? He worked with Clint. And Clint had left her with Camille.

When the door opened behind the counter, the woman returned with an older man.

"Ms. Bly, this is for you," he said in a French accent, sliding a phone across the counter to her. Then he glanced warily at Max. "And this is?"

"He's okay."

Why had she answered that way? Because she remembered how Max had saved her from Camille's thug outside. And because she still had hold of the gun in her purse.

"Very good," the manager said. "This is a prepaid mobile. Untraceable. So you don't have to worry about unwanted tracking."

"Thank you so much." Lexi grabbed the phone with her free hand. "Is there someplace private I could make a call?"

"Your suite is on the third floor," the manager answered, placing a key in front of her. "Ms. Everton booked it for you. Suite 303. The lift is to your right. Let us know if you need anything, Ms. Bly. Anything at all. Ms. Everton gave clear instructions to provide for your every request."

"I'm sure she did. Thank you again." Letting go of the gun, she placed the key and the phone in her purse. Then she walked to the elevator with Max still beside her. "I told you. I've got this."

"I know." He punched the elevator call button. "But I'm staying with you until Clint arrives."

Clint is coming. Her stomach did a flip-flop. What would she do when he showed up at her door? What would she say? A part of her was excited to see him again. Another part wanted to punch him for leaving her at Camille's.

And besides, how can I trust him?

She and Max rode the elevator to her floor and then walked to Room 303.

"You're not going in with me, Max." Since the hallway was empty, she brought out the gun to make her point crystal clear to him.

His hands shot up again. "That's okay. I'll stay out here and guard your door until Clint arrives."

"Call him. Tell him not to come. I'm fine." She unlocked the door and went inside, slamming it behind her and twisting the deadbolt into the locked position.

Breathing a sigh of relief, she flipped on the light.

Larger than her apartment in Dallas, the suite was gorgeous. Its twelve-foot ceilings, exotic artwork and high-end touches were meant for the rich and famous who expected the very best. To her right was a dining table with eight chairs. Off to the left was a large sectional sofa, wet bar and massive flat-screen TV. Straight ahead, a comfy king-sized bed seemed to invite her to collapse.

She was exhausted, but she wasn't here to rest or enjoy a vacation.

She took off the floppy hat she'd been wearing, allowing her hair to cascade down her back. Sitting on the sectional, she called Liz with the prepaid phone.

"I'm at the hotel, Liz. I'm safe."

"Thank God," Liz said. "I was so worried."

"Me, too. How much longer will you be?"

"GPS says just under ten hours from now, I'm afraid. You locked the door?"

"Yes. I'm safe." Lexi filled her in on what had happened after she'd left the parking garage. "I believe Max is telling the truth. Maybe I was wrong about Clint."

"It doesn't matter. I'm working on a plan to get you out of there and back home, but there is a problem."

"What problem?"

"Clint told you the truth. There *is* a Red Alert from Interpol out on you," Liz said. "And French authorities have also issued a warrant for you, so we'll have to jump through some hoops to get you back to the US."

Clint wasn't lying about that. "What about Steve? Did you find out anything?"

"There's no record of any victim of a gunshot wound being admitted in the last twenty-four hours to any hospitals in Paris."

"Where could Blake have taken him?" She recalled the image Blake had sent of Steve in a hospital bed. "We need to find him, Liz."

"We will, but my main concern right now is your safety. I want you to stay put at the hotel while I reach out to a friend of my parents."

"Who is he?"

"Not a he. Do you remember me talking about my mom's best friend Fran?"

"Of course. Isn't she the one who helps refugees in Europe?"

"That's right. I haven't seen her since I was twelve at mom's funeral, but she's stayed in touch through letters, emails and phone calls. I believe she can help get you transportation out of France."

"Where to? I can't show up back in Dallas without Steve. That will make things worse for me with Detective Sims."

"I know. Stay put. I'll meet you at the hotel. With Fran's help we can figure out the next steps."

Exhausted, Lexi said, "One step at a time is the best I can hope for at this moment."

"It's going to get better. I promise."

"I hope so. Please keep trying to find Steve."

"I will. You rest."

After ending the call with Liz, Lexi walked to the bed, stretched out on the mattress, placed the gun on the pillow next to her and then closed her eyes.

She was about to drift off when a couple of loud bangs from the hallway jolted her awake.

Grabbing the gun, she leapt off the bed and went to the door.

"Where is she, *dummkopf*?" The male voice had a German accent but sounded different than Camille's other man Carl to her.

She realized the voice had to come from the other guy who also worked for Camille, who Carl had called *Hans*. She had last seen his enraged face from the rear window of a taxi after the chase through the clothing store.

"She's long gone, asshole," Max yelled. "You're too late."

Another crash echoed in her ears followed by an awful groan.

"You will tell me where she is or you will die."

"Fuck you," Max shot back.

He wasn't giving her over to the creep, which proved Max was one of the good guys. Lexi couldn't remain on the other side of the door listening to Max being murdered.

"Too bad. Your funeral," Hans said.

Lexi jerked the door open and found him standing with his back to her pointing a gun at Max, who was on the floor bleeding from their battle.

Hans turned around, looked at the gun she held, and laughed. "You won't shoot me, Ms. Bly. You're not a killer."

As Hans held out his hand for the gun, Max's swollen eyes locked with hers. He was silently informing her that he was about to do something drastic and for her to be ready.

"Hand over the gun to me," Hans said in a forceful tone.

Max closed his eyes and bit the guy's ankle.

Hans screamed from the pain and jerked back around to face Max. "You're dead for sure, you motherfucker."

Lexi hit Hans at the back of the head as hard as she could with the butt of the gun.

He crumpled over, dropping to the floor next to Max.

"Nice one," Max choked out, as the double doors to the elevator dinged.

Lexi swung around, aiming her gun for the next attacker, but instead saw Clint running towards her.

10

"Seems like you two have been busy without me," Clint told Lexi, who was aiming a gun at his head.

"And yet we still managed to keep our clothes on. What the hell happened to your shirt?" she shot back at him. "If you're trying to be sexy, it's not going to work."

"I'm not trying to be sexy. I don't have to try."

Max laughed, but Lexi didn't move a muscle.

"Are you going to shoot me or would you like my help?"

"Help with what?" she shot back, lowering the weapon. "Seems to me that you're to blame for this guy coming for me, as well as his friend who Max knocked out on the street. They both work for your *girlfriend*, Camille."

Clint couldn't miss the sarcasm in her voice. *Is she jealous?*

"She's not my girlfriend, Lexi," he said, hoping to soften her up. "Camille is a colleague. Or was a colleague before today. I didn't know she'd flipped on me."

"Didn't know?" Lexi sharpened her tone. "Or were you too dumb to realize what was right in front of your face?"

"You're right."

Lexi's eyes widened at his admission.

So he continued, "I was too focused on capturing Koslova. I shouldn't have left you with Camille. I won't be making that mistake again."

"You better not." She pointed the gun at him once again as an obvious threat.

There's more to her than I realized.

She lowered the gun and then bent down to Max, who was on the floor. "Are you okay?"

"Ashamed that Camille's guy got the drop on me." Max's eyes were swollen, his nose was bleeding, and there was a deep gash on his forehead. He turned to Clint. "I guess I'm not ready for the field. Maybe I'll never be ready."

"Not sure I agree with you on that," Clint said. "You kept Lexi safe."

"He was terrific." Lexi put her shoulder under Max's arm, helping him to his feet.

"Let me do that," Clint told her.

"I'm more than capable."

He ignored her, and got on the other side of Max to give more support.

She rolled her eyes, but her tone softened when she addressed Max. "You saved my life for the second time today. I can't thank you enough."

"I think you had the biggest part in saving yourself." Max let out a slight chuckle, which was followed by a low groan. "And me. I was done for before you intervened."

"Slow down, soldier," Lexi said.

The prickliness she had for him didn't apply to Max.

Did she already forget that I saved her life, too? Come on, Clint. What is this? A contest? Damn, this woman is getting under my skin.

"You might have some broken ribs, buddy," Clint said.

"Let me help you into the room." Lexi opened the door a little wider. "You need some medical attention."

Max shook his head. "Lexi, there can't be any—"

"I know. I know. No doctors. Clint and I will do our best to get you fixed up. Right, Clint?"

"Of course."

"Damn right," she stated flatly. "It's the least I can do for my personal knight. You were so brave."

Clint was shocked at Lexi calling Max her *personal knight*. Was she falling for the guy? Of course he was glad Max had made it in time to keep her safe. But with every syllable she uttered about Max a singular emotion began to multiply inside him. *Jealousy?*

He and Lexi led Max to the bed.

"Lie down," she said.

After Max was stretched out, Clint turned to her. "I'll go get Camille's goon before someone spots him."

"Please don't kill the guy."

"The thought did enter my mind," he admitted, knowing the unconscious thug had meant to harm her.

"There's been enough damage done today," she said.

Clint was impressed at how merciful Lexi could be considering that this creep had tried to kidnap her.

She was unlike any person he'd ever known. His absolute darkness was no match for Lexi's pure light. For every pessimistic inclination inside him, he witnessed careful optimism from her. God, she was smart. And beautiful. Everything about her amazed him.

What the hell is the matter with me? She's part of a mission. That's all.

Once he had Camille's man inside the room, he placed zip ties on him.

Clint slipped the "Do Not Disturb" sign on the outside handle before locking the door.

Lexi opened the fridge next to the wet bar. "Good. There's an icemaker with plenty of ice. Clint, would you wet some cloths for me?"

Noticing her tone was beginning to soften with him, he gave her a nod and headed to the sink. As he turned on the faucet to soak the cloths, he heard her talking to Max.

"You may have suffered a concussion."

"I'm sure I'll be fine," Max answered.

"Stop trying to be Mr. Tough Guy," she said. "You saved me. For that I will be forever grateful and in your debt. Now lean back and let me get a good look at your injuries."

As he exited the bathroom with the wet cloths, Lexi said, "Clint, I remember what you did for Steve. You've had some medical training, correct?"

"Some. Yes. Here you go." When their hands touched as he offered her the cloths, they both locked eyes for a moment.

Lexi looked flushed, but took the cloths, turning her attention back to Max. "Clint, take a look at that gash on his forehead."

Max started to sit up. "Ouch."

"Lean back on the pillow," she ordered him.

Max nodded, and then looked at Clint. "We need to find Blake first and make him explain what he and Camille were up to."

"I agree."

"I don't care if you agree or not," she stated flatly. "Making sure Max is okay is *my* first priority."

"And mine, too. Let me have a look." Clint did a quick assessment of Max's injuries. "She's right, Max. You need professional attention."

"Why don't we take him to the same place Blake took Steve?" she suggested.

"Absolutely. The OC would be perfect."

"OC?"

"Our operations central. Doc is incredible, and should be back by the time we arrive. And I'm sure you would like to check in on Steve."

"Oh my God, yes. I have to see him. Not knowing where Steve's been is driving me crazy. Plus, it gets us out of here and away from everyone looking for me." She pointed at Camille's thug. "But what about Hans and his buddy Carl, who's still on the street?"

"Are you asking me to eliminate them?" he said with a grin, already knowing what her answer would be.

"Don't be ridiculous."

"We'll leave them. They don't know anything that can help your ex-boyfriend find you."

"Please don't refer to Roman as my *ex-boyfriend*. I feel stupid that I was so blind."

Understanding her pain, Clint looked her in the eyes. "Koslova is a professional. He's fooled some of the best. You shouldn't feel stupid."

She smiled, which unhinged him. "I did break up with him. Or tried."

"What do you mean?"

"Roman said he would never let go of me. Ever. His exact words were *'You're mine. Always.'* Back then I didn't know the extent of what he meant by that, but now I do. Look at all the damage that has happened. Steve took a bullet for me. Max was beaten severely." She closed her eyes tight and trembled. "I can't do this by myself."

Clint surrendered to the urge to comfort Lexi and put his arm around her.

He was glad she didn't pull away as he'd suspected she might. Instead she relaxed in his arms, leaning her head into his chest.

Squeezing her softly, he said, "Don't worry, Lexi. I've got this."

WHEN LEXI HEARD MAX GROAN, she opened her eyes and pulled away from Clint. "We've got to get him to the doctor, but what are we going to do with Hans?"

"He's not going anywhere, Lexi," Clint said. "Once we get away I'll call the police and say he broke into your hotel room. That should keep him out of our hair for awhile."

Anxious to get to Steve without being followed, she asked Max, "What about the guy you drugged on the street?"

"He'll be out for another hour," he answered. "We don't have to worry about him either. The police will likely discover him, if they haven't already."

"Come on, buddy." Clint helped Max off the bed.

Seeing how kind Clint was with Max and how he'd tried to comfort her, Lexi was beginning to wonder if she'd been wrong about him.

Could he be a good guy after all?

"Let me give you a hand." Lexi came to the other side of their patient.

Together, she and Clint guided Max out of the room.

"Not the elevator," Max whispered. "I'll attract too much attention in the lobby."

"You can't make the stairs in your condition," Clint said.

"Maybe there's a service elevator." Lexi glanced up and down the hallway, and saw the main elevator and the door to the stairs. "Damn, we have two options."

"Listen to me. Take the stairs," Max said. "With both of you helping, I can make it and we don't want to cause a scene."

"You got it, tough guy," Clint said.

Max winced and breathed unevenly on the trip down the stairs, but he never complained.

They exited out the back of the hotel.

"Stay here with Max," Clint told her. "I'll get us some transportation."

"My car is out front," Max told him.

"Yeah, next to the guy you drugged on the street. We'll come back for your car. You said it yourself. We need to be discreet and not attract attention."

"Stealing a car is going to bring a lot of attention." Max grinned.

"How about a taxi?" Lexi asked.

Clint shook his head. "That still puts us on the main street. Leave it to me."

She watched him run around the side of the building. When Clint was out of view, she let out a breath. "That man is so... so..."

"Skilled," Max said. "You can trust him, Lexi."

"Hardly, but at the moment I...we don't have any other choice."

She wanted to trust Clint. Wanted it with all her heart. But after her horrible history with Roman, that was impossible with any man—even a man like Clint.

Max groaned. "Damn, breathing is hard."

"Lean against me and the wall," she told him, pressing the damp cloth she'd kept from the room to his forehead.

"Thanks. I'm more shaky than I realized."

The photo of Steve in the hospital bed floated to the front of her mind.

"We'll get you to the OC's medical team and get you checked out. I'm sure you'll be okay."

"And you'll get to see your friend."

"That, too."

"Lexi, talk to me. Maybe that will help me not think about the pain."

"Okay. Umm. Let's see. How old are you? Do you have a girlfriend? Where do you live?"

"Slow down. I'm twenty-seven. Last girlfriend was two years ago. We didn't click. What was the other question?"

Where the hell is Clint with our transportation?

"Where are you from?"

"California. Canoga Park. What about you? Boyfriend?"

She grinned. "Are you hitting on me?"

"I wouldn't do that knowing Clint is interested in you."

"What? No. That can't be true.

"Yes. It's obvious to me at least. Do you know why Koslova is so obsessed with you?"

That was a question she'd tried to answer ever since the breakup. "Not really. Roman is a narcissistic, obsessive asshole, and those are his good qualities. I realized early on with him—"

Before she could finish her answer, Clint pulled up in a white van.

Clint jumped out of the driver's seat. "Let's get him inside."

Together, they ushered Max into the back of the vehicle.

The van had stacks of white laundry bags, which Lexi used to make her patient more comfortable.

"Clint, I'll stay back here with Max."

"Perfect. I'll get us to the OC as fast as I can." Clint shut the back doors, came around the van, and got back into the driver's seat. "Hold on tight."

As he sped them through Paris's streets, Lexi talked to Max. "So you're a California boy. Did you like going to the beach?"

"Yeah. Santa Monica State Beach was where my family loved to go."

"Tell me about your family. You have any brothers or sisters?"

"A brother and a sister. Nick is a year older than me. Abby is a year younger than me." He groaned as the van hit a bump.

"We're almost there," Clint yelled to her from the front.

"What about your parents, Max? Are they still in Canoga Park?"

"Dad died of cancer. Mom remarried and lives in Chicago."

The van came to a halt. A second later Clint opened the back doors.

Lexi saw that they were inside a warehouse. What shocked her were the two armed men that came up to the van.

"Max is injured and in the back," Clint told them.

Seconds later, a medical team rolled out a gurney for Max.

She and Clint followed as they wheeled him through double doors and into a large industrial space divided into three distinct areas.

To her left was a circular station that reminded her of NASA mission control with dozens of monitors and computers. Inside were two guys, who jumped up the moment they entered.

"What happened to Max?" one of them asked.

"He'll be fine, Ahmed," Clint told him. "He was great in the field."

The other looked directly at her. "Ms. Bly, you're here?"

"Yes. She's here, Geoff," the man in the doctor's white coat said. "Why don't you two get back to work on locating Koslova?"

The two of them returned to their computers, though they kept looking back at Max on the gurney.

Lexi glanced to her right and saw the man called Boris inside a cage.

"Hey, I could use a bio break," he yelled.

Everyone ignored him.

They moved straight ahead to a well-lit space that had been sealed off with thick, clear plastic. Inside the area was high-tech medical equipment.

That's when she spotted Steve just to the left. He was lying in a hospital bed hooked up to monitors.

Lexi ran to him and grabbed his hand. "Thank God, Blake didn't lie about bringing you here."

Steve's eyes were closed but he was breathing.

A woman in a nurse's uniform came up beside her and with an American accent said, "Hello, Ms. Bly. I'm Sandy. I've been taking care of your friend."

"How is he?"

"The surgery was a success. We removed the bullet and no organs were damaged. He's a very lucky guy. He'll be up and about before you know it."

"Thank you," Lexi said. "What about Blake, the man who brought my friend here? Where is he?"

"You'd have to ask Dr. Daniels about that," Sandy answered as she checked on Steve's vitals. "I don't know where Mr. Atlas is, but he might."

"How long ago was Blake here?"

"He left right after he brought in Mr. Torres."

"What time is it now?" Lexi asked.

Sandy looked at her phone. "Almost six."

What a whirlwind of a day it had been. Eight hours ago Lexi had been walking with Steve to meet with Pavel —*or so they had thought.*

She glanced at Clint as he talked to the doctor, and

then quietly reached into her purse and pulled out the burner phone.

"Not a good idea," Sandy said.

"I'd like to make a call to a friend. It's a pre-paid phone, so it can't be tracked."

"That's not quite true, Ms. Bly. Burners are anonymous, yes, but they still have internal GPS, which can be tracked with the right tech."

"The only person who knows I have the phone is someone I trust."

"You won't be able to make a call because this place has signal blocking. Calls in or out are not allowed."

"Allowed? Who are you people?"

"We are part of Mr. Atlas's team."

"I feel like Alice after she fell down the rabbit hole, but in this version all the rabbits are hired mercenaries."

Sandy touched Lexi's shoulder. "Hang in there. We're all here to protect you."

"I appreciate that." She was starting to believe they were. *But what about Blake?*

After Sandy walked away, Lexi pulled up a chair next to Steve's bed. She took a seat and held his hand.

"Steve, I'm so sorry I got you into this situation," she whispered so no one around could hear. "Roman has been two steps ahead of us. Why is he so obsessed with me? I want to trust Clint. I do. But I can't read him. What is his real motive in all of this? What do I do next?"

She squeezed Steve's hand, wishing he were awake.

GLANCING OVER AT LEXI, Clint listened to the news that

Dr. Eli Daniels, who everyone called *'Doc'* gave him about Max. Doc had once been with the Agency, too, though he'd never shared why he'd left.

"We took X-rays on his ribs, and unfortunately they revealed a couple breaks. Max will need about 6 weeks to fully mend and he'll be good as new."

"And what about Lexi's friend, Steve?"

"He went through the surgery just fine. I want to keep an eye on him for a couple of days, but he should have a full recovery, too."

"Where did you put Camille?"

"Sorry, Clint. When we got to her place, she was long gone."

"Damn it." Clint had a lot of questions for Camille. "Doc, any word from Blake?"

"No, which is unexpected. After Koslova didn't turn up at any of the airports, Blake called saying he was on his way back to interrogate our prisoner."

Clint recalled the encounter with Boris at Pavel's hotel. *Blake didn't act like a traitor then.*

Trying to make sense of it, Clint ran his hand through his hair. *None of this makes sense unless Blake is working with either Camille or Koslova, or both to kidnap Lexi.*

"Clint, do you think someone got the drop on Blake before he could get here?"

"I don't know." Unsure if he could fully trust Doc, Clint wasn't ready to tell him that Lexi had seen Blake on Camille's laptop.

"What about her?" Doc motioned toward Lexi. "You going to leave her here with us?"

"No. She stays with me." Clint wasn't about to let Lexi out of his sight again.

"Your research revealed how desperate she was to clear her name," Doc said. "But it seems there's a lot more to her story than what we read inside the dossier."

"Yep. Much more." All the intelligence he'd gathered on Lexi paled in comparison to what he'd discovered after spending time with her. "Keep me informed about Max and the detective. And if we hear anything from Blake, I want to know."

"You got it." Doc sighed. "The plan for this mission has really gone sideways. Blake is missing, and instead of following Ms. Bly to Koslova, she's here. Max is injured. What next?"

"Since Camille is still out, I'm going to start with Boris to get answers. But first, I want to check on Lexi."

As Clint took a single step Lexi's direction, he saw armed men rushing into the warehouse.

11

As six masked gunmen charged into the OC, Lexi stretched her body over an unconscious Steve, trying to protect him. She grabbed her gun from her purse, as Clint and the others fired at their attackers. To her shock, the medical staff were also armed and joined in the fray.

The noise was deafening.

Lexi saw one of the gunmen start to charge her direction.

Still covering Steve, she aimed her gun at the sprinting man. She and Clint fired their weapons simultaneously at him, and he fell to the floor.

"Stay behind me!" Clint shouted over the melee, using his body to screen her.

In horror, Lexi saw Steve's nurse, Sandy, drop to the floor.

Steve moaned. "Lexi? What are you doing? What's going on?"

"Hold on, Steve. Don't move."

Ahmed and Geoff took out two of their attackers, while Boris screamed to be released.

Then another medical staff member got shot.

And another attacker took a hit.

As the odds shifted to the medical staff's side, the remaining masked men retreated from where they'd entered.

The doctor and several of the team ran after them.

Lexi looked down and saw Steve's eyes widened in shock. "It's over now, Steve. You're okay."

His heart rate monitor, which had been beeping frantically during the chaos, slowly quieted to a steadier rhythm.

Clint turned to Lexi. "Are you okay?"

Shaken, she wrapped her arms around his shoulders. "You're always there when I need..."

Without a word, he grabbed her waist and pulled her in close.

She leaned her head into his shoulder, trying to tap into his strength. She didn't want to give into the tears welling in her eyes.

He touched her cheek and looked at her. "Lexi, it's over."

"I know, I'm just a little shaken." She looked up into his eyes.

"What's going on?" Steve asked. "Where are we?"

Lexi let go of Clint and stepped back to the bed. "We're at a medical facility. Do you remember being shot?"

"Yes. At Pavel's room. Two men. It's coming back to me now."

As Clint checked the monitors, she recounted to Steve about all that had happened since.

"Your vitals are stable, Detective," Clint told him. "You're in good shape."

"Thank God." Lexi breathed a sigh of relief. "I was so afraid a stray bullet would hit you, Steve."

"She protected you with her body." Clint came around the bed and stood next to her. "She's quite brave."

She liked hearing his praise for her, though deep down she wasn't sure it was deserved.

"She did what?" Steve looked stunned. "I'm supposed to be protecting you, young lady, not the other way around."

"I've learned that she's quite capable, Detective, and stubborn."

"Oh yes, I know," Steve said. "You should see her firing a gun. She hits the bull's-eye every time."

Lexi felt her heart skip a beat, thinking about the man she and Clint had shot.

Was it my bullet or his that delivered the deadly blow?

"Something the matter?" Clint asked. "You looked like you were far away in thought."

"I was thinking about us shooting that guy. I've never shot at a human being before, but I don't think we had a choice."

"You're right, Lexi," Clint said. "It was either you and the detective or that man."

"I know, but—"

Steve took her hand. "It sounds like you and this guy saved my life. Like I've always said, you've got the instincts of a cop. You did what had to be done."

Both Steve and Clint were making her feel better, but

the gravity of what had happened would stay with her for a very long time.

"Who were those people firing at us?" Steve asked.

"Likely some of Koslova's men," Clint answered.

"And who exactly are *you*?"

"Clint Richards, sir. I was a CIA officer."

"Was?"

"I had good reason for leaving the Agency."

Lexi turned to Steve. "One thing I've learned about him is he's not very forthcoming."

"That's how it is when you're dealing with spooks, Lexi." Steve still didn't seem convinced to trust Clint.

So Lexi added, "He's the man who saved your life at Pavel's."

Steve nodded, fixing his stare on Clint. "If she trusts you, I trust you. Besides, it seems like your main objective is to save my life, which is an excellent choice because I'm worth it."

Lexi nodded. "Damn right, you are."

Clint grinned. "I trust Lexi, and I know what you mean to her. Detective, I'll do whatever necessary to keep you and her safe."

"Okay. I like hearing that, but when I get out of this bed you can expect the same from me." Steve looked around the room, where the medical staff was tending to the fallen. "How did those masked guys find this place?"

"Who knows? Maybe someone saw me take the van and followed us here."

"Or maybe Blake is behind all of this." Lexi was angry, knowing Blake had lied about everything. "He's the one who brought Steve to this location, which would make it easy for him to send in those thugs."

"But that doesn't make sense," Steve said. "Why bring me here? Why not put a bullet in my head back at Pavel's? I was dead weight to him."

Clint put his arm protectively around Lexi shoulders. "Maybe to keep up appearances until he turned her over to Koslova."

"Maybe." Steve gingerly sat up, then swung his legs over the side of the bed. "Oh. Dizzy."

"Lie back down," she ordered. "You're in no shape to get up yet."

"You're right." Steve stretched back out on the bed.

"As soon as I can, I'm going to let Sara and Brad know what happened to you," Lexi said.

"No, young lady. It will only worry my kids, and you have more than you can say grace over already. We'll call them when this is over."

Lexi shook her head. "We don't know when that will be."

"If anyone is going to call them, it's going to be me. They don't have to know anything yet. There's nothing they can do. Plus, there's plenty of time for that later."

She grinned. "Talk about stubborn."

Steve winked at Clint, as one of the medical staff came over to check on him.

"I need to help with the injured," Clint said.

"I'm going with you." Lexi turned to Steve. "Don't you move, or you'll be sorry."

"I'll stay put."

Lexi and Clint went to help the others.

As her mind raced with dread, she bent over Sandy's body. Just moments earlier they'd been talking, and Sandy had been kind and understanding.

Now, Sandy was gone.

This is all my fault. Is there any place safe from Roman?

Clint was checking on another nurse a few feet from Lexi. "Need help over here. I've got a pulse."

Out of the corner of her eye, she saw Ahmed checking some of the others.

"This guy is breathing," he said, and two medics came over.

After examining all of the fallen, they discovered that the only fatality on their side had been Sandy.

Their side? Lexi realized she was getting entrenched with Clint and these mercenaries despite having seen Blake on Camille's screen. *More than entrenched.* Her feelings, no matter how foolish, were growing for Clint himself.

She returned to Steve's bed with Clint.

Steve looked at Clint. "You need to get Lexi out of here before those men return with reinforcements."

"No way. I'm not leaving you." She folded her arms in a show of defiance.

"You must." Steve took her hand. "It's not safe for you here."

"It's not safe for you either."

The doctor came over to them. "Don't worry, Ms. Bly. My team is already working on moving Mr. Torres and everyone else to our alternative facility."

"You have an alternative facility?"

Steve laughed. "Again, that's how spooks roll, kiddo. One second you see them, and the next they vanish without a trace. Isn't that right, Doc?"

"Part of the job. We'll be cleaned out of here in a flash."

"Well, I'm going wherever he's going," Lexi said.

"Steve is right," Clint said to her. "We need to go now before more of Koslova's goons return. You're the one he wants."

"And by staying, I'm putting everyone else in danger." She took in a deep breath. "Okay. But we're going where I say."

"You have a plan?" Clint asked.

"Yes." She brought out the burner phone. "Liz has a well-connected friend who will help you, me and Steve get out of the country."

He narrowed his eyes and his brow furrowed. "I'm not sure that's a good idea."

"What else can we do?"

"Fine. What's the friend's name?" Clint waved Geoff over. "I'll get him to run a background check on the guy."

"*Her* name is Fran. Liz didn't tell me her last name."

Geoff came with Max, who was bandaged up and looking much better than the last time she saw him.

"Max, how are you feeling?" Lexi asked. "Shouldn't you be resting?"

"I couldn't stay in bed with all this going on. I feel fine. Doc set me up with some pain killers." He turned to Clint. "What do you need from me and my team?"

Clint informed him about Liz's contact. "We need a flash background check on this Fran person."

Max nodded, pulled out an iPad from the backpack, and turned to Lexi. "Any other details from Liz you can remember about her?"

"She said Fran helped refugees find their way around Europe and sometimes used channels outside the legal system."

"Not a lot to go on, but it might be enough to get a match."

Geoff typed on the screen with Max at his side.

Lexi and Clint looked over Geoff's shoulder as screen after screen flashed by at lightning speed.

She wondered how Geoff and Max were able to take in the information so quickly, since she only got glimpses of pages with tons of data.

Geoff brought up systems of the FBI, the CIA, the Department of Defense, INTERPOL, the United Nations and more.

"How do you have access to all of these?" she asked.

"We have our ways," Max answered without looking up. "Hold on, Geoff. Back up. Yeah. Right there."

Suddenly the flashing screens stopped and settled on a single page from a French government system.

The photo was of an attractive woman, who looked to be in her fifties with auburn hair, green eyes and a warm smile. The only French words Liz could translate were *femme* and *adresse*.

"Here is Fran." Max turned and faced Lexi and Clint, holding the tablet so they could get a clear view of the screen. "Francine Binoche, age 54. Suspected of illegal transfers across Europe and Northern Africa."

"Illegal transfers?" Lexi didn't like the sound of that.

Geoff tapped the screen and another page popped up. "She works with human rights groups around the globe."

"That doesn't mean she's legit," Clint said.

"She's Liz's friend. That's good enough for me." Lexi looked over at Steve.

He was beginning to doze off again due to his meds. The staff was preparing to move him to another location.

She turned back to Clint. "I need a phone that I can call Liz from."

"Okay," Clint said, though it was clear he wasn't thrilled with the plan. "But we need to make it fast."

"It'll take less than a minute to set up an untraceable call," Max said.

Lexi followed him to the circular area with all the monitors.

Max took the burner phone from her, and typed in something onto his laptop before handing it back. "All set. Dial away."

"Hello?" Liz answered.

"It's me," Lexi said. "Change of plans here. I'm not at the hotel, but I did find Steve. He's fine."

"Thank God. I'm still six hours away. Where are you?"

"A lot has happened I need to let you know about, but it'll have to wait. First, tell me your friend Fran can help."

"Yes, she can. She's waiting for you at her house. I'll text you her address and meet you there."

"That'll be great. Liz, Clint is coming with me."

Her shocked tone followed. "Are you sure he's okay?"

"I wasn't at first, but I am now."

"Got it. I'll let Fran know to expect both you and Clint."

"I know I keep repeating this, but thanks. I love you."

"I love you. Stay safe, Lexi. See you shortly."

She hung up the phone. "Clint, I have the address. I want to let Steve know."

"Go."

She liked that Clint was all business, especially since the business was saving their lives. Being with him did make her feel protected and safe, even with all of Roman's men on the loose.

She left Clint and Max to hash out the details and went back to Steve's hospital bed. A nurse and the doctor were hurriedly preparing to transport Steve out of the warehouse.

"I need to speak to him," she told the doctor.

"Sure, but make it quick."

She grabbed Steve's hand. "Liz has a friend that will get us out of the country. As soon as I have all the details, Clint and I will come for you."

"Okay," he mumbled back. "But go and be safe, young lady."

She started to give the burner phone to Steve, but he held up his hand.

"No. You keep it. I'll find a phone. Don't worry about me." He squeezed her hand. "I'll be back on the beat before you know it."

She kissed his cheek.

As she and Clint left the warehouse, Lexi thought about all that had happened to her in Paris. Her original plan was to find Roman's location and pass it on to the authorities in the hopes her name would be cleared. Now, she prayed the new plan would work and she would find a way out of the monster's deadly web.

ONCE MORE CLINT kept Lexi close, scanning every direction for enemies as they exited the warehouse. His pulse thudded through his veins and he could feel the slight sweat on his forehead, despite the cool weather. So far, he found their path clear of attackers.

"Are you going to steal another car?" Lexi asked with a grin.

"Not necessary. Fran's address is right on one of the Metro lines. There's a stop not far from here. Since it's rush hour, Metro will be faster. Besides, it's best for us to disappear in crowds to get away from Koslova's goons."

"Looking like we're a couple enjoying Paris might help with that, too." She took hold of his hand, sending heat through his body, which surprised him.

Focus on the mission at hand, Clint.

"Spy stuff, right?" She looked into his eyes.

God, she's so cute. Despite the danger pursuing them, he couldn't help but grin. "You could say that."

"You're the expert in this kind of situation. Lead the way and I'll follow. But don't forget, we're coming back for Steve at the new location."

As they crossed the street, he couldn't get over how courageous and loyal she continued to be. "Lexi, I'll make sure Steve gets back to the US."

"Not good enough. I made a promise to Steve that *we* would come back for him. Now you promise me that's what will happen."

"I'll do my best," he answered, though a hundred scenarios rolled through his mind why he wasn't about to let her take that risk.

She was his first and sole priority. Once he got Lexi on Fran's plane and out of the country, then he would return for Steve.

Clint knew he would have a battle on his hands with

her about leaving Steve, but it was a battle he intended on winning. Her safety was all that mattered.

They found the entrance to the Metro and took the stairs down, passing Parisians he scrutinized along the way. So far he found no suspicious characters.

He led her past the ticket office windows to the green-colored, self-service machines.

After making the purchase, they walked through to the metal turnstiles, placing their tickets into the slot and retrieving them on the other end as the security bar unlocked.

Keeping a lookout the entire time, they made it to the correct platform for their train, which would arrive soon.

"So far, so good," Lexi said, still holding on tight to his hand.

"Since I tossed your personal phone and Max tricked out your burner, Koslova can't track you. So you can relax."

"Under the circumstances?" she smiled. "I'll try."

An elderly couple approached them.

Clint was certain they weren't part of Koslova's gang.

"*Pardon...uh...me...pour...vu...*," the woman read in broken French from the translator app on her phone. She looked up from the screen and said in a southern American accent, "I'm not getting this right, y'all. Do either of you speak English?"

"We both do," Lexi said before he could stop her.

The woman smiled and turned to the man. "Do you hear that, George? I told you we'd find people who could help."

"Yes, you did, Gayle. Yes, you did."

"What kind of help do you need?" Clint asked, hoping

the train would arrive so they could be free of the couple's distraction. He needed to sharpen his focus on their surroundings.

"Could you take our photo?" the woman asked, holding out her phone to Lexi. "This is our fiftieth anniversary."

"Of course we can." Lexi took the woman's phone. "Give me big smiles."

The man put his arm around his wife and they both grinned broadly.

"Perfect." Lexi clicked off several shots and then handed the phone back to the woman.

"Thank you so much, sweetie." The woman winked. "Would you like me to take a photo of you and your beau? You two are absolutely perfect together. Remember when we looked so young and in love, George?"

"I sure do, sweetheart. I sure do."

When Clint heard their train approaching, he thought they would be able to make their escape from these two well-meaning people. But he was wrong.

"I would love a photo of us," Lexi said, shocking him. "Wouldn't you, honey?"

"Uh...sure. Why not?"

She handed her phone to the woman.

"Not me. My George is the photographer in our family." Gayle passed Lexi's phone to George, just as the train pulled up and its doors opened.

"Let's get inside and I'll take the picture in the train before it leaves us," George said.

So much for our escape.

They all stepped off the platform and into the train.

George had them pose sitting, standing and with their arms around each other.

"For the final photo, give us a big kiss."

Grinning, Clint turned to Lexi, wanting to kiss her. He leaned in and whispered, "You got us into this, Ms. Spy Stuff."

She laughed, and he kissed her. The taste of her soft lips was so sweet. The kiss lingered a little longer than he thought it should have, but he couldn't bring himself to let her go.

"Beautiful," Gayle said, startling him.

Stepping apart, he and Lexi looked into each other's eyes. He could tell she enjoyed the kiss as much as he did. *What am I getting myself into?*

"Here you go," George said, passing the burner phone back to Lexi. "I didn't notice a ring on your pretty little finger. Young man, when are you going to ask her to get married?"

"George!" Gayle hit his arm.

"Well, they need to make this official."

"Oh, it's official," Lexi said, leaning into Clint. "We just haven't bought the ring yet."

Getting into the spirit of things, Clint offered, "We're thinking a June wedding would be nice."

"Remember that wonderful jewelry store we saw near our hotel," Gayle said. "We should take them there."

"Yes, darlin'. We should." George whispered to Clint. "They're a lot cheaper there than in the States."

Clint realized they were in deep with Gayle and George and needed an exit now.

Before he could respond to the man, Lexi said, "Unfortunately, this is Harold's and my last day in Paris, and we've made plans to meet up with a good friend of mine before we head to the airport."

"That's too bad, sweetheart." George handed Lexi a business card. "Look us up any time. We'd love to hear from you."

Gayle hugged Clint and Lexi. "And if you'd like to come and see us, we'd love to have you visit any time."

"Darlin', this is our stop," George said. "It was wonderful meeting y'all."

"Same here," Clint said, shaking his hand.

As Gayle and George stepped off the train and the doors closed, Lexi waved back at them through the windows. "They are adorable."

"I agree," Clint said.

Lexi looked at George's business card. "Oh my God, Clint. He's a minister and I lied to him. I'm going straight to hell for sure."

Clint laughed. "Not a chance. You might make a helluva spy, but do you really think I look like a Harold?"

She grinned and placed her hands on his chest. "As the future Mrs. Harold, I think so."

As he looked into her gorgeous eyes remembering the taste of her lips, he leaned in and kissed her until she melted into him. "That was great, *Mabel*."

She laughed and punched him in the arm. "Harold!"

12

During the entire walk to Fran's home, Lexi couldn't stop thinking about Clint's heat-inducing kisses. She'd never believed in the *butterflies-in-your-stomach* sensation before. But ever since his lips pressed to hers, a kaleidoscope of fluttering wings continued to consume her.

Staying in her spy character, she kept holding onto his hand, though deep down she knew there was more to it than that. She liked his touch and didn't want to let go —even if it was only pretend on his part.

The sun had already set and the street lamps illuminated their path. Noticing the addresses on the buildings they passed, she said, "Looks like we're almost there."

"Thank God, Mabel," Clint said in George's southern accent. "We got here without a hitch."

"Oh, Harold." She squeezed his hand.

Meeting Gayle and George had brought much needed levity and respite to what had been a horrible day. She'd enjoyed their company and longed for a time she might have their kind of relationship. But that could never be because of Roman. He was the cause of this entire nightmare. Just thinking about him made her shudder.

"Something wrong?" Clint asked.

Recalling Matthew's murder, Lexi released Clint's hand. "Just no need to keep up the spy game since we're so close to Fran's place."

She noticed the disappointed look on his face, but she had no choice. Roman had already proven he would kill anyone she had feelings for.

"Pretend time is over, Clint."

But it isn't. Not really. Despite having real feelings for him, she would have to hide them.

"I wasn't pretending, Lexi." Clint placed his hands on her shoulders. "You're unlike any woman I've ever known. Beautiful. Smart. Fun. Kind. Loyal. I want to get to know you better."

"When would we do that, Clint?" She shook her head, but didn't pull free from his hold. "I'm on the run from a murderous ex, plus I'm a suspect in a homicide. We can never be any more than we are right now."

"And what are we exactly?"

She took a step back from him. "You're on a mission. I'm just part of that. Once the mission is over we'll say our goodbyes and that will be that."

"I know you felt something when we kissed, just like I —" Clint stopped in mid-sentence, pulled out his gun, and then quietly said, "Lexi, hold on."

She nodded, as her heart lurched up to her throat.

An auburn haired woman came out from behind a hedge, mirroring Clint's aim of his gun at her with one of her own back at him. Lexi recognized her from the photo Max had shown them earlier.

"I'm Fran. I've been waiting for you and Ms. Bly." Her French accent had a lyrical quality that was easy on the ears. "I suggest we both put our weapons away, young man."

Clint hesitated for a moment, but then holstered his gun.

Fran lowered her gun at the same time and secured it in the back of her slacks. She wore a purple long-sleeved turtleneck top with a triple strand of pearls. Fran's makeup was flawless but understated. Her black slacks were tailored and her Prada heels were the same color as her top. The overall effect was regal.

"Liz told me some of what you've been through, my dear." Fran kept a watchful eye on Clint. "I suggest we get off the street."

Clint seemed to remain on guard with the woman as he moved closer to Lexi. "Where to?"

"This is my building." Fran pointed to a five-story modern structure behind her. "Come with me."

Fran turned and marched to the entrance.

As his eyes narrowed, he continued to stare at Fran's retreating back.

Lexi touched Clint's arm. "Liz has kept in touch with this woman over the years. I'm sure she's okay. Besides, she's all we have."

"No matter what happens next, keep close to me."

She nodded, and they both hurried after Fran, who was now inside the building.

They walked through the entrance and found her talking with the security guard, who was stationed behind a desk. The uniformed man looked to be in his seventies and had a thin mustache and twinkly eyes.

"*Merci beaucoup, Claude,*" Fran said to the man.

He answered, "*Je vous en prie, madame.*"

She turned their direction. "This is Claude, my dears. And Claude, these are my friends, Helen and Mike Wilkerson."

Lexi had to hold back a laugh, realizing this was the second alias she'd been given today. "Very nice to meet you, Claude."

Fran led them to the elevator and whispered. "Claude is very sweet but not much protection. Luckily, I've hacked into the building's CCTV, which will give us an advantage should any of your ex's men show up." She held out her phone with live feeds for all the entrances on her screen.

"Impressive," Clint said. "But I know we weren't followed."

"Even so, you can't be too cautious in these kinds of situations."

"Agreed." As the elevator doors opened, he said, "And you apparently have been in several situations yourself."

Fran grinned, walking into the lift. "As have you, Mr. Richards."

"True, and I have the scars to prove it."

"As do I," Fran said, as the doors closed.

Lexi got a kick out of their verbal sparring, though it seemed that they had mutual respect for each other.

"What floor is your apartment on?" Clint asked.

"I have the entire top floor of this building."

Lexi scanned the elevator's controls. "But there's no button for the top floor."

"Very perceptive." Fran opened a hidden panel, revealing a biometric scanner. She placed her hand on the device. "I'm the only one who can access it and allow people in."

A computer voice said something in French that Lexi once again couldn't translate.

As the elevator started to rise, Fran closed the panel. "So you can relax, my dear. My place is like a fortress."

There was a wall of glass that looked out onto a gorgeous balcony, and beyond that, a beautiful Parisian night. Even though it boasted the luxury of a palace, the space maintained an inviting and tranquil feel.

"Liz should be arriving a little after midnight." Fran opened a bottle of wine. "So that gives you a few hours to relax. May I pour you drinks?"

"I would love one," Lexi said.

"Clint?"

"Sure. What's the plan to get Lexi out of the country and to safety?"

"I have my jet on standby at a private airport." Fran filled three glasses with wine. "My pilot will fly Lexi and Liz to Morocco first thing in the morning."

Lexi took one of the glasses from Fran. "Not just Liz and me. My friend Steve, too." She wanted to turn to Clint and ask if he planned on flying with them, but she resisted.

"Not Steve," Clint said. "I talked to Doc, who says he won't be able to travel safely for another couple of days."

"Then I'm staying in Paris until he can." She took a long sip of the wine. "That's final."

"It's too dangerous for you to stay," Clint said. "Once

you're away I'll go straight to Steve. I won't leave his side until I can deliver him to you."

"Deliver him to me? In person?"

"Yes."

She couldn't imagine what it would feel like parting with Clint, so hearing that she would see him again thrilled her. "I still think I should stay. I'm the one who got him into this mess."

"He's a grown, capable man," Clint said. "Steve knew what he was getting into."

"Apparently, there's a lot more for you two to discuss, but I'm sure you both are exhausted after all your ordeals," Fran said. "Cook has prepared a delightful meal for you, but let me show you to your rooms where you can freshen up."

"Where is the cook? And are there other staff I need to be worried about?" Clint stayed close to Lexi.

She liked that he was here with her. It made her feel safe.

"Very good, young man." Fran smiled. "Cook and the other staff are gone for the rest of the day. We're all alone."

"Besides the elevator, what other entry points are there?" Clint asked.

"There's a service elevator, which requires my staff's biometrics, but I've disabled it." Fran looked at her. "This guy has some real skills."

"Yes, he does," she said with a smile.

"What about a fire escape?" Clint added.

Fran nodded. "It's near your rooms at the end of the hall. Follow me and I'll show it to you."

As they walked through the penthouse, she watched Clint assessing everything.

"Here is the fire escape for the penthouse," Fran said. "And as you can see, it doesn't connect to the lower floor until I push this." She pointed at a red button next to the window.

"Show me how it works," Clint said.

Lexi liked that he was in full-on protector mode.

"Of course." Fran pushed the button, and the stairs lowered to the building's escape route. "Happy, Mr. Richards?"

Clint took another five minutes scanning the device before he was satisfied. "Ms. Binoche, I'm impressed. You've thought of everything."

"Please, call me Fran."

"Gladly, if you will call me Clint."

"Deal. I'm impressed with you, Clint. Now, I'm sure Lexi would like to freshen up. Am I right?"

"Yes. And I just want to say thank you. I can't tell you how much I appreciate all you're doing for me," she said.

"Let me show you your rooms then."

"Rooms?" Clint held up his hand.

Fran grinned. "You're right next door to her."

Clint returned the smile. "Like I said before, you've thought of everything."

"Excellent." Fran led them to a door. "This is yours, my dear."

The warm colors and soft furnishing of the space's décor lured Lexi past the door and into the room.

"This is beautiful."

"I'm glad you like it. The en suite is through there." Fran

pointed at another door. "I always stock up on toiletries for my guests, so feel free to use anything at all. Take your time. If there's something else you need, just let me know."

As Fran gave her the tour of the bedroom suite that was larger than Lexi's apartment, Clint inspected the windows, the closet, and every other square inch of the place.

"Satisfied, young man?" Fran asked.

"This door is locked. What's it to?"

Fran walked over to the door and used a key to unlock it. "Your room. This door connects the two spaces, though you can access your room from the hallway as well." She handed the key to Lexi and then turned back to Clint. "Come with me, so she can have some privacy. Lexi, take all the time you need. Dinner will be ready whenever you'd like."

Fran walked through the connecting door into the other bedroom.

Hanging back, Clint grabbed Lexi's hands and squeezed. "Keep the door unlocked. I'll only be a few feet away."

He released her and followed Fran into the other room, leaving her alone.

Lexi let out a long sigh, and felt exhaustion sweep through her body. Knowing Clint was in the next room made her feel better. He was her North Star in all of this, something constant she could depend on. As much as she wished they could be more than friends, she knew they couldn't.

Damn you, Roman!

JUST A LITTLE AFTER TEN, Clint looked in on Lexi, who was asleep. He knew she needed this chance to recharge.

Seeing her caused primal urges to boil deep inside him. Her gorgeous body lying in the middle of the massive bed was mesmerizing. The pale pink nightgown Fran had given her to sleep in only added to her beauty. As much as he wanted to make love to Lexi, he didn't want to push her. She'd been through so much.

He stepped back into his room, leaving the door to Lexi's slightly ajar. Thank God, Fran had provided a bottle of his favorite Scotch, which he poured into a glass to calm his desires. Normally, he would savor the warm liquid but he downed it instead. Then he refilled the glass, which he did sip slowly.

He'd enjoyed the meal Fran, or Cook, actually, had provided—grilled chicken, asparagus, and a refreshing salad.

He'd listened intently to Lexi share some stories about her life, hoping to learn even more *about her*.

Though he already knew she'd lost her parents from his research, it broke his heart hearing her deflect when Fran asked about them.

"Could I have a little more wine," she'd said, avoiding the question. *"And enough about me. Tell me more about you, Fran."*

Why was Lexi so guarded? Was the pain so deep it was hard for her to talk about losing her parents?

When she talked about times she'd spent with Liz, her eyes lit up. It was obvious Liz filled a void in her life. They were more like sisters rather than just friends.

Fran told some funny stories about her escapades with old boyfriends that made them all laugh. She seemed open and truthful, which tamped down his suspicions. He liked that side of her. It made her seem more genuine to him. He also appreciated the other side of Fran—the skilled woman, who worked to make the world a better place. Some of Fran's stories about the refugees she'd helped were heart wrenching.

Despite everything, he would still be cautious. Lexi was his only concern and trusting Fran completely wasn't a good idea. *At least not yet.*

Feeling more in charge, Clint called Max to get an update.

"Hey, Clint. I'm glad you called because we're all settled into the new location and Torres was just asking about Lexi."

"She's fine. Max, any word on Blake's whereabouts?"

"Nothing. It's like he's vanished. There's no digital trail. None of his contacts I've reached out to know anything."

"That's so strange." Clint believed if Blake wanted to kidnap Lexi that he had all the intelligence necessary and would have already tried something. "What have we learned from Boris?"

"Unfortunately he's not talking."

"You need to make him talk, Max. He has to know something that can lead us to Blake, Camille and Koslova."

"On the Koslova issue, I intercepted more chatter about him on the Dark Web. Seems like he's in Paris for more than Lexi."

"What do you mean?"

"Someone took out a contract on a high level target."

"That sounds just like something Koslova would be interested in."

"I agree," Max said. "The only thing I know is it's supposed to happen tomorrow around noon."

"Keep digging, buddy. We need a location and a name."

"I'm on it."

Clint remembered what Max had gone through protecting Lexi. "How are you feeling?"

"Better. Doc keeps telling me to rest, but there's too much on the line for that."

"I appreciate that, but don't overdo it."

"I'm being careful."

Clint took a sip of his drink and then told Max Fran's plan to get Lexi out of the country. "Can you get me the tail number for Fran's jet?"

"Actually, she has two jets." Max gave him both tail numbers.

"Perfect. I'm going to text you a contact of mine. Maddox MacKinnon, though he has several aliases I'm sure you can find if necessary. Tell Madd to meet the plane when it lands in Morocco. Once Lexi is safe and secure, I want to know."

"Got it," Max said. "Anything else?"

Before Clint could answer, he heard Lexi scream.

13

With abject fear coursing through her, Lexi ran down a darkened alley. She glanced back and saw Roman charging her direction.

The pounding of Roman's footsteps behind her seemed to be getting closer. She was exhausted from running, but she couldn't stop. She had to get away from him.

She saw a possible escape to her right—a building with a security guard inside. She dashed to the entrance, through the door and found the guard.

"Hi Mabel," he said with a grin, tipping his hat.

"Clint?"

As he stepped into the light, she could see his handsome face. "What are you doing here?"

"I'm here to protect you from Roman," he said, pulling her into his body.

She melted into him.

Roman blasted through the doors. "She's mine, asshole."

Clint stepped forward, placing his body between her and

Roman. "She never was yours. She never wanted you. She loves me and I love her."

Just as Lexi tried to absorb Clint's declaration of his feelings for her, everything seemed to go into slow motion.

Roman fired his gun at Clint.

Frozen in place, she watched as the bullet took a straight line to Clint's heart.

As he fell to the floor, she screamed and screamed...

"LEXI? LEXI?"

SHE KNELT DOWN NEXT to him and watched the life disappear from his eyes. "Please don't leave me, Clint. I can't lose you. I love you. Please stay."

His eyes closed and she knew he was gone.

Grief and rage rolled through her like twin tsunamis. She hurtled toward Roman and beat him on the chest.

"LEXI?"

"I HATE YOU! I hate you! I hate you!" she continued pounding him.

"LEXI? WAKE UP."

"I'LL NEVER BE YOURS, Roman. Never." With every ounce of

strength she could muster, she hit him again and again, wishing she could kill him with her fists.

"Ow. That hurts." Clint grabbed her wrists and said loudly, "You're having a nightmare."

She opened her eyes. "Oh my God, Clint. You're alive."

Sitting close, he put his arms around her. "It's okay, sweetheart. I'm right here."

Trembling with tears streaming down her cheeks, she rested her head on his shoulder. "I thought Roman killed you."

"I'm okay. I'm here with you." As the nightmare's hold faded away, Clint guided her to face him. "We're both safe."

His dark, piercing eyes were filled with extreme passion.

Did I say 'I love you' aloud?

Clint leaned in and kissed her. With warm tingles sizzling in her body, she kissed him back passionately.

Clint pulled the strap of the silky nightgown off her shoulder, lightly kissing her neck.

"Stop, Clint." She leaned back from him. "I can't do this. Roman will kill you. He murdered a guy I was dating back in Dallas. It's all my fault." As she shared the horrible memories with Clint, she began to cry. "I should have known what Roman was capable of. He's crazy and obsessed. When I tried to break up with him, he told me I was his. I just didn't believe him at the time." She looked up at him, her face wet with tears. "I couldn't bear it if he killed you too."

"Sweetheart, you don't have to feel guilty about any of that."

"But Matth would still be alive if I—"

"Stop, Lexi." Clint pulled her in tight to his body. "You said yourself he is crazy, and you are right. That's where I have the advantage. Trust me. I will stop the son of a bitch. He will never hurt you again."

"But I remember you telling me Blake hired you to find Roman. Why did you agree to that?"

"Koslova and I have history. I saw him kill a close friend of mine."

As Clint continued telling her the entire story about his friend Gary, Lexi's heart melted for him and her hatred for Roman multiplied.

"Lexi, that's why I left the Agency. When Blake showed up saying he had new intel on Koslova, I jumped at the chance to get revenge for Gary."

"I'm sorry that you had to go through all that."

He ran his hand down her arm. "But even though revenge was the reason I took this mission, things have changed."

"What do you mean?"

He smiled. "I fell in love with Mabel. She changed everything for me."

"Oh Clint, I'm just so scared."

"You don't have to be, sweetheart."

"But—"

He placed his fingers to her lips. "Shh. I will take care of you."

Her chaotic mind swung like a pendulum—back and forth. From her boundless desire for his touch to her crushing fear of what Roman might do to him.

How could she make Clint understand? "I know you will keep me safe, but I'm still worried about you. Roman is crazy. That's why he is so dangerous. You can't predict what he will do."

"I've been through many tough situations facing enemies like Koslova. I'm trained to take care of myself." He threaded his fingers through her hair. "You don't have to worry about me or about yourself. I will not let Koslova hurt you. Trust me."

Once again, he made her feel safe and protected. "I do trust you."

The more he touched and kissed her, the more her heart beat like mad inside her chest. She felt so connected to him. How was that even possible? They'd only just met. Yes, they'd already been through so much together, but was that enough for such strong emotions? Lexi had no idea but she couldn't deny her feelings for him.

"I love you," he said, as if he'd been reading her thoughts.

"I love you, too," she confessed. "But even that scares me. I can't let Roman hurt you either."

"He won't." Clint kissed her. "I want you, sweetheart."

"I want you, too, with all my heart."

He kissed her again, this time deeper.

She felt tingles roll through her body.

"God, you're so beautiful," he said.

She traced his jawline with her fingers. "And you are so handsome."

He laughed, which thrilled her from head to toe. "No one has ever told me that before."

"Liar," she teased, enjoying the feel of his muscles.

"Sweetheart, I will never lie to you." Clint brushed his lips lightly to her ear, causing her pulse to quicken.

"I believe you." Lexi felt the tension she'd been carrying forever began to let go as she relaxed into him. "And I will never lie to you either."

He stopped his wandering kisses and looked at her with those devastating, knowing eyes. She could feel his warm breath on her skin.

A tremble rolled through her. Everything about him called to something deep inside her. Clint was good and kind. He was also strong and intense. A masculine combination that unlocked emotions— emotions she'd believed were impossible for her to feel.

She nestled her head into the crook of his neck, inhaling his scent of musk and earth. "You smell good." His aroma made her sense how strong and in charge he was, a powerful invitation to welcome his touch.

He sniffed her hair. "You smell like honey and coconut, but what I'm really breathing in is you, sweetheart. God, you're so sexy."

When she brushed her lips lightly against his, sparks shot up and down her spine.

He responded by placing his hands on her waist, causing her to shiver with anticipation.

Their bodies entwined and became one, the physical evidence of what their hearts had already done.

She got lost in the incredible ecstasy he gave her. He took her to heights of pleasure and love she hadn't known were possible for her.

To catch her breath, she slid her body in tight to his. He put his arms around her and held her.

Having him so close, she felt like the luckiest woman in the world.

He pressed his lips to hers. "I love you."

"I love you, too." Attempting to give him her best Scarlet O'Hara, she said, "Well, I do declare, Harold, where did you learn your incredible skills in lovemaking?"

He laughed.

Smiling, she closed her eyes and drifted off to sleep.

CLINT LISTENED INTENTLY to Lexi's rhythmic breathing. He enjoyed holding her tight next to him, skin to skin, but being with her was so much more than just physical. He'd never felt such intimacy. Her falling asleep in his arms proved she trusted him completely.

God, I love her so much.

When he'd spoken those three important words to her, he'd shocked himself. He'd never believed he would ever fall in love. And what about love at first sight? Before Lexi he would have called such a thing BS. Boy, was he wrong. *Mabel has me wrapped around her finger.*

He had to hold back a laugh, fearing he might disturb Lexi.

How long has it been since I felt like laughing?

She had the best sense of humor, besides all her other incredible qualities.

She's everything I could ever want.

Clint realized how much she'd changed him in such a short time.

He'd always been so serious. In college he was focused on his grades. At the Agency all that had mattered was his career. After Gary's murder, he was consumed with revenge. But now, all he cared about was keeping her safe and doing whatever he could to make her happy.

He glanced at the clock on the nightstand. 12:45 am, just a few hours before they had to leave for the airfield. Had Liz already arrived?

His gut wrenched for a moment, realizing he would have to part with Lexi in order to follow through with his promise to her about Steve. Clint vowed to himself that when this was over, he would never part from her again.

Carefully, he moved his arms in order not to awaken her. He quietly left the bed and walked to his room. Again, he kept the door open. He wanted to take a shower and clear his mind about what he needed to do to ensure Lexi remained safe.

Clint checked his phone for text messages, hoping Max had gotten something actionable out of Boris.

There was no text. *Damn.*

He walked into the bathroom and turned on the shower's faucet. Once he was satisfied with the water's temperature, he stepped in and mentally ticked off the areas of this mission that were still in flux that needed his attention.

They were no closer to apprehending Koslova than when this had all begun. *They?* Where the hell was Blake? Clint still couldn't wrap his head around what Lexi had seen at Camille's. Blake working jointly with Camille to help Koslova just didn't make any sense.

As he squirted out shampoo into his hand, Clint knew what he had to do.

First, he wanted to make sure Madd was ready to meet Lexi when Fran's jet landed in Morocco. He wanted someone he trusted to ensure they weren't landing with any hostiles nearby.

Second, he needed to get Lexi safely on Fran's jet and out of the country.

Third, he had to follow through on his promise to Lexi about Steve.

Fourth, he had to find Blake and figure out what was going on with him.

And finally, he would have to locate Koslova, but not any longer to seek revenge. All that mattered to him now was Lexi. And because of that fact Koslova had to be eliminated.

14

Lexi was startled awake from the buzzing of the burner phone. She reached for Clint in the bed, but realized he was gone. The door between their rooms was wide open.

Wrapping the sheet around her naked body, she walked to the door and heard his shower running.

The phone buzzed again, pulling her attention back.

Glancing at the clock, she reached for the phone, wondering if it was a message from Liz. Surely, she'd already arrived. God, she wanted to see her.

The message *was* from Liz's phone. When Lexi opened up the text, she felt her entire body go numb.

Surprise! Not Liz. Roman.

Where's Liz?

She's with me, but her continued safety depends on you.

Don't you dare hurt her.

Ha! That doesn't sound like my Lexi. You've been spending too much time with that CIA agent.

How did he know about Clint? Through Camille? What else did Roman know? Had he been watching her the whole time?

How did you get this number?

It was the only French number that Liz had called. Got some techies to locate the burner via its GPS. Look out your window, baby.

Lexi ran to the window and saw four thugs on the street looking up at her.

Do exactly as I say and Liz and the CIA agent will live. Don't and they die.

What do you want from me?

Right now, you have exactly 2 minutes, my love, to get to my men or I'll blow Liz's head off and then I'll come for that CIA agent. Come alone, understand?

I'll do it, Roman, just don't hurt Liz.

She didn't wait for a response, but dressed quickly. Her mind raced with a million outcomes to this nightmare, and all of them ended in tragedy.

Roman will never give me up. Never.

Steve had been shot, and Liz was already in danger because of her. And soon, Clint would be too. She couldn't bear Roman hurting the people she loved. The image from her dream where Roman killed Clint replayed in her mind. She had to warn him somehow. She looked at Roman's message on the burner phone's screen, and then placed it on her pillow.

With her heart beating like mad, she ran down the hallway to the fire escape.

She opened the window, climbed out onto the tucked stairs, reached back and hit the red button.

As a loud alarm blared inside Fran's penthouse, Lexi

raced down the moving stairs holding on tight as it latched onto the lower fire escape. Glancing at Roman's men below, she sped down the remainder of the stairs to the street.

THE INSTANT CLINT heard an alarm he shot out of the shower, grabbing a robe and his gun.

He ran into Lexi's bedroom.

She was gone.

Fear for her consumed him, and he blasted into the hallway.

Fran stood there in a nightgown with a gun in her hand and her eyes wide. "It's the fire escape alarm."

They ran to the open window and saw Lexi step off the last rung of the fire escape and onto the street.

He yelled, "Lexi?"

She looked up at him from the street but didn't say a word. To his utter shock, she ran to four men—*Koslova's men.*

Clint leapt through the window and charged down the stairs.

Although the thugs shot at him, he wouldn't take a chance returning fire at this distance for fear of hitting Lexi.

Jumping down flight to flight, he watched in horror as her attackers placed a hood over her head and handcuffs on her wrists.

Ducking the shots, he saw two of the men shove her into a black van.

With Lexi out of his line of fire, Clint ran into the

street, shooting at the other two men still outside the vehicle.

Both dropped to the ground as the van sped away.

He memorized the license plate as he kicked the guns away from the two fallen thugs. It was out of habit, but he needn't have bothered—they were obviously dead.

Fran ran out of the building. "Over here, Clint."

Still in her nightgown, she jumped into a black Mercedes parked just outside.

Clint got in on the passenger's side.

She floored it, leaving rubber on the street. "I don't see them anywhere, do you?"

He glanced down every street they passed, but came up empty.

After several minutes passed with no sign of the black van, she said, "Damn it. They got away."

He pounded his fists on the dashboard. "Fuck!"

She placed her hand on his arm. "I know you're worried, but it's going to be okay."

"The hell it is. Lexi is in danger because of my mistake. I shouldn't have left her side for even a single second."

"You couldn't have known. Right now, we need to get back to my place, get dressed and see if there are any clues that made Lexi leave so suddenly and without warning. Something must have happened."

"I agree. Lexi is too smart to walk right into a trap." Clint's gut tightened. "If Koslova hurts her..."

"He won't. From what you and Lexi told me about him last night, it's obvious to me Koslova sees her as his property." Fran turned left. "Let's head back and figure out our next steps."

Praying Fran was right about Koslova not hurting Lexi, Clint fought back the black hole trying to devour him.

15

L exi bounced from side to side as the van raced through Paris.

She couldn't stop replaying the image of Clint leaning out of the window yelling her name. Everything inside her had wanted to call back to him, but she couldn't risk endangering him or Fran.

She prayed Clint would find the burner phone with Roman's message and understand why. Would he ever forgive her? Of course he would. He'd told her he loved her. She'd never known that a love like the one she shared with him existed until now. She realized Clint would not stop looking for her. But what if he succeeded and found her? She knew what Roman was capable of. He'd already killed one man because of her.

"We got the girl, boss," one of the thugs said. "But the CIA guy shot Carl and Hans."

"Are they dead?"

Lexi recognized Blake's voice from the phone's

speaker. "You asshole! How could you betray Clint like this?"

"Foolish girl." He laughed. "You don't know what you're talking about."

"Boss, that guy was a helluva shot. I can't be sure, but I doubt our guys survived."

"I'll take care of the clean up. Get to the designated drop-off as fast as you can. Camille will be waiting to deliver her to Roman."

"Yes, sir. We're ten minutes out."

"Excellent."

Lexi heard the man click his phone off. "Almost to your boyfriend, sweetheart."

The other thug laughed. "Koslova is going to get him some tonight."

When she felt him run his hand down her arm, she jerked away.

"Get your filthy hands off of me."

"Better listen to her," the driver said. "You know what will happen if you touch the boss's merchandise."

"Fine." Thankfully, the man shifted away from her. "But you have to admit she's a looker."

The remainder of the drive the two men didn't say another word, which left Lexi to her own thoughts.

She reminded herself, she had no other choice. So many people had suffered because of her. Matt was dead. Steve was shot. Liz kidnapped. And Clint threatened.

This has to stop.

The only way she knew it would was to give in to Roman's demands and hope for the best.

I hate him.

But she wouldn't show it if it could mean Liz would be set free.

Will I ever see Clint again?

WHEN FRAN PULLED to the curb outside of her building, Clint saw that the two men he'd shot were gone.

"That was a fast clean up," Fran said. "Is Roman that powerful?"

"I didn't think so until now," he said, as they got out of her car. "Or maybe he's working for someone that powerful."

She nodded and they ran to the entrance doors.

"Madame?" the security guard stood, his eyes full of concern. "I didn't know whether I should call the police or not."

"Toujours discrétion, Claude," Fran said, as they rushed past him to the elevator.

As the doors opened, she shouted back to Claude, *"Merci beaucoup.* You did right. Always discretion."

In a flash, Fran opened the secret panel and placed her hand on the bio scanner.

Every moment without Lexi felt like an unbearable eternity. "Can't this damn elevator go any faster?"

"Be patient, Clint. It is just seconds away."

The doors opened and he bolted to the room where he'd left Lexi earlier. Fran followed closely behind.

Instantly, he spotted the burner phone on the pillow. He picked it up and read Roman's message.

"What is it?" Fran asked.

He handed her the phone, as a mix of guilt and anger swelled inside him.

"Oh my God, Clint. He has Liz, too." Fran shook her head. "Lexi was trying to protect you and Liz."

"I've got to get her back."

"And Liz, too. Wait for me. I'm getting dressed and coming with you."

As Fran raced to her room, Clint ran through the connecting door to retrieve his phone.

Grabbing his clothes and slipping out of the robe, he called Max and told him what had happened. "I need you to run this plate." He recited what he'd memorized earlier as he'd watched those bastards take Lexi away from him.

"I'm on it," Max said.

"And what have you learned from Boris?"

"Still nothing. Doc and I have tried everything, but he won't spill the beans."

"He will to me. I'm on my way." Clint put his phone away.

WHEN LEXI FELT the van stop and heard a garage door opening, she knew the journey was almost over. When would it finally end? Or would this nightmare with Roman *ever* end?

I must save Liz.

More than anything, Lexi longed for Clint to be by her side. He would have known exactly what to do. But Roman had made it clear he would kill him, so she didn't have a choice.

Despite being completely shaken, she needed to put on a brave face once her captors took off the hood. She wasn't sure what was going to happen to her, but she hoped that by giving into Roman's demands, Liz would be spared.

The van moved a few feet and stopped.

The sound of the garage door closing echoed in her ears.

I wonder if I'll see Roman now.

She started shaking uncontrollably at the thought of being in the same room with him. She prayed the two men wouldn't notice. Clint would have calmed her down.

I wish he could be here.

Her captors grabbed her by the arms and forced her out of the van.

Steeling her resolve, she said, "How about taking off this damn hood so I can see where I'm going?"

"Not a chance, sweet cheeks. Not a chance."

"You're lucky you have these handcuffs on me, because if I didn't, I'd make sure you never talked to me or any other woman like that again."

His sickening laugh fueled her anger and kept her focused on being strong. She vowed that she would get the last laugh.

The two men marched her forward.

She tried to count her steps, hoping that any bit of information that she could get might help her and Liz escape—and to find her way back to Clint.

God, please let there be a way.

After ninety-two steps, Lexi heard her captors open a door.

"In you go."

Six more steps, and then they slammed her down into what felt like a metal chair.

"Lexi? Are...you...okay?"

She recognized Blake's voice, though he sounded drunk. "You asshole!"

When the hood was finally removed, Lexi had to blink several times to adjust her eyes to the sudden flood of light.

She sat in the middle of a large, sterile-looking room —gray walls and no furnishings except for the chairs she and Blake sat in. On the wall in front of her was a large, blank screen. Next to it was a camera pointed at her and Blake.

The two men from the van stood a few feet from her left, posted on either side of the door they'd just entered.

There was another door off to her right. She wondered where it might lead. Was Liz behind that door or was Roman? Could it be a way for her and Liz to escape?

"You...hurt her...and you'll...be sorry," Blake slurred at her attackers.

She glanced over at him to get a better look. Seeing his state, she realized that he was a prisoner just like her. *Why?* Blake was tied to his chair. Both his eyes were black and his lips were swollen. Blood soaked his shirt.

"What's going on?" Confused, she stared at him. "Weren't you the one who ordered them to bring me here?"

He shook his head. "Not me. There's a...lot to...tell you..."

Camille entered the room from the door to the right.

"Are you awake again, Blake? We can't have that now, can we?"

Helpless to stop her, Lexi watched in horror as Camille brought out a syringe.

"What are you doing to him?"

Camille wink at her. "You'll see."

She slammed the needle into Blake's neck and pressed the plunger.

A few seconds later, Blake's eyes closed and his head dropped.

"He's just asleep, Lexi. It's better that way. Easier to control Blakey-boy." Camille patted Blake on the top of the head.

Plainly, he had put up quite the fight.

How was this possible? She had seen his face on Camille's laptop. Just minutes ago, she had heard his voice on the phone. There had to be some explanation. *But what?*

Either way, not only did she want to save Liz, now she also wanted to save Blake. She wished she could let Clint know that Blake hadn't betrayed them.

"Roman and I made a deal," Lexi said. "Where is he?"

"Oh, you made a deal with him? Interesting." Camille smirked. "He'll be here very soon. He's been dying to see you again. But first there's someone I want you to meet." She clicked a button on her phone.

To Lexi's utter shock the big screen in front of her filled with an image of a man that looked exactly like Blake.

"Hello, Ms. Bly."

Lexi looked at Blake and back at the man on the screen. "Oh. So you're twins."

"That's right. I'm exactly four minutes older than my baby brother, Blake. I'm Drake Atlas. Pleased to meet you."

"You were the one I saw talking with Camille."

"Yes. Aren't you a bright one now?" His voice dripped with condescension. "I'm also the one who orchestrated your trip to Paris via an unsuspecting Pavel."

"Why? What have I ever done to you?"

"Let's just say that you are part of a difficult negotiation I made with your boyfriend."

"Roman is not my boyfriend."

"I'm sure you are aware he feels differently about you."

With everything she could muster, Lexi tried to keep her fear from showing. "Where is my friend Liz? Whatever Roman promised you, I will get more."

"I doubt that's possible for a pauper like you, sweetheart," Camille laughed, calling her bluff.

Drake snapped, "That's enough, my dear."

"I'm sorry, *mon prince.*"

Lexi looked directly at the camera. "You've got her well-trained, don't you?"

Camille glared at her, but Drake grinned.

"Interesting. You're different than what Roman described," he said. "First things first. You asked about your friend."

The screen switched to an image of a terrified but defiant Liz, who was tied to a chair.

What have I got my best friend into?

Liz had always been there for Lexi. But look how she was repaying Liz.

"You'll be sorry for this, whoever you are," Liz yelled from the screen.

Thank God, she seemed unharmed. At least for now, but Lexi had to find a way to get them out of here before something worse happened.

"Liz, it's me. Lexi. Are you okay?"

The screen switched back to Drake. "I'm afraid she can't hear you, Ms. Bly, but she is just fine. I promise you."

How could she trust a man who was willing to kidnap two women and beat up his own brother? Once again, she didn't have much of a choice since Drake had the upper hand.

But somehow she had to find a way to flip the script. "Listen to me, Drake. Roman and I made a deal. If I came alone he would let Liz go. And I expect that to happen. Now."

The door to the right opened, and Roman entered.

All those years of worry and fear about seeing him again vanished. The only thing she wanted was for Liz to be let go. Though she knew the depths of evil that Roman could sink to, Lexi also knew she was not the same naïve girl who'd tried to break it off with him back in college. She was stronger. Much stronger.

"I'm here. Like you asked. Let. Liz. Go."

"Not my call, baby." Roman leaned forward to kiss her forehead.

She butted his head as hard as she could. "Liar!"

"Ow, bitch. That fucking hurt." Glaring at her, Roman rubbed his forehead. "I'll have to work on improving your manners."

Fury blasted through her. "Let Liz go or I swear I'll kill you myself."

Roman looked amused, which infuriated her even more. "Again, not my call. It's his." He pointed to Drake on the screen.

"I'll release her, Ms. Bly, once you and your boyfriend fulfill his commitment to me," Drake said.

"Why should I believe you?"

"I'm a man of my word is why you should believe me."

"So am I," Roman said. "We'll complete the contract."

"What contract? What commitment? What is this all about?" She needed more information.

Roman came up behind her and placed his hands on her shoulders and squeezed. "That's none of your business."

"Get your damn hands off of me."

To her shock, Roman let go of her and stepped back.

"And you better tell me what your scheme is right now, or don't expect me to cooperate, whatever it is."

"Oh, you'll cooperate," Drake said. "Or your pretty little friend Liz won't be quite so pretty when I'm through with her."

"If you harm her in any way, I *will* kill you."

"Okay," Drake said. "Since that's settled, I'll expect you both at the event at eight."

"We'll be there," Roman said. "Won't we, love?"

"I just better find my friend in one piece."

"Once your boyfriend completes his job, I will release Liz as agreed."

She hoped that was true, but regardless she was between the proverbial rock and hard place.

"Make sure she gets ready, Camille," Drake said.

"Of course, my darling."

Drake smiled and the screen went black.

"Uncuff her. I'm sure Lexi will behave to save her friend. Won't you?" Camille waved a gun at her.

She nodded, and the men removed the handcuffs.

"I'll be waiting for you, my love." Roman exited through the door to the left.

Camille led her through the door to the right and down a hallway.

She rubbed her wrists. "Camille, what am I supposed to be getting ready for?"

"You'll see."

Once again, Lexi longed to feel Clint's arms protectively around her. She had no doubt that he was searching for her, because that was the kind of man he was. As much as it hurt to admit, she hoped he wouldn't find her. She loved him too much. They'd just *found* each other, and she couldn't risk losing him.

Even though I'm on my own, I can do this. I must do this.

16

U nable to stop his mind from replaying the image of Lexi's abduction, Clint weaved in and out of traffic.

Fran held onto the arm rests. "I know I agreed to let you drive my car, but remember to keep focused. We won't be able to help Lexi if we're in a wreck or stopped by the police."

"I'm not stopping for anyone. Just hold on. I'll get us there."

The GPS on his phone indicated the trip to the new OC would normally take twenty minutes. But that was if he drove the speed limit, which he definitely wasn't.

Arriving eleven minutes later, he parked Fran's Mercedes as close as he could to the main entrance of a restaurant. The restaurant was a front for the new OC.

He jumped out of the car and raced for the door with Fran following close behind.

The restaurant was located in a non-descript building

with a lone sign next to the entrance that simply read: *Le Café.*

When he and Fran walked through the door, they were met by the *maître d'.* Clint recognized him as one of the operatives on the team who worked for Doc as a medic.

"Doc and Max are expecting you."

He led them through the spartan dining room, which only had a few patrons.

They followed him past the double doors to the kitchen. Clint knew all the chefs had weapons under their aprons. He wondered if they were chefs acting as operatives or operatives acting as chefs. Either way it was a great setup.

"This way." The man took them through a door into a large storage area with rows of shelves filled with produce. To the casual observer it might look benign, but not to Clint. He saw the intentional spacing of every item that provided camouflage and cover.

When the guy stopped and entered a code into his phone, the shelves to their right began to move, revealing a secret elevator beyond.

"They are waiting for you on level three," he told them.

Clint and Fran walked past him into the lift. Immediately, the unique shelves closed.

"Very James Bond." Fran pressed the button for the floor they needed. "I guess that makes me a perfect M to your 007."

In any other circumstance Clint would have laughed at her joke, but all he could focus on was rescuing Lexi. Koslova had taken away the love of his life.

As the elevator came to a stop, he felt his rage rising once again. If Koslova hurt her in any way, he would rip the bastard's heart out and shove it down his throat.

When the elevator doors opened, he and Fran stepped forward into an expansive space beyond.

Like the original OC, the new one had three designated areas.

To the right was the command station. Max sat in the middle of the space with Ahmed and Geoff, typing on keyboards and staring at the massive monitors on the walls.

Straight ahead was the medical area. Steve was sitting in a chair, looking much better than he had yesterday.

To the left, Boris paced in the same 6 by 6 foot cage. Clint was impressed with how thorough the team had made the transition from the original OC to this one.

"Who's in charge?" Fran asked Clint.

Since Blake was working against them, he wasn't sure what the real answer was.

"Right now, I suppose Max is running things," Clint said. "And I bet he has the keys for the cage."

"Why do you need the keys to interrogate the prisoner if the cell is made of chain link?"

"You'll see why." Determined to get information out of Boris that he could use to find Lexi, Clint headed straight for the command area with Fran.

"You must be Max," she said. "I'm Fran. I'm here to help any way I can to find Lexi and Liz."

Max stood. "Nice to meet—"

"Max, give me the keys to Boris's cage," he interrupted. "I need to interrogate him myself."

"Sure thing." Max opened a drawer and tossed him a set of keys.

Still in a hospital gown, Steve marched directly to them with a medic chasing after him.

"It's okay, Jones," Doc said, walking up behind the medic and his patient. "Let him go."

Steve glared at Clint. "Where is Lexi?"

Guilt slammed into the middle of his chest as he recounted what had happened at Fran's penthouse.

"Why the hell did you let her out of your sight knowing Koslova was after her?"

Clint didn't have an answer, since he agreed with him. "I'm going to find her, Steve, even if I have to beat her location out of that asshole in the cage."

"What are we waiting for? Let's go."

Clint charged to the cage with Fran, Steve, Max and Doc following.

"I brought my medical bag when you get done with him," Doc yelled. "We don't want his blood everywhere."

Boris stepped to the back of the cage with his eyes wide.

Clint unlatched the lock and opened the gate. He blasted inside, grabbing Boris by the throat.

"Max tells me you don't want to talk. I'm giving you to the count of three, Boris, to spill everything. If you don't, I will make it so you never talk again. One."

From behind him, Fran said calmly. "I'd listen to him if I were you."

Steve chimed in. "She's right. The guy's crazy."

"Two."

Boris choked out, "I don't know anything. I swear."

"Three." Clint cocked his arm and landed his fist into the thug's face.

Blood and a tooth shot out of Boris's mouth.

"Okay. Okay. Okay. I'll talk. I'll talk." His voice was slightly muffled, and he bent over to spit out more blood. "Just don't kill me."

"Don't make me." Clint liked seeing the fear in Boris's eyes.

"I remember what you did to Stan at Pavel's. I just want to live."

Clint kept a tight hold on the man. "Where is your boss?"

"Drake isn't in France," Boris blurted out. "Nobody knows where he is. But I do know who's running the operation here in Paris, if that helps. Camille. She's in charge."

"I already know about Camille. What about this Drake person? He's your boss, not Koslova?"

Boris shook his head. "Roman Koslova is just a hired hand for Drake."

Realizing there was a new player in the mix, Clint's gut tightened. "*Drake* who?"

"Drake Atlas. He's my boss."

Clint shoved Boris away as the truth became clear to him.

"Drake Atlas? Blake Atlas's twin brother?" Fran asked in a shocked tone.

Clint turned to her. "You know Blake?"

"Know him? He and I have had each other's backs for years."

Though Clint had more questions about their connection to each other, it would have to wait.

Boris continued revealing the facts. "Drake is every-one's boss, including his girlfriend Camille."

"Who is Drake Atlas?" Steve asked.

"Blake's twin brother," Clint answered. "A man who is supposed to be dead."

"Dead?" Fran prodded. "For how long?"

"Years. This is crazy." Max shook his head in disbelief. "Drake also worked at the agency. But he was supposedly killed during a mission gone bad."

"If this guy is telling the truth, it looks like Blake's twin is very much alive," Steve said, leaning against the fencing.

Max pulled over a chair for Steve, who sat and took a deep breath.

"You need to take it easy," Max said in a low voice.

"Not until we find Lexi," Steve said.

Clint admired his determination despite recovering from surgery. The loyalty that Lexi had shown for him ran both ways.

Boris looked warily at him and then at Steve. "Drake Atlas is alive. He's the man in charge. I swear."

"That must explain why Blake is missing."

Boris nodded. "When I saw him at Pavel's hotel I knew he was the boss's twin brother."

Fran turned to Doc. "Do you mind checking on our prisoner? He took a pretty powerful hit to the face."

"I lost a tooth."

"If you hadn't spoken up, you would have lost much more than a single tooth, asshole," Clint growled.

"Now, now, Clint," Fran said, playing *good cop* to his *bad*. "Boris has been forthcoming, and I'm sure there's more he wants to tell us, isn't that right?"

"I'll tell you everything, but you have to swear to protect me from Drake. He will kill me."

As Doc opened his medical bag, Fran impressed Clint with her interrogation skills.

"I'll make sure you're safe, Boris. You just have to answer my questions," Fran told him in a sweet tone. "First, you said Koslova was a hired hand. What did you mean by that?"

"All I know is Drake hired him to assassinate a woman at a charity event tonight," Boris said.

Doc swabbed the cut on his lip. "You'll be fine. I recommend a trip to the dentist after this is all over."

"What woman is Koslova supposed to kill?" Fran asked.

"I don't know. I'm just the muscle. I swear."

Clint smirked. "Muscle?"

"And the location for the charity event and the time?" Fran pressed.

Boris shook his head. "They never gave me any details."

Fran smiled. "You're doing great, Boris. Did you ever hear anyone mention the charity *Les Droits des Femmes?*"

Clint wasn't sure where Fran's line of questioning was going, but he trusted she knew what she was doing. It was clear how skilled an interrogator she was. It seemed there was much more to Fran than what Max had uncovered. Clint believed she must have been a spy, or still was.

"No," Boris said. "I'm sorry. No. My only job was to kidnap Lexi Bly at Pavel's hotel. Our instructions were that she was to be handled with kid gloves."

Hearing that Drake wanted to treat Lexi delicately made Clint feel a little better, but he wondered if that was only a temporary situation. Until he had her back in his arms he would not rest.

After Fran finished with her questions, the five of them left Boris in the cage and returned to the command area.

"Fran, that was fantastic interrogating," Max said.

Steve found another chair and asked her, "Where did you learn how to do that?"

She grinned. "Let's just say that I've been around."

"I'm glad we know that Blake isn't a traitor," Doc said. "I've worked for him for years. I couldn't believe he would betray us."

"But your boss is a hostage, which means we have work to do," Fran said flatly. "Though we don't know the name of Koslova's target, the good news is the only high profile charity event in Paris this evening is for *Les Droits des Femmes*—Women's Rights, to which I happen to have an invitation. Clint, you can be my plus one."

"What time?" Steve asked.

"Eight. It's black tie, but I can call in a favor and have a tuxedo delivered to my place." She pulled out her phone and looked at Clint. "What size are you?"

After he rattled off his measurements, Steve said, "I still don't understand what Lexi has to do with all of this. I know that she *was* Koslova's girlfriend, but how does that fit into Drake's plan to assassinate someone?"

While texting on her phone, Fran gave the most compelling answer. "Likely this Drake fellow wanted to make sure Koslova followed through with the plan and used Lexi as leverage."

"It seems like our mission now includes preventing an assassination," Max said.

"And rescuing Lexi," Steve stated emphatically.

Clint couldn't agree more. While stopping a woman from being killed was noble, his singular focus was to save Lexi. The new intel Fran had pulled out of Boris had intersected these two goals. Not only would he get Lexi back, he would make sure Koslova never saw the light of day again.

"Your tuxedo will be delivered in an hour." Fran put her phone away.

"You said the event starts at eight, which gives us three hours." Hoping to discover something that might locate Lexi earlier, Clint asked, "Max, did you find out anything about the van's license yet?"

Max shook his head. "It's a puzzle—one shell company after another. Drake Atlas seems to have quite the network, but trust me, we will get to the bottom of this."

"Wait a second," Ahmed said. "I just got a hit."

Max leaned over him and looked at his laptop's screen. "Great work. Do we have an address?"

"Yes we do." Geoff handed a slip of paper to Max.

"Excellent, guys." Max passed the slip to Clint. "This is the warehouse where the van should be stored."

"What are you waiting for?" Steve moved to the seat between Ahmed and the Geoff. "I'll hold down the fort with these two fellas. The rest of you go find Lexi and bring her back."

"Yes, sir." Fran whispered to Clint. "Now, that's the real man in charge."

Clint didn't respond but ran to the elevator. Fran, Max and Doc raced after him.

17

L exi felt the barrel of Camille's gun pressing hard against the middle of her back.

"Move, *mon petit poulet,*" Camille said with obvious sarcasm.

She had no idea what Camille had just called her, but she continued moving forward. "You don't need the gun. I don't have any intentions of trying to escape."

"Don't give me that. I know you don't give a damn about Roman. He's the one who is obsessed with you. You'll make a break for it the first chance you get."

"Suit yourself." She didn't care if Camille believed her or not. She wasn't going anywhere until Liz was released.

And what about Blake? She wasn't sure how to save him yet, but she was determined to figure out a way.

She had no doubt Clint was still searching for her. Would he succeed? With Max's hacking talent and Clint's covert skills and mindset she was certain they would eventually find her.

As much as she longed for Clint's embrace to help her

through this horror, she couldn't shake the dread that Roman would kill him once he arrived. But she knew there was no stopping Clint.

Maybe the whole OC team would be with him giving him a numeric advantage against Roman. But the more she played the likely scenarios in her mind, the more the image of the nightmare of Roman shooting Clint burned blistering hot.

She *had* to do this on her own before Clint found her. *But how?* Her frustration multiplied.

Camille led her out of the warehouse to the street, where the red Porsche convertible was parked.

"There's your car. I sure did enjoy driving it," Lexi said with a smirk.

"You're lucky it was in one piece. Get in. You'll have to drive because I'm keeping the gun on you."

"Oh great. I get to drive it again."

"Shut up, or you and your friend Liz may not get to drive anything else ever."

"Come on, Camille. Be real. You won't do anything without Drake's permission." Lexi didn't wait for her to snap back, but instead opened the driver's side door and got behind the wheel. "You coming or are you just going to stand there with your mouth open all day?"

"Fine." Camille tucked the gun away in her jacket, and got in on the other side of the car. "Just drive."

Unable to stop herself, Lexi licked the tip of her finger and drew an invisible mark in the air to show she'd one-upped Camille. "Where to?"

"There's more to you than what I first thought," Camille said, typing in an address on the car's GPS. "I can see why Clint was so impressed with you. He likes sassy women, but believe me, Lexi, you are not the first nor will you be the last." Camille copied Lexi's gesture of marking her win.

She grinned. "You know, Camille, another place and another time we might have been friends. Clint spoke highly of you. What happened to change you?"

"Just drive." Camille pointed to the screen with the directions.

"Okay." Lexi started the car and pulled out onto the street. Hoping to soften up Camille, she asked, "Can you tell me what I'm getting ready for at least?"

"Oh, Lexi. It's going to be so grand. It's a charity ball to support women's rights. You're going to love the beautiful black evening gown I've chosen for you."

Lexi recalled the plunging red number Camille wore during their first meeting at her house. Lexi usually sported yoga pants when she was home alone. "I kind of hate to admit it, but you do have great taste."

"*Merci.* You will have so much fun. Roman is no Drake, but I'm sure he will show you a good time."

A good time? Is she crazy? "You know, Camille, riding in this car with you reminds me of that movie with Susan Sarandon and Geena Davis, though we're missing our Brad Pitt."

"What was the name of that movie?" Camille asked. "I don't remember, but my Brad Pitt would definitely be Drake Atlas."

"Drake Atlas?" She laughed. "Now you've ruined the whole thing for me."

"Not if you knew him like I do."

"How did you two meet?" Lexi wanted to keep Camille talking in the hopes of making sense of what and why this was happening. And perhaps she might let some detail slip that might help with an escape.

"That's such a romantic story." Camille's tone softened. "Did Clint tell you that I worked for French Intelligence with the DGSE? That's how I met Drake. I was working on a joint mission where he was the lead for the CIA."

"Drake was with the CIA?"

"Oh yes. He was an incredible agent. And you saw him. Sexy."

"He and Blake look so much alike."

"But Blake isn't anything like Drake. In fact, Blake is a monster."

Lexi was confused about Camille's viewpoint on Blake, but decided it was best to keep her talking on the subject of Drake—*the real monster.* "So your boyfriend is sexy, huh?"

"He knows just how to make a woman feel like she's the only person in the world. We were and still are so in love."

"So what happened? Did you both leave your respective agencies?"

"Actually, everyone thought Drake had been killed in a black ops mission where Blake was in charge. When I heard, I just wanted to die. I couldn't imagine living a single day without Drake."

Lexi was beginning to understand Camille. Clint had changed everything for her, just like Drake had for Camille. But why had she and Drake gone bad?

Stopping at a universal red light, Lexi asked, "So that's when you left your agency?"

"No, Lexi. I'm still DGSE, though my loyalties are with Drake alone now."

"A double agent then? Sounds like a movie."

"It feels like one too—one where the girl and guy fall madly in love."

"But go back. You thought Drake was dead. Then what?"

"I was working on a big operation in Ukraine when Drake knocked on my door."

"I can't imagine what a shock and relief that would have been." Lexi's mind once again replayed the image of Roman killing Clint.

"You're right about that. Drake told me that Blake had botched the mission intentionally to make sure he was killed."

"Why would he do that?"

"Because Drake had learned that his monster of a brother had killed their parents."

"Oh my God."

"Their parents were very wealthy and had a massive estate in the Rocky Mountains in Colorado. Everyone believed that Mr. & Mrs. Atlas died in a car accident. But it wasn't true. Blake had drained the brake fluid on their car because he wanted their money. The road from their mansion was windy and narrow. When the brakes failed, they drove off the side of a cliff and were killed."

"Drake told you all of that?"

"Yes. Drake learned about it while working on that last mission with Blake. When he confronted him about it, Blake threatened to kill him. Drake was determined to let the authorities know, but Blake used his position as lead of the mission to set a trap for him. Drake barely got away with his life."

"Why didn't he let the higher ups at the CIA know what had happened?"

"He couldn't trust them. Blake had fooled everyone."

Lexi wasn't so sure. It seemed to her that Camille had been fooled.

"That's why Drake faked his death to leave the CIA and start anew. He's brilliant, Lexi."

"It would take someone brilliant to pull that off."

"Drake showed me that all governments are corrupt. We have to work outside of the normal structures to make a real difference. He wants to change the world for the better."

"By kidnapping women and torturing his twin brother, and God only knows what else?"

"Blake deserves everything that's coming to him."

"And what about me and Liz?"

"Change comes at a cost. You couldn't understand."

"I understand that you love him and would do anything for him."

"Yes. I would." Camille pointed ahead. "There's the hotel."

"It is grand," Lexi said, as she drove into the parking garage. "Tell me one thing. Will Drake let Liz go once this is over?"

"Of course. He's not a monster."

Lexi knew better, but she couldn't let herself sink into despair. She had to stay focused and strong.

Hers, Liz and Blake's lives depended on it.

∾

AVOIDING the security cameras around the warehouse, Clint led Fran, Doc and Max to the fence that surrounded the entire perimeter. From the street, the building looked abandoned, which he knew wasn't true. He prayed Lexi was inside, as well as Liz and Blake.

Clint and his three companions wore black from head to toe and were armed with tools and weapons from the team's arsenal.

Max snapped through the chain link with bolt cutters.

Quietly, they shot through the opening one at a time and headed to the loading dock.

When Clint spotted a single guard who was scanning the area, he motioned to the other three.

They were careful to stay in the shadows out of the man's line of sight, while moving closer and closer.

Clint gave instructions via hand signals to the team. Doc and Fran went right, and he and Max headed left.

When they were all in position, Fran jumped up and said, "*Bonjour monsieur.*"

"*Madame?*" the guard said, drawing his weapon.

Before he could utter another word or fire his gun, Clint came up behind him and put him in a sleeper chokehold, knocking him out.

He then secured the guard with zip ties on his wrists, while Fran tied his ankles. Max placed a gag over the man's mouth in case he came to. Doc took the man's gun and communication device, which was quiet at the moment.

More hand signals followed between Clint and the others. They entered the building, working together like a well-oiled machine.

With his senses completely focused on their dangerous surroundings, Clint walked into a large open space filled with black vans identical to the one Lexi had been shoved into.

As they hurried through the area, he looked in each of the vehicles they passed for any sign of her, Liz or Blake but found none.

When they heard boisterous laughter off to the left, they stopped behind a van.

Clint peered around the vehicle and spotted four armed men, smoking and playing cards.

He held up four fingers to let the other three know. Silently, they came up with a plan. They each would neutralize one man.

When he looked at Fran, he could see excitement in her eyes, which continued to indicate there was much more to her than Max had uncovered.

First chance I get, I'm going to find out where she got her skills.

Using the parked vans as cover, they each made their way to their specific target. From the shadows, Clint made eye contact with the team. On the count of three, they rushed the four thugs.

Fran's target twisted around in his chair to attack her.

"Not today, asshole," she said, hitting him over the head with her gun.

Max and Doc knocked out their targets, while Clint slammed his against the wall.

"Where is she?" he growled at the terrified guard.

"I don't know what you're talking about."

Clint bashed the man's head against the wall. "I. Said. Where. Is. She?"

"Down that hallway," he blurted out, pointing to the other side of the warehouse.

Clint secured and gagged the man, which the other three had already done to their targets.

They hurried to the other side of the warehouse and found a long hallway.

This has to be where Lexi is.

Anxious to have her safe and back in his arms, Clint went down the hallway, and the team followed.

He and Max checked the rooms to their left, while Fran and Doc did the same for the ones on the right. They used their hand signals to indicate when a room was empty.

Where are you Lexi? You have to be here.

The next set of doors on his and Max's side were restrooms.

He and Max entered the men's room, and found a guard standing at a urinal.

"*Merde!*" the man blurted out, as they rushed him before he could react, slamming him to the ground.

Clint secured the guy to the radiator. In record speed, Max tied up the guard's ankles and placed a gag over his mouth.

Clint nodded his approval. "You might have been trained to be an analyst, but you sure have mad skills in the field."

Max shrugged. "I didn't know I had it in me either."

"Well, you do. How are those ribs doing?"

"Doc wrapped them real tight. They hurt a little, but I'm doing okay."

Clint sent him an approving nod. He took the guard's

communication device and weapon, and he and Max exited the restroom.

Fran and Doc let them know that they'd found the women's room empty.

There were only four more rooms to check—two on the left and two on the right.

He opened one of the doors and discovered Liz tied to a chair—*but no Lexi.*

A relieved Fran ran past him, and cut Liz's restraints.

"Liz, it's me, Fran."

"Fran? It's really you?"

"Yes, sweetheart. You look so much like your mother."

Liz hugged her. "I'm so glad to see you. But where's Lexi? Is she safe? She's supposed to be with you."

Clint realized she'd not seen Lexi.

"Lexi is missing, but we're still searching for her. Don't worry." Fran put her arm around Liz. "We're going to find her. Have you seen anyone else that's in the same situation as you?"

Liz shook her head. "I've only seen the two men who jumped me when I was getting gas and shoved me into a van. No one else."

"Same M.O. as Lexi's," Max said.

"Who are you exactly?" Liz didn't wait for him to answer, but instead turned her attention to Fran. "Do these three men work for you?"

"No, but I trust them. Did your *kidnappeurs* hurt you, *mon chéri*?"

"No, I've just been locked up in here ever since."

Realizing Liz had provided all the intel she could, Clint raced out of the room to continue his desperate search for Lexi with Max following close behind.

Dread began to consume him, as the next two rooms were empty.

The last door was his *last* chance to find Lexi.

Please let her be inside and okay.

With his gun in one hand, he opened the door with his other. When he saw she wasn't inside his heart seized in his chest.

The room was the largest off the hallway, at 20 feet by 20 feet. In the middle of the room was Blake, who was bloodied, bruised and tied to a metal chair.

Max ran to Blake and knelt down in front of him. "We're here, boss."

There was no response.

"Doc, get in here," Clint called out, knowing there were no guards close enough to hear.

While he was cutting Blake's restraints and Max was trying to revive him, Doc, Fran and Liz rushed into the room.

"That's Blake Atlas," Fran said in a shocked tone.

"You know him?"

"Know him. He and I have had each others backs for years."

Though Clint had more questions about their connection to each other, it would have to wait. "Doc, is there any way to bring Blake to?"

"I don't have anything like that with me," he answered.

Fran touched Clint's shoulder. "You'll just have to carry him."

Liz looked directly at him. "So you're Clint."

He nodded, and lifted Blake over his shoulders. "Let's go."

"Max and Doc can take Blake and Liz to the OC, because Clint and I need to get back to my place," Fran ordered. "Will have just enough time to get ready for the event Koslova will be attending. He's the key to us finding Lexi."

Having Fran close helped Clint stay focused and hopeful. "You're right. Lead the way."

They rushed out of the warehouse without encountering any more guards. But every step along the way, Clint's only thoughts were about finding Lexi.

18

Despite now being the best chance to get away, Lexi remained close to Camille through the lobby of the luxurious hotel. What other choice did she have but to comply with her captors until Liz was released? But would Drake honor his promise? If not, all she could do was keep moving forward until she found another way to secure Liz's escape and safety.

The lobby's fantastic flooring of inlaid white marble had touches of gold, creating a perfect balance with the frames of antique mirrors on the walls. Above, massive crystal chandeliers lit the space. Completing the look were white and gold leather sofas.

Without stopping at the registration desk, Camille turned to her. "What do you think so far?"

"It's incredible and makes me wonder what kind of room you're taking me to?"

Camille grinned. "My Drake always demands the best."

As they trekked their way to the elevators, Lexi

noticed a sign in both English and French that read: *"Global Women's Rights Initiative."*

The photo of the guest of honor showed an attractive woman with long blonde hair. The caption identified her as Lila Cross, the Executive Director of Cyber Security for the European Union.

"Camille, what's Roman supposed to do for Drake at this event? Is it about power or money? Or both?"

Camille hit the call button for the elevator. "You'll see soon enough, but first we have to get you ready."

Lexi realized she wasn't going to get any more details from the woman.

When the doors closed, Camille entered a code onto a keypad next to the bank of buttons. Once completed, the top button with the letters SP lit up.

"What does SP stand for?" Lexi asked.

"Suite Présidentielle," Camille said with a broad grin. "The presidential suite. Like I told you, my guy requires the best."

They rode the lift all the way to the top floor, and then the doors opened to the lavish suite. Even more extravagant than the lobby below, the rooms were decorated in an elegant, modern motif.

Camille led her to the bedroom, where a black evening gown was draped across the king-sized bed. Next to the dress was a matching clutch, stilettos, and an exquisite set of diamond necklace and earrings.

"Camille, that's such a gorgeous dress."

The woman lifted it up for her to get a better look. "I knew you would love it."

The strapless, sequined gown had a split leg and low-back design that made it extremely sexy.

Lexi wished she could wear the outfit for Clint instead of Roman.

Camille left her alone in the opulent bathroom, allowing her time to get her hair and makeup done. There was a wide assortment of cosmetics stretched out on the counter that she could choose from.

She decided to go for a dramatic smokey eye. It was more than she was used to wearing, but this was a formal event.

Now, what to do with my hair?

She used the curling iron and put her hair up, deciding it would be best with the dress.

Gazing at her reflection, she was satisfied. Her imagination created an image of Clint behind her placing his hands around her waist and pressing his lips to the back of her neck.

She moved her hand to where the imaginary kiss had landed, wishing he were with her right now to help her through the next few hours. *But that's impossible.*

She hated not having a gun. At the moment she would continue to follow directions, but if things turned south she would need to defend herself. What could she use as a weapon that Roman and Camille would overlook? She scanned the items on the vanity, and picked up the travel-size hairspray the hotel provided. She knew it would sting the eyes, as she'd done it before to herself accidentally. It wasn't mace, but it would suffice. She grabbed a comb and a lipstick to help hide her real motive for the hairspray.

Camille walked in holding the dress and shoes. "You look absolutely beautiful. Roman will be so pleased."

"Thanks, Camille, but I don't care what he thinks. I'm

doing this for Liz." Lexi took the dress from Camille. "Where is the purse? I want to add these for emergencies."

"Good thinking. You'll want to look your best all evening." Camille exited the bathroom.

When Lexi put on the dress, she was glad the fit was just right. *But how?* She was shocked to find the shoes were also her specific size. How would Camille know her exact sizes?

Roman! That's how.

She remembered finding him in her closet back in college. The monster had lied that he was only checking out her clothes to help him find her a present, but she'd seen through him. He'd been so controlling when they were dating, even about what she wore. That and many other things had led her to breakup with him back then.

Camille returned with the handbag and jewelry. "I knew that dress would look good on you."

Lexi took the handbag, placing the items she'd selected inside, and then she put on the jewelry. Glancing once again at her reflection, she thought to herself that any other time dressing up like this would have thrilled her. But now she just wanted to get it over with. "Okay, let's do this."

Camille nodded.

Lexi grabbed the purse and walked out of the bathroom with her.

"My love, you look stunning." Roman wore a tuxedo and stood next to the window.

There was no denying how handsome he looked in the tux. Most women would die to go on a date with him. But they didn't know him.

AFTER PUTTING on the tuxedo jacket, Clint went through the door that connected his room to Lexi's. He stared at the empty bed, remembering the feel of her soft body next to his.

Lexi, I'll find you. I promise.

He rushed into the hallway and saw Fran in a red evening gown.

As they ran to the elevator, he said, "You look great, Fran."

"And you look nice." Once inside the descending elevator, she patted her handbag. "And I'm packing, too, just in case."

He brought out the comms from Max, handing one set to her. "We can hear and speak with the rest of the team with these."

"These are much smaller than any I've used before," she said, once again piquing his curiosity about her past. "They're virtually invisible."

"Blake doesn't skimp on tech."

"You think the others are already in place?"

"Soon. We'll check with them on the way."

Before heading to the hotel, the entire team had donned outfits that would let them blend in with the guests, security and staff.

Once on the ground floor of her building and churning with anxiety, Clint and Fran rushed past the security guard.

"Enjoy your evening," Claude called after them.

They got in the black Mercedes and Clint blasted down the street.

"I wish this could be an enjoyable evening instead of what we're facing," Fran said.

"Lexi. She's all that matters. Finding her."

"We *will* find her." Fran was kind, and he prayed she was right.

Ten minutes later, he exited off of the *Boulevard Périphérique* and onto the road that would take them to the event's location.

Something at the back of his mind told him he was getting closer to Lexi. Was the connection he had with her so strong he could actually sense her presence?

It's probably just wishful thinking.

Koslova knew where she was and if he had to beat it out of him, so be it.

Clint hit the button on the comms in his ear. "Is everyone in position?"

He was surprised at the voice that answered.

"Yes. They are." Blake's deep tone came through loud and clear. "Audio is working great."

"Hello, Blake. This is Fran. I'm glad we're working together again."

"It's been a long time, Fran. Max got me up to speed about all you've done for the team. I always can depend on you."

"Same here, my friend."

"Blake, did you see Lexi at the warehouse?" Clint asked.

"I did. She's alive."

"Thank God."

"It's all foggy because of the drugs Camille gave me, but I remember Lexi sitting next to me."

"Was she hurt?" Clint demanded.

"No. She seemed fine."

Fran touched the back of Clint's hand. "Lexi knows how to survive. I have no doubt we're going to find her."

"We *must* find her." Clint drove the car to the hotel's parking valet stand. They had arrived.

t the top of the grand staircase that led to the event in the ballroom, Lexi watched as Roman held out his arm for her.

"Shall we, my love?" His grin sickened her.

She hated complying, but she had to in order to get as much information as possible.

"Why are you hesitating?" Roman asked with a frown. "Does it have something to do with that guy who brought you to Camille's? Wasn't his name Clint?"

Dread shot through Lexi like a hot knife.

"Oh Roman." She took his arm, plastering a smile on her face. "That man means nothing to me."

His eyes were full of anger and doubt. "You expect me to believe that?"

"Why wouldn't you?" Her heart jumped like mad in her chest, though she tried to keep her panic from showing. "I'm so lucky to be with you again. You look so handsome tonight."

"We will be the most attractive couple at the event."

His demeanor swung to warmth in a flash, reminding her about how quickly he could turn from blistering hot to icy cold.

As they descended the stairs, she wondered if Clint was still searching for her? Of course he was.

She pressed her fingers against the handbag, feeling the hairspray inside. If Roman made one wrong move, she would use it to blind him and escape.

Roman had mentioned Clint by name. She prayed he didn't suspect the truth that she loved Clint, because if Roman knew he would kill him just like in her dream—*and just like he'd killed Matth.*

As Roman led her to the registration desk, she did her best to keep up the acting. "I can't believe I'm here with you after all these years. It feels like a fairy tale."

"I knew you would like it." His smile broadened, and he turned to a young woman behind the table. "Mr. and Mrs. Roman Koslova."

Even though the pit in her stomach twisted at his words, Lexi knew she couldn't say anything.

"*Bonjour.*" The woman looked at a printed list of guests. "Here you are. Roman Koslova with your beautiful wife as your plus one."

"She is beautiful, isn't she?" Roman put his arm around Lexi's waist.

Despite her disgust, she smiled, continuing to play the role. She glanced at the growing line behind them. "Seems like we got here before the crowd."

"*Oui, madame.* We are expecting two thousand guests this evening. You and your husband were smart to come early." The young woman handed them two pink, plastic bracelets. "These will get you into the ballroom and your table number is printed on them—number 33. Welcome and enjoy."

"We will," Roman said.

He led Lexi to the two men at the double doors, who were checking guests for the plastic bracelets and handing out programs.

Once inside the ballroom, Lexi took a deep breath. *So far, so good.*

"Well, what do you think, my love?" Roman asked, motioning to the grandeur around them.

She took it all in, searching for possible ways to escape and also for any sign of Clint or the team.

Harkening back to an earlier age, the space's primary palette was a decadent gold. In the center of its 30-foot ceiling hung a massive crystal chandelier. Circling above were several balconies, and underneath each of them were alcoves where drinks were being served.

"I've never seen such an elegant place. It's so beautiful." She glanced at the bracelet on her wrist. "Over there is table number 33. Shall we?"

"We're not here for the meal, my love." He grabbed her hand and led her to a far corner of the room.

JUST OUTSIDE THE BALLROOM, Clint hung back scanning the large crowd for any sign of Koslova, while Fran stood in the long line to get them registered.

Using his comms, he asked, "Max, any sign of our target?"

"The ballroom is filling up fast, but I haven't spotted Koslova yet. Hold on. Here comes one of the managers."

Clint could hear the woman's voice through his comms.

In French she said, "I need you behind the bar in that alcove. Now."

"*Oui, madame,*" Max answered her and then in a low tone said, "Don't worry, team. That location gives me a wide view of the—"

"Wait a minute, Max," Clint said after spotting Camille. His pulse burned in his veins. "Team, I've got eyes on Camille Moreau. She's coming down the main stairs with a suitcase."

"I'm in the lobby," Doc said. "But headed that direction now."

Being careful to blend into the crowd, Clint made his way to intercept Camille.

Just as she got to the ground floor, he came up next to her, grabbing her arm and shoving his gun into her side. "Don't make a scene, Camille."

"Oh *mon chéri.* I knew you still cared," she said with a laugh.

"Where is Lexi?"

"What is it with you and that girl? How would I know where she is?"

He pressed the barrel of his gun harder into her side. "I want to know where she is and I want to know now."

Camille shook her head, until Fran came up beside him. Then her eyes widened. "You! You're with him?"

"Why hello Camille," Fran said in a singsong tone. "It's been ages and ages. But we can catch up another time, because I think you better answer Clint's question."

The mystery of Fran's past continued to puzzle him. How did she and Camille know each other? Camille was clearly terrified of Fran. Why? Right now, he didn't care. He only wanted answers that would lead him to Lexi.

"She's with Roman," Camille blurted out.

Roman is here, so that means Lexi is here. In this very place.

SHE WAS SO CLOSE, just like he'd been feeling. He could sense her presence. Their connection was real.

"That's all I know, Francine. I swear."

"Where is Roman?" Fran asked in what sounded like a non-threatening tone to him, but had different undercurrents that Camille feared.

"He's inside." She shakily pointed at the ballroom's double doors. "They're both inside."

Doc came over to them with one of his medics, placing Camille between them. "I understand from Clint that you took quite the blow to your head."

"I'm fine," she answered, though keeping her eyes locked on Fran.

"We'll take her back to the OC," Doc said to him and Fran.

"It's good to see you again, Camille," Fran placed a pink plastic bracelet on Clint's wrist. "I look forward to catching up with you later."

Camille winced at her words.

As Doc and the medic took her away, Clint and Fran hurried to the doors that led into the ballroom—*and to Lexi.*

LEXI FOLLOWED Roman past a sign that read—*Ne Pas Entrer.* "Doesn't that mean we're not supposed to enter?"

Still holding tight to her hand, he led her up the stairs to the balconies. "My love, it doesn't matter. I'm Mr. Koslova. No one tells me what to do."

Since it was clear that they weren't going to attend the event, she wondered what was the real reason they were here.

"You mentioned a contract, but Drake called it a commitment. What are we doing here, Roman?"

"You keep that pretty little mouth of yours quiet and do as I tell you, understand?"

I'll do as he says for now. "Yes. I understand."

"That's better." He steered her past several doors to the balconies, which were all numbered.

When they came to number 7, he opened the door, motioning her inside.

He pulled over one of the chairs. "Sit, my love. This won't take long."

Just breathe, Lexi. "Thank you." She smiled and sat.

Roman cupped her chin. "You're perfect for me. I have a plane waiting that will take us to my private island once this task is completed." He stepped back from her, and bent down next to an intake grille for the air conditioning. "You will love it there. Just imagine. The two of us, all alone, in paradise."

Far from paradise. More like hell.

There was no way she was getting on a plane with Roman. But her time was running out.

He removed the grille and pulled out a black case. "I've already got the house stocked with enough food and wine that we won't have to lay eyes on another soul for a year."

Even though Roman continued rambling about what future he wanted, his words faded into the background. Her concern was finding answers that would help her save Liz and lead her back to Clint. Did the contents of the black case have the answers she desperately needed?

When Roman lifted the case's lid, she gasped. Inside were parts of a rifle.

"What the hell?"

Roman's happy mood vanished, and he glared hard at her. "I. Told. You. To. Be. Quiet. I have a job to do."

Back to acting.

She took a deep breath. "Sorry, Roman. I'll be good."

I can't let him kill again.

"That's my girl." Roman ran his hands through her hair, flipping back in his Jekyll and Hyde routine to his previous jovial mood. "You are mine, my love. All mine."

As Roman quickly assembled the sniper rifle, Lexi could feel her heart pounding fast inside her chest.

What do I do? What do I do?

After hearing the emcee begin to address the crowd below, she peered over the edge of the balcony and realized there was a direct line of sight to the podium.

CLINT AND FRAN went in opposite directions through the crowd, who were taking their seats at the tables.

"*Mesdames et messieurs, bienvenue à...*"

Clint tuned out the applause that followed the emcee

addressing the audience. No matter where he looked, he could not find Lexi.

Where are you?

As CONFLICTING THOUGHTS and emotions raced through her mind, Lexi watched as Roman peered through the scope of the rifle, now fully assembled.

I have to stop him, but what happens to Liz?

Lexi carefully retrieved the hairspray from the handbag.

"...we'll drink piña coladas and watch the sunset every night, my love." Abruptly, Roman's rambling ended.

Lexi knew time was up. She had to act now.

Seeing Roman's finger curl around the trigger, she leapt at him, spraying the blinding mist into his eyes a split-second before the gun fired.

Bang!

When the crowd below screamed, Lexi believed that she'd failed.

"You bitch!" With his eyes swelling and closed, Roman grabbed her arm. "You'll pay for this."

When Clint turned the direction of the shooter that had fired the shot, he saw Koslova grab Lexi.

Like rocket fuel, the onslaught of pure rage and the primal need to protect Lexi raced through his body as he shot through the terrified crowd and up the stairs.

LEXI TRIED to get free from Roman's hold, but his grip was too strong.

Her one advantage was he couldn't hold his eyes open, and tears streamed down his face from the burn.

"You're mine! Stop fighting me!"

"Never!" She watched as he pulled out a pistol from his jacket.

"If I can't have you, no one can."

Charged with adrenaline, she bit his forearm as hard as she could.

"Fuck!" Roman shoved her to the floor, knocking the wind out of her.

He got on top of her, pinning her down. "That's it. You're dead."

Lexi closed her eyes and prayed...

"Koslova!" Clint's voice came through like he was really there.

"You!" Roman yelled.

Bang!

20

As the hotel alarms blared, Clint pulled Roman's body off of Lexi and lifted her into his arms.

"Lexi. Lexi. It's me. Clint. Open your eyes, sweetheart."

She looked up at him. "Clint, it is you." She put her arms around his shoulders, melting into him. Her tears began to flow. "I'm so glad you're here. I'm so exhausted."

"Of course you are after all you've been through. But you're going to be okay now, sweetheart." He kissed her forehead tenderly. "It's all over. You're safe."

"But what about Liz?" she asked in a panicky tone.

"She's safe, too. She's with Steve."

"And Blake? He didn't betray us."

"I know. He's safe, too."

Relief showed on her face. "Thank God."

Blake's voice came through the comms. "Authorities are on their way, three minutes out."

He looked at Lexi. "We've got to go."

"You don't have to carry me. Put me down and I'll follow you."

"No. You said it yourself. You're exhausted. This will be faster. Trust me."

"I do trust you." She held on a little tighter to him.

"Clint, bring Lexi to the alley." Max was out of breath from running. "I'll be waiting in the Cadillac."

"On my way," Clint answered, rushing to the stairs with Lexi in his arms.

"The rest of the team take the other vehicles and meet back at Command," Blake instructed.

"Fran, where are you?" Max asked.

"I'm close to the exit. I'll meet you at the Cadillac."

When Clint made it to the emergency exit, he saw that it had been propped open, likely by Fran or Max.

He ran out of the building and straight to the Cadillac. Max was already behind the wheel and Fran held the back door open for them.

Still holding onto Lexi, Clint got in the back.

Fran jumped in the front. "Hit it, Max."

He sped the Cadillac away.

Sirens sounded behind them.

"We got out of there just in time," Max said, weaving effortlessly in and out of traffic.

"Great driving, buddy." Clint ran his hands through Lexi's hair.

Still in his arms, she touched his face, whispering. "I'm sorry for leaving, but Roman—"

"I know, sweetheart," he said in a quiet tone so that only she could hear. "I saw his message. Koslova is a career criminal, an assassin who is skilled at manipulating people." Clint pulled her up into a gentle kiss. "I was afraid I was going to lose you," he confessed, his voice cracking with raw emotion.

"I knew you wouldn't stop looking for me."

"I shouldn't have let you out of my sight."

"Baby, you have nothing to be guilty about. I'm so sorry I caused you so much worry. If anyone is to blame for what happened, it's me."

"Don't do that to yourself, sweetheart. You've been blaming yourself for things beyond your control for far too long." He knew a thing or two about that as he'd done the same concerning Gary. "That guy's murder in Dallas wasn't your fault. That was Koslova's. Steve getting shot? Again, all Koslova's doing. Liz being kidnapped? That was him not you. When you left Fran's, you did it to protect Liz and me. Lexi, you're amazing. Every decision you've made has come from your heart. There's only one person to blame. Koslova. Just him. Not you. Not me. He's the guilty party in all of this."

A weak smile spread across her lips. "I know you're right, it's just so—"

He kissed her before she could protest more. "I am right. You're the most incredible woman I've ever known."

"And you are safe," Lexi told him. "And Roman is really gone. It's finally over."

Feeling like he'd conquered the world, Clint gazed at her. "You've changed my entire life, sweetheart. Every dream or want inside me belongs to you. Your happiness is all that matters to me, and I will spend the rest of my life making sure you have everything you ever desire. I love you so much."

"I love you, too," she whispered back.

He never dreamed a woman like her could fall in love with a man like him.

s the Cadillac came to a stop, Lexi held on tight to Clint and looked out the front windshield.

To her surprise, the wall full of graffiti ahead suddenly split in two, leaving an opening just wide enough for Max to drive the vehicle through.

Once the Cadillac passed the divided wall, it closed, returning back to a singular structure. Now, their presence would remain secret from those on the streets outside.

There were several cars inside the clandestine parking garage.

"That spy wall isn't something a person sees every day," she said to Clint.

He chuckled. "That's because it's a spy wall, sweetheart."

She liked this side of Clint, where he let his guard down and could laugh.

"It's necessary to keep anyone from finding us," Max said, "including the authorities. Ahmed and Geoff have been monitoring the police bands and it looks like we're in the clear."

Lexi smiled. "Seems like I have a lot of people to thank for helping me out of this mess, especially the artist who painted the graffiti. I was impressed with the giant unicorn."

Everyone laughed, which felt good to her.

Clint squeezed her tight. "I'm glad you're feeling better."

"I am. Very much so, thanks to you." She felt like his energy was feeding into hers, making her stronger and stronger.

"Lexi!" Liz ran out to meet them at the Cadillac.

She let go of Clint and hopped out of the car, wrapping Liz in her arms. "Thank God, you're okay."

"And you, too." Liz turned to Clint. "Thank you so much. I owe you."

He put his arm around Lexi. "No one owes me anything, Liz."

Liz's eyes widened. "Hmm. Well, I'm in debt whether you like it or not."

Fran smiled. "You are so much like your mother, Liz. Generous to a fault."

Liz hugged her. "I don't know what I would have done if you or Lexi had been hurt."

"Good thing we made it through unscathed then."

"Come on inside," Liz said, leading them to a door. "Blake has information for all of you."

"He's okay, too?" Lexi asked, remembering the state she'd last seen him in.

"He is. Blake is just fine." Liz had a glimmer in her eyes that Lexi couldn't remember ever seeing before.

Liz led them through a door that opened up to a large area.

Lexi scanned the space, which was so similar to the OC she'd seen before.

To her left was Boris inside a cage.

Straight ahead was a medical area with an empty bed.

"Lexi!" Steve walked towards her from the tech area. He hugged her tight. "God, it's good to see you."

"It's good to see you up and walking around." She smiled, then saw over his shoulder that Blake and Doc were headed their way.

Steve let her go and held out his hand to Clint. "You did it. I can't thank you enough."

Clint shook his hand. "It took all of us, including Lexi herself. She used skills and instincts that few operatives have."

"She's a natural, is she?" Steve smiled at her with pride.

"I don't know about all of that." Lexi felt heat in her cheeks.

"Well, I do know. I saw you in action." Clint put his arm around her shoulder. "Koslova would have succeeded and killed his target had you not acted when you did."

"Oh my gosh. She's really alive?"

"She is. Koslova missed, and she was rushed out. You saved her."

"I had to do something. Anyone would have done the same."

"Sweetheart, a lot of agents have tried to stop Koslova before and failed." Clint squeezed her. "You did what no one else has ever been able to do. You succeeded."

"You give me more credit than I deserve. Like you said, it took all of us. The real concern for me is why was Roman targeting that woman? And how would Drake benefit from her assassination?"

"We're not entirely sure," Blake answered. "Lila Cross is the Executive Director of Cyber Security for the European Union. What we don't know is why my brother was after her."

"Where did you put Camille?" Clint asked. "She likely has the answers we need."

"She's tied up in my office, nice and tight," Doc said. "I've got two men guarding the door. She's not going anywhere."

"I'm not so sure about that," Fran interjected.

"She's right there," Ahmed pointed to his screen, which showed an image of Camille sitting in a chair with her wrists and ankles secured with zip ties.

"Maybe she is. Maybe she isn't," Fran said wryly.

"What do you mean by that?" Doc asked.

"I know you did your best to secure her, but Camille isn't your average operative. I've known her to wiggle free from the impossible on more than a few occasions. In fact, she's known in many circles as Houdini."

"Now you've got me worried." Doc immediately turned and ran to a hallway past the hospital bed.

Everyone followed, and was shocked to find no guards at his office door.

When they went in, they discovered the two men were knocked out on the floor and Camille was long gone.

Doc bent down to check on his men. "They'll be fine, but damn it! How did she manage to do this?"

Fran shrugged. "I trained her well."

"You what?" Steve asked.

"It's a long story for another time." Fran turned to Clint.

"I look forward to hearing about those stories and more from you," he said.

"All I ask is for a nice cup of tea."

"You've got a deal, Fran."

Lexi could tell that Clint and Fran respected each other.

"Let's check the monitors to figure out what she did," Max said.

Leaving Doc to attend to the fallen men, the rest returned to the high-tech area.

"Ahmed, put up camera six's feed on monitor four," Max instructed, pointing to the largest screen on the wall.

Along with the others, Lexi saw the same image they'd just viewed only minutes ago with Camille tied up in the chair.

"What the hell!" Steve exclaimed. "How is that possible?"

"It's a previous video loop," Fran told him. "Can you roll back the feed, Max?"

"Sure." He hit some buttons on the keyboard and the video reversed.

"Stop. There." Fran nodded. "See that. Her hands are free right before the screen scrambles for a split second."

"I didn't see anything," Liz said.

Fran leaned forward. "Max, try rolling the video in slow motion."

Lexi focused on Camille's hands, which did seem like

they were farther apart from each other than a second earlier.

"Like I told you before. They call her Houdini," Fran said. "Her rings are much more than jewelry. They're tools. I'm betting one of Camille's rings had a tiny retractable knife and another had a jammer that let her take control of the camera."

"Wow," Liz said. "Just like a James Bond movie."

"You're a girl after my own heart," Fran said. "But this is the twenty-first century after all."

Doc returned with the two guards, who were humiliated.

"Camille tricked them, claiming she needed to use the bathroom," he said. "When they opened the door, she got the jump on them. I'm not sure how she got out the back without tripping the alarm, but she's long gone."

"Back to Drake, no doubt," Clint said, as Max checked the other feeds.

There were no images of Camille.

"Damn, she is Houdini," Geoff said.

"Could she still be in the building?" Ahmed asked.

Clint, Doc and some others searched the building for her, while Max and his team did an inspection of the alarm system.

After looking in every possible hiding place with no sign of Camille, everyone turned to Max for an answer.

"Somehow, she was able to override our system," he said. "She turned off the alarm to the west exit. Like she'd done in Doc's office, she was able to scramble the feeds once again."

"Impressive," Blake said. "I wish my brother hadn't corrupted her."

"Did you know Drake was alive?" Clint asked.

"No. I didn't." Blake's face darkened. "But obviously he's been playing me all along."

Clint placed his hand on Blake's shoulder. "What happened between you and your brother? How did he survive that final mission you ran? We all thought he was dead."

"So did I. My last words to Drake were accusing him of killing our parents." Blake's tone was heartbreaking.

From every syllable he spoke, Lexi could sense the ancient pain he'd been carrying. She recalled what Camille had told her about blaming Blake. Now, the real truth and real culprit was about to be revealed.

"I was lead on a mission to capture a high level target. Drake was one of four operatives. I dismissed his suggestion of bleeding the target's brakes, since it was a capture, not eliminate mission. But I couldn't shake the similarities of what had happened to our parents. They died in a car accident years earlier. Their brakes failed. At the time, no one suspected the brake fluid had been drained, including me, until Drake mentioned his idea. So I confronted him right before the mission. Drake exploded, screaming that I just wanted to keep him from his inheritance."

Lexi recalled Drake's cruelty to Blake. Not only had he kept him drugged, but he'd also had him beaten. The bruises were still evident. How could anyone do that to someone, let alone his own brother?

"On the night of the mission, Drake and another operative ran into a building. We had proof that the target was hiding there. An explosion erupted, and the entire place went up in flames. There seemed to be no escape. I thought he was dead, but I was wrong."

"Did you recover bodies?" Steve asked.

"That was a black ops, not on friendly soil. I had to get the rest of my men to safety. And after seeing the total destruction of that building, I still don't know how Drake survived."

"Do you think the other operative could have made it out too?" Fran asked.

"No one ever heard from him either, but who knows now?" Blake looked at Clint. "I know you told me that you would only work on the one mission to bring down Koslova, but I hope you'll consider joining the team permanently."

"I get it," Clint said. "But all that matters to me now is Lexi."

"I don't know what my brother's plans are," Blake said, "but I need you and her on this team to stop him."

"Me?" Lexi was shocked to hear him include her in his pitch.

Clint shook his head. "No way, Blake. I don't want her to be in danger ever again."

"Danger?" She turned to Clint. "I've never felt so alive in my life. I think I want to do this. Today I stopped an assassination. Can you believe that?"

Fran laughed. "I understand. You remind me of myself many years ago. Clint, here's a friendly suggestion. Don't try to stop her. Instead, make sure you're always beside her."

"Clint, we could be the new Mr. and Mrs. Smith, but I promise I wouldn't try to kill you."

"Is that a proposal?" he asked with a grin.

She felt her face flush with warmth. "No. I'm... no."

"Why not? Aren't I husband material?"

"No. Well. I don't know. We... um... I..." She looked into his devilish, laughing eyes. "Can we just talk about this later?"

"Yes, sweetheart." He kissed her, and she heard everyone clapping.

Ahmed looked up from his monitor. "Guys, we have a problem."

"What kind of problem?" Clint pulled her in closer.

Blake and Max leaned in to get a good look at Ahmed and Geoff's screens.

"The heat has been turned up on Lexi," Ahmed said.

Geoff added, "We weren't the only ones hacking into the hotel's security cameras."

"Who else?" Steve asked.

"My brother," Blake answered, still scanning the monitors. "And it appears he anonymously turned over some doctored footage to Interpol."

"What kind of doctored footage?" Clint asked.

Suddenly, a video popped up on one of the screens showing her and Roman entering the event. Another feed began, that showed her on the balcony with the barrel of Roman's gun pointed at the podium.

Lexi felt the blood drain out of her face. "So does that mean they're still looking to arrest me?"

Blake nodded.

Clint turned to Fran. "Is your plan of getting her out of the country still active?"

"It is." Fran nodded. "The pilot can have my jet *wheels-up* at a moment's notice. Lexi can be in Morocco in under three hours."

s the others worked out the details for Lexi to escape the country, she followed Liz to the break room.

Before entering, she glanced back across the hallway at Doc's open door, wishing Camille hadn't escaped.

Was the woman returning to Drake? Most likely, yes. Camille was so in love with him, but Lexi doubted he felt the same for her.

What else could Drake be up to?

Whatever his plans might be, she knew they were no good and would need to be stopped.

Lexi entered the break room, which looked like it could be a part of any typical office, though the OC was far from typical. The space had a water cooler, cabinets, a sink, a microwave, and a refrigerator. On the counter was a coffee pot with a variety of creamers and sweeteners, plus a wide assortment of muffins.

"Liz, don't those muffins look delicious?" Lexi asked. "And that coffee smells so good."

"I bet you're hungry. When was the last chance you had to eat?"

"At Fran's last night."

"My God, you must be starving."

She felt her stomach rumble. "Yep. Pretty hungry."

"Grab a muffin and I'll pour us some fresh coffee." Liz pulled out two cups from the cabinets. "Seems like Ahmed and Geoff have an addiction to caffeine. When everyone left to find you, they kept the coffee going."

"I'm sure Steve appreciates that." Lexi took a bite of a blueberry muffin, which was heavenly.

"Him and me both." Liz handed her a cup with cream and sugar, just the way she liked it.

Lexi took a long sip. "Mm. I needed this to keep me going. Are you all set for the trip?"

"Actually, I'm staying. Fran says there's things I can be working on for you from France, where I have a lot of contacts. In Morocco I don't have any. Also, if the police show up at her place looking for you, she said that we can tell them that it was me staying there, not you."

"I would have never thought of that. Fran is brilliant."

"And apparently there's more to her than just helping refugees."

"No doubt about that." Lexi took another sip of the coffee, glad for the warmth it gave her. "And I want to know more about her past with Camille."

"Me, too. Staying will give me the opportunity to have a long talk with her. After all, I haven't seen her since I was twelve."

"All I know right now is Fran is not only brilliant but brave, too." She finished the muffin and couldn't resist getting another. "Her instincts are spot on every time. But

I'm worried about you staying behind with Camille and Drake still out there."

Liz refilled their cups. "I see no reason why they'd be interested in me. And now that Roman is gone, I bet their attention has moved away from you. But you need to get to Morocco just to be safe until we can clear your name."

"How is that even possible now? Drake fed that video of me with Roman at the event. Roman is dead. Matt is dead. It won't be long before they connect me to their deaths."

"Lexi, you've proven your ability to adapt and survive. Leave it to Blake's team, Fran and me to fix the rest of this mess. From what I've already seen from the team, it won't take long. Don't you agree?"

"Yes. I do. And I can't wait to have a clean record."

"You may not keep a clean record if you're going to be a spy or an agent or whatever Blake's team calls themselves. Are you sure about joining them?"

"Liz, all I can say is I've never felt more alive since losing mom and dad. I went to college but had no purpose. Now I do. Clint has helped me see what is possible. We can make the world a better place."

"Does he know about your parents?"

She and Liz had initially bonded because they both had lost their parents at young ages.

"I believe he knows some, but I haven't had a chance to share much about my life with him yet. He has shared some with me, but I want to learn more."

"That's another reason I'm not going. You need a chance to be alone with him, and I hear Morocco is a romantic country." She winked at her.

Clint entered. "Hey, babe. It's time to leave. Blake sent

Ahmed to retrieve your luggage from your hotel room. He'll meet us at the airstrip."

"You think my luggage is still there?" Lexi asked.

"Probably, but if not Fran says she'll have some things delivered to the place she's set up for us in Morocco."

She and Liz looked at each other and in unison said, "Brilliant."

They both laughed.

"Am I missing something?" Clint asked.

"Nope. Just our admiration for Fran," Lexi said, moving closer to Clint. "Would you like a cup of coffee to take with us?"

"And some muffins?" Liz added. "I suppose you haven't eaten either since last night."

"You're right. I haven't." He rubbed his stomach. "I simply forgot."

"Not that we had the time to eat," Lexi said.

"Yes to coffee and muffins. That would be great, Liz. Thanks."

Lexi was glad they seemed to be warming up to each other nicely.

"By the looks of this crumb at the corner of your mouth, it seems you enjoyed a muffin."

She raised her hand to wipe it, but he stopped her.

"Let me get that for you." He kissed her lightly.

She grinned. "Two actually, and I could easily eat another."

Liz placed several muffins in a container she'd retrieved from the cabinets. "There's a blueberry, two banana, a lemon and two poppy seeds for your trip."

"Liz, it's only a three-hour trip," she said with a laugh.

"Well, you're both hungry. And you can have them for breakfast if there are any left."

Max walked in. "You two ready?"

"We are." Lexi grabbed the container of muffins.

Clint took the cup of coffee. "Thanks, Liz."

"Take care of her."

"I will."

Liz turned to her. "Be safe."

"You, too."

Clint put his arm around her and they followed Max to the parking garage.

CLINT GLANCED at the digital clock on the Cadillac's dashboard.

3:11 am.

They were still a few minutes from the airstrip where Fran's jet waited.

Lexi broke off a piece of a muffin and placed it in his mouth. "Good, huh?"

"Delicious." He liked the intimacy of her feeding him. "Best damn muffin I've ever eaten."

"Just got a text from Ahmed," Max said from the backseat. "He's five minutes ahead of us and has your luggage."

"So my room was untouched?" Lexi asked.

"Not exactly. Someone had broken in earlier likely looking for a clue to your location. They dumped your suitcase out, but Ahmed repacked everything."

Lexi nodded. "Clint, you were right about us not going back. We would have run right into them."

"I'm just glad you'll have your things in Morocco."

"What about you? You don't have a bag?"

"Actually, Ahmed stopped at my hotel first and grabbed my stuff since it was on the way to yours. You and I are all set." Clint was looking forward to spending more time alone with Lexi. They would have three hours together. Three hours without interruption. Three hours without threats.

Three wonderful hours alone.

"Max, would you mind doing me a favor?" Lexi asked.

"Sure. What do you need?"

"Could you check on Liz and Fran after you drop us off at the airstrip?"

"I'm way ahead of you, Lexi," Max answered. "I have already discussed this with Blake and Fran. I'm going to be staying at her place until we're sure it's safe. I promise I won't let anything happen to her or Liz."

"Thank you. You don't know how much I appreciate that. One more thing."

"What?"

"Would you also ask Doc to let me know how Steve is doing? He was so exhausted after things settled down. I want him to get all the rest he needs."

"I'll let Doc know."

Clint smiled. He learning that no matter what, Lexi would make sure her friends were okay.

And Max? He was turning out to be quite the operative—*and a great friend.*

Clint saw the sign for the private airstrip, which was located in a remote area outside of Paris. He turned in, passing the gate.

At the end of a long drive was a lone hangar. A Learjet

sat next to the building with its engines running. Off to the side were two vehicles.

Ahmed stood next to the jet's stairs.

Clint, Lexi and Max exited the Cadillac and stepped onto the tarmac.

"I put your luggage inside," Ahmed said. "The pilot is in the cockpit ready to go. And Fran told me to tell you the bar is fully stocked with drinks and snacks."

"I doubt if we need any booze," Lexi said. "The coffee is what's keeping us awake. But the snacks sound good. And thanks for repacking my things."

"I did my best, but they were a little wrinkled."

"That's okay. I'll figure it out. I just appreciate what you did for me. Not just the luggage, but everything."

"All in a day's work," Ahmed said. "And welcome to the team, Lexi."

"Thanks. I've got a lot to learn but I am so excited."

Clint wasn't so sure about her joining the team. In fact, he wasn't sure what he was going to do. But he couldn't shake what she'd told him when Blake had made the offer to her.

"I've never felt so alive in my life. I think I want to do this. Today I stopped an assassination. Can you believe that?"

REMEMBERING the look in her eyes, he knew how excited she was. One thing he was certain of—*he wasn't ever leaving her again.* If she joined, he would join.

Clint was glad for the flight, which would give them time to discuss their future.

"Safe travels," Max said, as he and Ahmed stepped back.

"I've never been in a private jet before." Lexi bounded through the door.

Clint grinned, following her into the jet. "You're going to love it, sweetheart."

23

Lexi was amazed at the jet's interior of plush leather seats and warm mahogany accents. "Clint, can you believe how luxurious this is?"

"Considering it's Fran's, I wouldn't expect anything less."

A uniformed pilot came out from the cockpit door. Where Clint had rugged good looks, the pilot leaned to the classic. He was quite handsome with his closely trimmed beard, dark hair and even darker eyes. She guessed him to be about the same age as she was—late twenties.

"*Bonjour,* Ms. Bly. Mr. Knight. Grab yourself a drink from the galley, and then please have a seat and buckle up. We'll be taking off in five minutes."

"Thank you," Clint said. "And your name is...?"

"Captain Andre Leclair, at your service."

"I assume Fran told you of the sensitivity of this flight?"

Lexi could tell that Clint wasn't leaving anything to

chance.

"No cause to worry, Mr. Knight. I've been with Ms. Binoche for a very long time. As far as anyone else knows, I'm flying the jet alone to Spain for scheduled maintenance. No passengers."

Lexi wondered how long it would be before she could travel freely again with a clear name. "But aren't we supposed to be going to Morocco not Spain?"

"Yes, we are flying to Morocco," Andre said with a smile. "Ms. Binoche's other jet, which is a twin to this one, will be taking our place in Spain while we make our detour to Morocco. We'll be landing at a private airfield just outside of Casablanca."

Clint nodded. "That'll work."

"I'm glad you approve. Once we are in the air you can move about the cabin. I've promised Ms. Binoche to see to your every need."

"She is brilliant and generous," Lexi said.

"That she is, *madame*. There are several types of drinks as well as a fruit and cheese plate for you in the galley."

"Fran has thought of everything," Clint said.

"There are also facilities in the back of the cabin. The chairs can recline." Andre demonstrated that function for them, and then pointed to the sofa. "And this can pull out into a bed, should you decide to sleep. Make yourself at home. If you need anything, just press one of the call buttons."

"Thank you, Andre," Clint said. "We'll be fine."

Andre returned to the cockpit, shutting the door behind him.

"I think we're in good hands, don't you, Clint?" Lexi

asked.

"Seems quite capable and loyal to Fran. Yes. I like him." He moved to the galley. "I know you said the coffee would do, but how about a glass of wine before takeoff to help you relax?"

"Yes, please." She sat on the sofa, glad to be off her feet. "If there is white, that would be great."

"There is." He filled two glasses and handed her one.

"Please fasten your seatbelts." Andre's voice came through the hidden speakers. "And prepare for takeoff."

Clint sat next to her. "Hand me your drink so you can buckle up."

She did and then took his, so he could do the same.

The takeoff impressed her, smoother than any commercial flight she'd ever been on.

"A girl could get used to this kind of treatment," she said, taking a sip of the wine.

After a few minutes, Andre informed them from the cockpit, "We've reached our cruising altitude. You're free to move about the cabin. Enjoy the flight."

"Clint, I feel quite comfortable right where I am, as long as I'm next to you." Lexi leaned her head on his shoulder.

"I'm glad you do, because I feel the same way. I've never met anyone who has affected me the way you have." He moved in close. "Do you believe in love at first sight?"

"I didn't until I met you, but I do now."

"Same for me, sweetheart. I love you so much."

"I love you, too even though you know more about me than I do about you."

"I just know a few facts, what Max and the team were

able to find. But I want to know everything about your life. And I want to hear it from you." Clint's soft tone and the way he stroked her hair made her drift back into the past.

"My parents were killed in a car accident when I was twelve. I was at my friend's sleepover when..."

I GIGGLED with the other girls at Krista pretending to be Paul, the cutest boy in the eighth grade, who had a big crush on Liz.

"Give me a kiss," Krista said in a deep tone.

"Stop it," Liz said laughing.

The bedroom door suddenly opened, and Krista's mom walked in with a strange look on her face.

"Lexi, will you come with me?"

"What's wrong, Mom?" Krista asked.

"Shh. I'll talk to you in a little bit."

I walked out of the room with Krista's mom. "Did I do something wrong?"

"Of course not, sweetheart." She led me to the living room, where Sheriff Johnson stood.

"What's going on?" I asked.

The sheriff took my hand. "It's about your mom and dad, Lexi. There's been an accident."

As he told me my parents were dead, I felt everything slow to a crawl. His voice sounded distant as though coming from a far off place. My legs buckled and I fell to the floor.

"Dave, get me a wet cloth!" Krista's mom yelled to her husband, as I felt the Sheriff lift me to the sofa.

"Should we call an ambulance?" Krista's mom asked, as my focus began to return.

"No. Please. I'm fine." Despite my words, I could feel the

tears flowing from my eyes. "I just need to go home."

I saw Liz and the other girls running into the room.

"What's going on, Mom?" Krista asked.

"You girls go back into your bedroom."

I felt Liz squeeze my hand, and I put my arms around her.

She didn't say anything, but kept hold of me while I cried and cried.

As the painful memory receded, Lexi held on tight to Clint. "Liz's grandparents took me in, and just like they'd done for her when her parents had died, they got custody of me. The last time I was in my house was when Liz's grandparents took me to get some of my stuff. They put all my mom and dad's things in storage, thinking I would go through them when I was older. But I haven't, Clint. I still pay the storage bill, but I've never opened the door. Not once."

"Sweetheart, I didn't mean to make you relive such a terrible ordeal." Clint's eyes glistened with compassionate tears. "I remember Fran asking about your parents and how you avoided her questions. If this is too much—"

"But I want to tell you. I've held a lot of these feelings inside of me because I've been unable to express myself. It's hard for me to open up to anyone. Liz and I are very close, like sisters. And even she doesn't know I've never gone to the storage unit. You're the first person I've ever told."

He kissed her forehead.

"Maybe it's because I lost my parents when I was twelve and I didn't know how to express myself. Whatever the reason, it's easy for me to tell you everything."

"It makes me feel happy that you can trust me. I want to be there for you, now and forever."

"I feel like a weight has been lifted that I didn't even know I'd been carrying all this time. I want to share everything with you. After losing my parents in the car accident, I didn't believe in *happily ever afters*. I was so alone. But being with you has changed that for me."

"For me, too, sweetheart." He refilled their glasses. "So are you close with Liz's grandparents?"

"Yes, I was. They treated me just like they did Liz. There was no difference between us. We lost Grammy five years ago and Grampy a year later. I miss them very much. But what about you, Clint? What about your family? Do you have brothers and sisters?"

CLINT HAD BEEN TRAINED to keep personal details to himself, but with Lexi he wanted to share everything. Actually it was much more than that. He *needed* to share everything, especially after she trusted him and opened up about her own life.

"I have one sister. She's three years younger than me."

"What's your sister's name?"

"Shayla. She lives in Montana with her husband and her five year old twins, a boy and girl. They have a horse ranch." He brought out his phone and showed her photos from Shayla's ranch.

"It's so beautiful. I bet you love visiting your sister."

"Actually, these photos are from her Facebook page. I've never been, though she's begged me to come every summer. I always had a mission. At least that was my excuse."

Her gorgeous green eyes locked with his. "Why did you need an excuse?"

"Being in the Agency didn't allow me to share what I was doing. They drilled into us from day one the importance of secrecy. We had to keep our family life separate in order to protect them."

"That makes perfect sense to me."

"But I took it to the extreme level. I quit calling, writing, and keeping in touch. I haven't seen my parents or Shayla since I joined the Agency. And I've never seen my nephews in person."

"Well, mister, that's not right. And I'm going to make sure we fix it."

He laughed. "Oh you are, are you?"

"Yes, I am. I would give anything to be able to see my parents."

"So you're pulling out the big guns, are you?"

"Yes. If I have to. Family is more important than any job."

"It's just that—"

She pressed her fingers to his lips. "There's no *just thats* about it. I can't wait to meet your family." She kissed him lightly.

"No fair using kisses to convince me."

"I don't play fair, mister." She grinned. "So what do your parents and Shayla think you do?"

"They believe I work for an international investment agency."

"Good one. That sounds very important and vague and explains why you have to travel abroad."

"Exactly. It's worked all these years. And when you do meet them, you have to play along, okay?"

"I may be new to the spy game, but I'm a damn good actress, Harold."

"Yes, you are, Mabel. Yes you are. And I know my family is going to love you."

"So you do want me to meet them?"

"Yes. I lost this argument before it began."

"Now that we've got that straight, do your parents live near Shayla?"

"Not yet, but I bet eventually they'll want to be close to their grandkids. Right now, Mom and Dad live in Springfield, Missouri. Dad is a firefighter and Mom is a pediatric nurse." He pulled up a photo of his parents on his phone to show her.

"Wow. I see where you get your good looks. And it sounds like giving back is in your blood, too."

"I never thought about it that way, but maybe you're right—at least about trying to give back."

"So, you're throwing the modest card out there." She grinned. "Are you saying I don't have good taste in men?"

"I can't win with you, can I?"

"You're finally catching on."

He stood, picking up the bottle of wine and their empty glasses. "We finished this bottle. Want some more or would you like something else?"

"I'm a little tipsy, so a soda would be nice. And some food, *s'il vous plait.* Those muffins did not last."

He bent at the waist and in a quirky French accent said, "*Oui, madame.* One soda with a fruit and cheese platter coming right up?"

"*Merci beaucoup.*"

He returned with their snacks, placing them on the table in front of her and continuing his act as a French waiter. "I understand you ordered our premier service, *madame.*"

"*Oui.*"

He leaned down and kissed her, loving the taste of her lips.

"Your service is *extraordinaire, monsieur.* I will definitely be back for more."

He sat next to her. "Excellent, and I hope you'll leave us a glowing Yelp review."

She laughed, placing a grape at his lips.

"You look radiant," he said. "Happier."

"Roman has taken up space in my head for years. Every knock on the door, every creak in the middle of the night, I'd think, *He's back.* Now he's dead. He can't ever hurt me again. I feel free." She squeezed his hand. "What about you? You told me Roman killed your friend. How are you feeling?"

"My best friend is gone. He's not coming back." Clint felt a long sigh pass over his lips. "I just hope Gary knows I got Koslova in the end."

"I'm sure he does."

The rest of the flight he and Lexi talked and talked. About everything. Big things. Little things. He learned she hated coconut because of the texture, and he told her about his dislike of cilantro because it tasted like soap to him. They both were excited to discover they had a joint love of the band Phish. And on and on. He didn't want the flight to end.

But Andre's voice finally came through the speakers. "Please fasten your seatbelts. We're about to land."

 s the sun began to rise over the Casablanca skyline, Lexi stepped down the jet's stairs to the tarmac with Clint and Andre.

A tall, muscled man with red hair greeted them with a distinct Scottish accent. "*Fàilte* to Casablanca."

"What's the status here, Madd?" Clint asked.

"All clear. No sign of hostiles, including Drake, Camille, their operatives, or any unwanted authorities."

"I knew I could count on you." Clint and the man hugged each other.

Lexi could tell their bond was strong.

"It's been a very long time, Clint."

"Yes it has. That last time I saw you was that mission in Nepal." When they let go, Clint put his arm around Lexi. "Madd, this is Lexi Bly. Lexi, this is Maddox MacKinnon, a trusted friend."

Madd bent slightly at the waist. "A pleasure to meet such a bonnie lass as you, Miss Bly."

"Please call me *Lexi*."

"And you call me Madd. Remind me to tell you some stories about this lad."

"Believe me, I will remind you. I want to know everything I can about Clint." She instantly liked Madd. "Thank you for all your help."

Madd handed her a colorful scarf. "To keep you from standing out. The dress for women in Morocco is on the conservative side of things."

"This matches my outfit perfectly. How did you know?"

"Fran," he said.

"That doesn't surprise me." Lexi wrapped the scarf around her head. "Is this okay?"

Madd nodded. "I doubt if you'll need it since we're going straight to the villa. But just in case..."

Clint motioned to Andre. "Madd, this is our pilot An—"

"Yes, I know Andre. He and I have worked on a couple of things for Fran before." Madd shook Andre's hand.

Clint seemed confused. "Madd, you know Fran?"

"*Aye*, and I'm surprised you don't."

"Hmm. I know her some now, but I plan on learning everything about her. She's agreed to fill me in over tea."

Madd laughed. "It'll take more than just an afternoon of tea to learn everything."

Andre nodded. "That's for certain."

Madd slapped him on the back in agreement. "You'd have to drink all the tea the colonists poured out in Boston before you could learn all of Fran's secrets."

Lexi appreciated the respect these men had for Fran. Like Clint, she wanted to learn more about the woman whose footsteps she hoped to follow.

Madd said, "I have a car waiting to take us to Fran's villa."

"It'll just be Clint and Lexi," Andre said. "Fran wanted me to head straight back to Paris, so the jet wouldn't be missed."

"Thank you, Andre," Clint said.

Lexi added, "For everything."

"My pleasure. I'm sure we'll meet again. Good luck." Andre went back into the jet, pulling the door closed.

Madd led her and Clint to a black Mercedes.

Twenty-five minutes later, they came to a large security gate in an isolated area.

"This is quite remote." Lexi said.

"Better for keeping you off the grid." Madd typed in a code on his phone, and the large metal gate opened. "There's also a safe room in the lower floor I'll show you after you're settled."

"Safe room?" she asked.

"Fran always hopes for the best but plans for the worst."

"Sounds like a great philosophy to me," Clint said.

Madd drove down a long driveway, which was lined with palm trees.

Once the villa came into view, Lexi couldn't believe how palatial it looked with its white stucco walls and red-tiled roof. The keyhole Moorish arch that was above the dark, double doors created a grand entrance.

When Madd parked near the walkway, the front doors opened and three young men dressed in white came out.

"The staff will get your luggage," Madd said. "If you would like breakfast, I can have the chef prepare something for you. But if you'd rather go to your suite, I can take you there. I understand you haven't had much sleep."

As the young men got their things out of the back, Clint turned to her. "Are you hungry, sweetheart?"

"No. I just want to sleep." Lexi couldn't hold back a yawn.

Clint followed suit and also yawned.

"I heard yawning was contagious," Madd said with a grin. "And now you've proved it for me."

"We're both tired." She felt so at ease being here with Clint inside Fran's fortress palace. "And this is the first time we've had that we could let our guard down and relax."

"You heard the lady, Madd. Please, take us to our suite."

"Of course. This way."

The interior of the villa was stunning. The pattern of the tiled floors, the plush white sofas, the many colorful pillows, and the silky draperies made Lexi feel like she had entered an Arabian Nights story.

With the three young men following behind with their luggage, Madd led her and Clint past a large expanse of floor-to-ceiling windows with a view of a massive infinity pool that seemed to blend into the Atlantic Ocean beyond.

Once she got some much-needed sleep, Lexi wanted to enjoy a swim. "My God, Clint, this place is beautiful."

He took her hand. "Fran does have impeccable taste."

"Here we are," Madd said, opening the door to the suite.

Though the space was just as gorgeous as the rest of

the villa, Lexi couldn't take her eyes off of the grand, comfy-looking bed, which seemed to be at least double the size of a normal king-sized one.

"Lexi, would you like the staff to unpack your things for you?" Madd asked.

"No thank you. I can do that later." She turned to the young men. "Just place them over there near the bed."

"*Oui, madame*," one of them answered.

After the three young men finished with their luggage and left, Madd turned to her and Clint. "This wing of the house is all yours. If you need anything, just press one of the call buttons which you will find throughout the rooms."

"You're satisfied with the security measures here?" Clint asked.

"I am. Fran has the best in all her homes. Sleep well." Madd left, closing the door behind him.

"I'm so tired, Clint."

Clint pulled the covers down on the bed, as she slipped out of her clothes.

Lexi got in the bed, relishing its softness. After another yawn, she whispered, "I love you, Clint."

"I love you, too." He pulled the covers over her and stripped out of his clothes, lying down beside her.

Drifting off, she loved the feel of his body next to her.

STILL ASLEEP, Clint stretched out his arm to touch Lexi. When his hand couldn't find her, he opened his eyes. "Lexi?"

She didn't answer.

A horrible dread rolled through him, and he jumped out of the bed. "Lexi. Lexi."

"In here, honey," she called to him. "I'm taking a bath. Come join me."

He ran into the bathroom and saw her in the middle of a large tub, soaking under soapy bubbles. "Sweetheart, you scared me half to death. I couldn't find you."

"I'm sorry. You were sleeping so soundly I didn't want to wake you."

He sat on the side of the tub, running his hand through her wet locks. "It's weird for me to pass out like that. I don't know about you, but I felt so relaxed. I can't remember when I've ever slept that well."

"Me, too. I feel so much better." She grinned and splashed a little water at him.

"So, that's how you want to play it." He laughed and splashed her right back.

She grabbed him, pulling him in the water before he could react. Bubbles and water went everywhere, as he fell in on top of her.

"You asked for it, missy." He took the shower wand and sprayed her with cold water.

"You devil." Laughing, she splashed him even more until he grabbed her hands by the wrist.

"Have you ever kissed a devil?" He devoured her lips, thrilled to have her in his arms again.

She kissed him back, wrapping her wet, soapy arms around his neck.

25

Wearing a white robe, Lexi sat in the middle of the bed with Clint, who was also in a robe. They were enjoying the food he had requested from the chef.

"This is so good," she said. "Where do you think Fran's chef learned to make hamburgers?"

"It was probably a requirement to get the job." Clint fed her a French fry.

She was still glowing from the bath they'd shared. "This feels more like a vacation than me hiding out from the law."

"So are you hoping they don't clear this up soon?"

"If I could stay here with you, the answer is *yes*. But we know we have such a good team working on clearing my name it won't take them long."

"Speaking of team, I suppose you've made up your mind about joining?"

"Yes, I have. I can't imagine not being a part of something so important. And the best part is I'll be working with you."

"You do realize that you can't join me in the field until you've had a ton of training."

"I get it, honey. I will do everything necessary to make sure I'm prepared." She grabbed his hand and squeezed. "I can tell you're apprehensive about me joining the team."

"I've waited a lifetime for you. I don't want you heading into a dangerous mission."

"I feel the same way. That's why us being together is so important. We've already proven what we're capable of. You believe in me, don't you?"

"Of course I do. I just want to make sure you're safe. How can I do that now and especially after we're married and have kids?"

"Married? Kids? Why Harold, you haven't even proposed yet?"

"There's no winning with you, Mabel, is there?"

Her heart skipped several beats. "You want to marry me?"

He slipped off the bed and got on one knee, while keeping hold of her hands.

"You're the most amazing woman I've ever met in my life. I've fallen deeply in love with you. Will you make me the happiest man in the world and marry me, Lexi Bly?"

"You're serious?"

"Of course I am."

As warmth spread over her entire body, she wrapped her arms around him. "Yes. Yes. Yes. I will marry you, Clint Knight. I love you so much."

SITTING on the side of the pool with his legs in the water, Clint intently watched Lexi swim laps. It had been two days since she'd accepted his proposal and he was still flying high.

How could this beautiful, amazing woman want to be my wife?

He'd given up trying to convince her not to join Blake's team. Besides being gorgeous, Lexi was stubborn. So he changed tactics, and started training her.

Madd came up to him. "What lap is she on?"

"Seventy-four of a hundred."

"Damn, your fiancée is impressive. She'll be through the training regimen in record time if she keeps this up."

"Oh, I'm sure she will, but this is *my* training regimen, not the Agency's. She'll pass when I'm convinced she's ready. Tomorrow, we're doing a ten-mile hike in the desert with full gear that the staff got for her and me."

Madd laughed. "You're tough. I hope you allow her water."

"Well, of course I'm going to allow her water. I'm not a monster. In fact, I love her."

"I know you do, but do you know that Lexi is going to surpass every test you give her? I've never seen any one more determined than her."

Lexi flipped on the side of the pool to start her seventy-fifth lap.

"Damn it, me either. I just don't want anything to happen to her."

"You can't hold her back, Clint, but I understand how

you feel. Well, if you two are joining Fran and Blake's team, I guess I will, too."

"What? What do you mean *Fran and Blake's* team? What's going on?"

"I just got off the phone with them. They've decided to join forces. And that's not all. Not only did Interpol rescind their warrant for Lexi, but her name has been completely cleared of the murder back in Dallas."

"Are you serious?"

"Yep. Boris squealed like a pig and after new evidence from Koslova's gun matched the ballistics, Lexi's record is completely cleared."

"Lexi, come here please!" he shouted, unable to hold back his excitement. "Great news."

She swam over. "I've got twenty-four more laps to go. What's the news?"

He pulled her out of the pool and onto his lap. "You're a free woman, sweetheart."

"I'll get the champagne while you explain everything to her." Madd walked into the house, leaving them alone.

"Are you serious, Clint?"

"Totally serious." He told her everything that Madd had shared, including the bit about Fran and Blake joining forces.

"Oh my God, that's wonderful. Do we have to leave now?"

He laughed. "Not right away, but soon. After your training is finished."

She kissed him. "I've got quite a few more laps to go, which I'll knock out before I drink a sip of champagne."

She dove back into the pool, continuing her laps.

Madd returned with three glasses and a bottle of

champagne. "You're quite the taskmaster, Clint. She can't even take a break to celebrate?"

"Wasn't me, Madd." He took the glass from him. "It was Lexi. There's no stopping that woman when she's made up her mind. You'll see. She'll be through in fifteen minutes."

As they watched Lexi finish her workout, Madd let him know what else he'd learned on the call.

"Blake and Fran finished their interrogation of Boris and got some important intel that should help in our efforts to stop Drake. They turned Boris over to a contact Blake has at Interpol. Good thing for our side that Boris had warrants in Spain, Germany, Belarus and the UK."

"What about the woman Koslova was supposed to kill? Has the team figured out why Drake wanted her taken out?"

"Not yet, but even though she has her own security detail Blake has assigned Doc and Geoff to shadow her. So far, it's been quiet."

"Any sign of Drake or Camille yet?"

"Nope. They're in the wind."

"I'm glad you're joining the team. I look forward to us working together again."

"Me, too, my friend." Madd clinked their glasses together. "Me, too."

After Lexi finished her laps, she swam up to them. "All done. I'll take that champagne now."

26

W hen the alarm clock went off at 5 am, Lexi hit the *off* button and leapt from the bed hoping to beat Clint to the bathroom. But he charged past her, getting to the bathroom door a split-second before she did.

"Damn it. Turning off the alarm slowed me down."

"You almost made it, sweetheart." He gave her a quick kiss. "After you pee, drop and give me twenty, rookie."

"You just wait, mister. I was so close to beating you. Tomorrow, you turn off the damn alarm clock, then per our deal you'll have to do the pushups."

"Alarm clock or not, you still have to beat me."

She raced through the morning routine he'd set up for her training. Pee. Pushups, because she'd lost again. Brush teeth. Dress. Coffee. Stretch.

"Good job, rookie," he said.

"Thanks, but I've been giving this training program some thought. You're an operative. Don't you need to qualify, too?"

"Yes. Periodically. Where are you going with this, Mabel?"

"Well, Harold, today you're not following me in the golf cart on the run. You're joining me, so put on your running shoes, mister."

"God, you're such a spitfire. This'll be a piece of cake for me."

"Oh we won't be finished after the run, honey. You're going to join me in every bit of this training. You want me at top performance before I start missions. I want the same from you."

He tied his shoes. "I've been doing this for years. I know what is necessary for any mission we have to undertake. And I'm always ready."

"Prove it." She ran out the door.

Moments later, he caught up with her, carrying her backpack. "Forget something, rookie?"

Without slowing, she grabbed the backpack from him, which had water, a pistol and ammo. "I know. Always be prepared for anything. I just wanted to get a head start on you."

"You're doing great. I'll meet you at the finish line." He increased his pace, leaving her in the dust on the mile-long circular track.

He and Madd had set up the track inside the property's walls for her training.

Beating Clint wasn't possible, but she would do her damnedest to keep him from lapping her.

She increased her speed, though careful not to push too hard in order to conserve enough energy to finish.

Clint's training had made her stronger and faster than she'd ever been before. She was in the best shape of her life, which got her excited about shopping for a wedding dress.

Don't jump the gun, rookie.

Yes, he'd proposed and she'd accepted, but there was a lot to discuss before they settled on a date. Meeting his family was one of the first milestones she wanted to get to.

Seeing Clint pass the finish line, Lexi tapped into every ounce of energy left in her and raced to complete the final distance.

"Wow." Clint looked at his watch, as she ran up to him. "You shaved another ninety seconds off your time."

"That is fast," she panted out. "Maybe I'll beat you yet."

"You just might."

She got the water bottle out of the backpack. "You rested enough for the hand-to-hand training, Harold?"

"Bring it—"

She knocked him off his feet with a sweeping sidekick.

He laughed, dusting his clothes as he got back up on his feet. "Mabel, I just taught you that move yesterday."

"How did I do, Harold?"

"I landed on my ass, so I think it's obvious, don't you?"

Before she could respond, he made a move that flipped her onto her back with him on top of her, pinning her to the ground. "That's the next move I want you to learn."

She smiled, pressing her lips to his. "I rather like that move. Can you show it to me again?"

As he opened his mouth to answer, she twisted,

getting free from him and ending up with her foot on his throat.

"I've never seen anyone pick up hand-to-hand so fast," Madd said as he approached them from the house.

"Thanks for the compliment, Madd." She stepped back as Clint got off the ground.

"Sorry to interrupt the training, but just got off the phone with Fran. Andre is flying her, Liz and Steve here."

"That's great news," Lexi said. "But it's only been two weeks since Steve's surgery. Did Doc give his blessing for him to travel?"

"He did. The only restriction now is he's not allowed to lift anything over ten pounds. They will arrive midafternoon. Fran wants to have tea."

Lexi turned to Clint. "Does that mean I get a pass on training after lunch?"

"I guess a girl has to have time to get ready." He smiled. "But we still have time before lunch for shooting practice."

She hugged him. "That's one area where I know I can beat you."

"You don't give up, do you?"

"Never."

Madd laughed. "That's why she's going to be one of the best operatives on the team."

CLINT WALKED into the west garden with Lexi at his side. As always, she looked spectacular. The outfit she'd selected for Fran's afternoon tea was a light green cotton dress.

They rounded the corner and walked through the arch into the garden. The place had more of an English feel than Moroccan with its manicured hedges and colorful rosebushes.

In the center of the lawn was a fountain. Next to the fountain was a large round table, where Liz, Steve, Madd and Andre were already seated. In front of each chair was a pot of tea with cream, sugar and honey.

On another table nearby was an assortment of finger sandwiches, dainty scones, sweet cakes, and other tempting nibbles.

"Hey, everyone." Lexi went straight to Steve, giving him a hug. "I'm glad you're here and looking so good."

"Feeling good, too. Fran has been taking good care of me."

The other night Lexi had mentioned that she thought there might be a spark between Steve and Fran.

Clint thought she might be right.

Lexi wrapped Liz in her arms. "I missed you."

"Same here. Are you doing okay?"

"Oh yes, I am. My name is cleared, and I'm in training with my fiancé."

"Your fiancé?" Fran walked over to the table.

"Oops." Lexi laughed and turned to him. "I didn't mean to let that slip, honey. Sorry."

"You didn't do anything wrong." He pulled out a chair for her. "I'm proud to let the whole world know."

Everyone congratulated them, as he and Fran took their seats.

"Have you settled on a date?" Liz asked. "Because you know I want to help with the planning."

"I'm counting on it," Lexi said. "No date yet, but once we settle on one all of you will be the first to know."

"Excellent," Fran said. "I hope you don't mind. I did give the staff the rest of the afternoon off, so we're on our own."

"Perfectly fine, Fran. I believe most of us are more familiar helping ourselves." Clint filled his cup from the pot closest to him. "Mm. Earl Grey. My favorite. How did you know?"

"I did a little research," Fran admitted. "I hope I got your favorite tea right for each of you."

"It's been ages since I've had a proper cup of Chai," Liz said. "Thank you, Fran."

Fran turned to Steve. "And since I know you're not a fan of tea, there's Folgers in your pot."

"Thank you." Steve grinned and winked at her. "Fran, you always think of everything."

From the reactions around the table, Clint realized it wasn't just him and Lexi who were catching on to the mutual attraction between Steve and Fran.

"So as you know, Blake and I have combined our resources for the new team," Fran said. "He and I go way back. My first encounter with him and his brother was right after they joined the CIA. I'd been with French intelligence for nearly a decade when we were assigned to a joint task force. Since then, Blake has always had my back and I've always had his. He's someone I can trust implicitly."

"Are you serious? You're a spy?" Liz seemed shocked and a little irritated. "I get you didn't tell me you were a spy before all this, but you couldn't tell me the truth in the past couple of weeks I've been staying with you in Paris?"

"I'm sorry, sweetheart, but I had to wrap up some loose ends in my organization first. Plus, I thought it would be best to tell you and Lexi together."

"Fran, why did you choose the spy biz?" Lexi asked. "Are you still with French intelligence? If not, why did you leave? And what—"

"Hold on, dear. That's a lot of questions to start with, but let me try to answer. First of all, I became a spy, as you say, after I lost my sister."

"You had a sister?" Liz asked. "You never mentioned that before?"

"It's painful for me, but you deserve to know. My little sister Gisele worked at a bank. She was unaware her boss was an undercover operative for Russia until she discovered some documents he'd left on his desk. Gisele wanted to do the right thing, the patriotic thing, and turn him in. But before she could, the bastard flipped the tables on her doctoring some forms that made it look like she was the spy, not him. Gisele went to prison."

"Oh my God, Fran," Lexi said. "That's horrible."

"I wanted to save Gisele, but I didn't know how. After the Russians had Gisele killed in prison, new evidence came to light that cleared her name. Too late. She was still dead. That's when I joined French intelligence. I hunted down Gisele's boss and proved his guilt. He will die in prison. But it's not enough." Fran closed her eyes. "Gisele deserved more."

Steve took her hand. "Go on."

Fran opened her eyes. "So, I've kept doing all that I can do to try to stop evil people like her boss, like

Koslova, like Drake, like Camille. That's why Blake and I have joined forces. That's why this team is so important. We have to do all we can before more innocent people are killed."

Clint's appreciation for Fran continued to grow the more he learned about her. "But you're no longer with French intelligence. Why?"

"I've been out on my own for fifteen years. There was a point the agency required more paperwork than getting the job done. So I left the agency. Some like-minded friends followed me, and we ran our own missions. Being outside of normal channels allowed us freedom and flexibility that has brought down a fair share of bad people. With the vast resources I inherited from my parents, I'm able to fund a variety of missions. Now, with Blake's family fortune and expertise added to mine, there's no terrorist attack, whether cyber or explosive, that we can't stop."

"You mentioned knowing his twin brother Drake," Steve said. "What can you tell us about him?"

"I was an external contractor on that failed mission where the building exploded and we all thought Drake had died. Blake would have died, too, had I not been there to get him clear of the wreckage."

Clint realized how deep the ties between Fran and Blake went.

"Since I was an ordained minister, Blake had me conduct Drake's funeral. I knew he was devastated and felt guilty about his brother. After he left the CIA I tried to reconnect with him, but Blake had already set up his own clandestine operation. I'm glad we're working together now." Fran looked around the table. "I'm glad we're all working together. Any questions?"

Clint leaned in close to Lexi and whispered softly. "Would you be okay with Fran officiating our wedding?"

She nodded and raised her hand. "We have a question, Fran."

"Okay?"

"Since you're an ordained minister, we would love for you to officiate our wedding?"

Fran's eyes welled up. "Nothing would make me happier, Lexi. I would love to."

"Thank you, Fran," Clint said. "We really appreciate it."

They talked until the orange sun sat low in the sky. Clint felt more connected with the team than ever before.

Liz stood. "It's been a wonderful afternoon, but if you don't mind, I would like to finish unpacking my things."

Lexi left her chair. "I'll go with you. It'll give us time to discuss your maid of honor dress."

As the two of them walked towards the house, he heard Liz say, "Just please, no ruffles. That's all I ask."

Lexi laughed. "I wouldn't do that to you."

When they disappeared from view, a loud blast shook the ground, and all hell broke loose.

Just as Lexi stepped inside with Liz, an explosion rocked the house.

"What the hell was that?" Liz yelled.

"Shh." Lexi brought out her gun, whispering, "Get down and stay close."

As gunfire erupted outside, she ran through all their options. It was impossible to know the full extent of the threat, but Liz was unarmed and untrained. She needed to get her to safety and out of the line of fire.

"I'm taking you to Fran's safe room. Follow me."

Just as she and Liz got to the stairs, a man jumped out and aimed a gun at them.

Without hesitation, she fired her weapon and the guy went down.

Liz screamed, "Behind you!"

Lexi twisted around, kicking the attacker in the face and then punching him in the hand, knocking his gun away.

"You bitch!" He started to charge her, but she did a flying sidekick into his throat that made him fall.

On his way down, his head hit the edge of a marble table and he landed on his back. He was completely out.

"Let's go," she told Liz.

As they ran down the stairs, the gunfire suddenly stopped.

"Lexi!" Clint yelled.

"Is it all clear?" she called back.

"Yes. Where are you?"

"At the door to the safe room."

A second later, he bounded down the stairs, pulling her into his arms. He just held her tight, never letting go.

She held onto him. "I'm okay, honey. Are you?"

"Now that I know you're okay, I'm okay."

She grinned. "As Matthew McConaughey says, okay, okay, okay."

Liz shook her head. "That's not right, Lexi. It was alright, alright, alright."

"That's right," Lexi said.

They all burst out laughing, still feeling the adrenaline coursing through their veins.

"Honey, what about the rest of the team?" she asked.

"No casualties on our side, but there are six dead on their side."

Madd stood at the top of the stairs. "Clint, come up here. You've got to see this."

Clint led her and Liz to the main floor.

Madd stood over the two men she'd taken out.

Liz looked at Madd. "Your leg is bleeding."

"It's nothing," Madd told her, then turned his attention to Clint. "These two make a total of eight hostiles, but they are still alive."

"You should have seen your fiancée, Clint." Liz's jittery tone and rapid tempo made it clear she was still rattled from all they'd just been through. "That man pointed a gun straight at us, and Lexi fired at him before he could shoot us. And this other guy came up behind us, and she looked like Bruce Lee in a martial arts film." She turned and faced her. "Where did you learn to do that?"

Lexi smiled, "I had a great instructor."

"Great instructor or incredible student?" Madd laughed. "Clint, you have to admit she's ready now."

Clint locked eyes with hers. "You think?"

****

Clint walked out to the table where the team had been enjoying tea before the attack twenty-four hours ago. Fran was seated with a laptop in front of her.

"West gate still secure," Madd's voice came through his comms.

"Copy that," he sent back and then addressed Fran. "Mind if I have a seat?"

"Please. Be my guest." She motioned to the chair next to her. "I'd like to discuss what happened and what the team needs to do next with you."

He sat. "Have you heard from Andre yet?"

"He and Steve secured the prisoners for transport. They took off ten minutes ago for Paris and Blake has already informed Interpol to be ready." Fran stared hard at him. "Clint, what's wrong?"

"I could have lost her. In one brief moment she could have been gone. How am I going to deal with her being an operative and constantly fear for her life?"

"She's found her passion. I know it's scary but you can't take that away from her."

"I know, but it's hard. I love her so much."

"And she loves you. She will feel the same way when you go out on a mission. But this is the life you have both chosen. What we do is important. By the way, where is she?"

"She's insistent that Liz learns self-defense."

"I agree with that, and you have to admit that Lexi is more than capable."

"She is. She's already proven to be a helluva operative."

"Front door secure," Madd's voice came through the comms.

"Copy that," he sent back.

"How's his leg doing?" Fran asked.

"He's still limping, but it was only a graze."

"Good. Blake and I are going to assign him as Liz's bodyguard for the time being."

"Do you really think Drake and Camille would go after her?"

"What we learned from the two prisoners tells me they are willing to do whatever it takes to destroy our team, which means our family and friends might be in danger."

Clint thought about his own family. Were they safe? He would make sure they were.

Fran filled two cups with tea. "My other pilot is on his way here with the other jet. This place is burned, as is Operation Central in Paris. We've got to figure out how he finds our locations. When we do, we can set up a new OC."

They'd been shocked to learn that the OC had been attacked at the exact same time as here in Morocco. Drake was sending a clear message. The war was on. In Paris, the team had beaten back the attacks but one member on their side had been shot.

"Any word on Geoff?"

"Still in critical condition, but Doc is hopeful." Fran's face darkened. "The bastard shot him in the back. He didn't have a chance."

"What about Lila Cross, who Drake wanted Koslova to kill?"

"Max and Ahmed are keeping tabs on her, even though she does have her own security detail. So far there hasn't been any sign of Drake or Camille near her."

"I think we need to dig deeper into why her execution might be important to Drake's bigger plan."

"I'm glad you think so. Blake and I want you and Lexi to go undercover and get close to her."

Clint felt his gut tighten.

"Before you say anything, think. Isn't it better you are with her for her first op?"

28

L exi checked her hair and makeup using the mirror on the underside of the sun visor. "Clint, we're just ten minutes away. Are you sure I look okay? Should I have worn a dress instead of these pants? Do you think these earrings are too dangly? I have a smaller pair in my purse."

"Slow down, babe." Clint glanced at her from behind the steering wheel. "You look absolutely gorgeous. They're going to love you."

"I'm just nervous meeting your family for the first time. I want to make a good impression."

"You don't have to try. You will. Just be yourself. I'm the one who should worry. I haven't seen them in years."

"They'll be so happy to see you. You'll see."

"You good with the cover story?" he asked.

"Yes, I am. We met at work. BAII. Binoche & Atlas International Investments."

Fran and Blake had set up the company to operate as a front for the team. While there were real world investments in BAII, the bulk of the funds fed missions. She was still on her first undercover assignment with Clint at Cyber Security for the European Union. After months of work they were still trying to figure out why Drake wanted Lila Cross, the director, killed.

Lexi continued rattling off their cover story, which also had a large portion of the truth. "You manage portfolios and I am in mergers and acquisitions. We met in Paris eight months ago, which is true. But, that the meeting was at a company party, isn't."

"Go on."

"We've dated for several months, and now are engaged—also true." She held up her left hand with the diamond ring he'd given her after they'd left Morocco.

"You got it, sweetheart." He reached over and patted her leg. "Seriously, they're going to go crazy for you."

Lexi spotted the sign to his sister's place. "There's the turnoff for the N & S Ranch."

"Finally. I'm beat after that long drive."

"Billings to Clearwater is quite the distance, but what wonderful country we got to see." She was in awe at how beautiful everything here was. "The trees, the mountains, the wildlife, and the wide open skies are like nowhere else I've ever been."

"Me either. Shayla is very lucky to live here with Nick and the twins."

Clint drove through the ranch's cattle guard. "Security is non-existent out here. They should at least install a keypad."

"I know you're worried about Drake and Camille targeting to your family, but remember that Fran and Blake have hired private security to keep an eye on them. Besides, your family isn't in our line of work, honey."

"Even so, it's very isolated out here. I'm going to suggest they beef up their security."

"Maybe it would be better not to lead with that. It has been some time since you've seen your sister, let alone your mom and dad."

Clint's parents had arrived at the ranch two days earlier. This was going to be a big family reunion as well as Lexi being introduced to all of them. She could tell that Clint was a little anxious, too.

As he pulled the rental car up to the front of the large log cabin, two large German Shepherds ran towards them.

"Looks like your sister and brother-in-law have security after all."

"Seems so."

His family filed out onto the wide porch, which spanned the entire front of the house. She recognized each of them from photos Clint had shared with her.

Shayla had long dark hair and was next to the five year-old twins, Brian and Brianna.

Then came Nick, who was several inches taller than his wife and sported a beard. He yelled commands at the two dogs. "*Halt, Shatzi. Halt, Wolf. Sitzen. Bleibe.*"

They sat down with their tails wagging.

Bringing up the rear were Clint's parents, Sam and Paula Knight. They were an attractive couple.

"Wow, Clint. You look just like your dad and Shayla looks like your mom. Their smiles are warm and welcoming." Lexi took one last quick look in the mirror. "Ready or not, Harold?"

"Here we go, Mabel."

As they got out of the car, Clint's family descended on them with hugs.

"Lexi, you're even more beautiful in person," Mrs. Knight told her. "I'm so glad to finally meet you."

"It's wonderful meeting you, too."

"And she got our boy to finally make a trip to see us after all these years." Mr. Knight said.

Mrs. Knight smiled. "Come here, son."

Clint stepped forward, as his parents greeted him with a combined bear hug. "God, I missed you both."

"It sure is good to see you, son," his dad said with tears welling in his eyes.

"I'm sorry it's been so long, but you and mom haven't changed a bit."

"Oh go on. Tell me more," his dad said. "I've been considering taking up modeling as a second career."

As they all laughed, his mom turned to his dad. "Oh Sam. Be serious."

"Please don't stop him, Mrs. Knight," Lexi said. "I just love his humor. I love all of this."

Clint bent down to the same height as his niece and teased, "You must be Brian." Then he turned to his nephew. "And you must be Brianna."

"Nope," Brianna said first. "I'm a girl. Brianna. He's my brother. Brian."

"Smart and pretty," Clint said.

"Uncle Clint, do you like to fish?" Brian asked. "Because Daddy said we could go fishing if you wanted to."

"I love to fish, Brian. That would be fun."

Brian gave him a big hug. "See, Daddy. Uncle Clint likes fishing."

"I like fishing too," Brianna said, not wanting to miss out.

As Lexi enjoyed watching Clint with the twins, she imagined how great he would be with their own kids someday.

"Brother, I can't believe you waited this long to come see me." Shayla shook her head. "I should be mad."

"Yes, you should. I'm sorry."

She hugged him. "All's forgiven now, but if you take as long between visits as the last one, know that I will come hunt you down."

"I won't, Sis. I promise." He put his arm around Lexi. "Besides, she won't allow me to wait too long."

Shayla smiled. "After we talked on the phone, I knew I was going to like you. I'm a hugger."

"Me, too." Lexi spread her arms wide, and she and Shayla embraced.

Shayla whispered in her ear. "Thank you for bringing my brother back to us. I missed him so much."

"This is what family is all about." Fond memories of Lexi's parents flooded into her mind. "Being together. Enjoying each and every moment you can."

"Lexi is right," Mr. Knight said. " And what better way to enjoy this moment than with a slice or two or three of the pies that Paula whipped up for us and a cup of coffee."

"Mom, tell me you made my favorite?" Clint said.

"Oh honey, I forgot what your favorite was," his mom teased. "I made apple, because you told me that was Lexi's favorite. I made chocolate cream, because that's Shayla's favorite. Banana cream for Nick and the kids. Mm? And yours is…? Lexi, do you know what his favorite is?"

Lexi loved the sense of humor Clint's parents had. "I believe he likes coconut cream with cilantro."

Again, they all laughed.

"Come on, everyone," Shayla said. "Actually, Mom put the cilantro on the side."

More laughs followed, as they entered the house.

Carrying another string of fish, Clint walked up from the stream's bank to Nick. "Here's some more, buddy."

"Man, they sure are biting today," Nick said. "Put them on the table with the rest."

"I'll help you clean them, but the other three fishermen aren't ready to give it up yet."

"That doesn't surprise me one bit. When the twins heard you and Lexi were coming, Brian wouldn't stop asking if we could take you fishing. And whatever Brian wants, Brianna wants it, too. And your dad loves to spoil them rotten, as does your mom."

"I sure hope Mom still knows how to fry fish."

"I know Mom is good, but Shayla is fantastic at frying them. My mouth is just watering thinking about it."

Clint realized he'd missed so much staying away from his family. He wasn't going to let that happen again. "You've built something special here, Nick."

"Your sister and I did," Nick told him. "When you and Lexi get tired of all that travel with your big jobs, we hope you'll consider settling down here. There's a hundred acres next to our land that I'm sure you could buy any time."

"Maybe someday."

Nick was a good man, a good husband and a good father. Clint hoped he could be just as good for Lexi and their new life together.

"I love it out here. It's so quiet and tranquil. But since you are so far away from anyone, have you thought about beefing up your security?"

"That's the point, Clint. We are so far away from anyone. We don't need any more security than the two dogs."

"You may be secluded, but you never know what could happen. Would you please just consider adding a little more security? I have some expertise in that area I could help you with."

"Okay. I'll consider it. Let me talk to Shayla."

"There's something else that Lexi and I talked about that I would like to discuss with you."

"You're sounding quite mysterious, Clint. What's up?"

"First, would it be okay if we had our wedding here at the ranch?"

Nick smiled. "Are you kidding? That sounds great to me, and I know Shayla would love it."

"Lexi wants a small, intimate ceremony. Only close friends and family."

"Whatever you guys want, we're happy to do our part."

"There's one other thing. Lexi is going to ask Shayla to be her matron of honor, and I would like you to be one of my best men."

"Of course." Nick grinned. "One of?"

"Yeah, my buddy Madd is going to be the other. Co-best men, if you will. Lexi is going to have Shayla as her matron of honor and her best friend Liz as her maid of honor."

"Sounds like fun to me, Clint. Have you settled on a date yet?"

"It's Montana, Nick. It has to be summer."

Nick laughed. "Even though I've really only been around you these past few days, you're more than just a brother-in-law to me now. You're a good friend."

"Buddy, I feel the same way about you."

"I just can't understand why you stayed away so long."

"There's a lot to that story I wish I could share with you, but I can't now. Someday? Maybe I can tell you. But know this, Lexi and I won't be staying away ever again."

Lexi felt so relaxed sitting on the back porch and drinking lemonade with Clint's sister and mom. "Did you see how Clint gobbled up the last of the coconut cream pie before they left on the fishing trip this morning? You have to give me your recipe, Mrs. Knight."

"If you don't mind, I would love for you to call me *mom*."

"I don't mind at all. Thank you...Mom."

"I feel so honored, sweetheart."

Lexi reached over and squeezed her hand. "That means so much to me. I haven't been able to call anyone mom since I was twelve."

"How awful," Shayla said. "What happened to your mother?"

"Both my mom and dad were killed in a car wreck." Lexi went on to tell them what had happened.

"Oh Lexi." Clint's mom wiped her eyes. "I'm so sorry."

"Do you have any other family?" Shayla asked.

"Only Liz, who is like a sister to me. She's going to be my maid of honor. Her grandparents took me in after the accident. Unfortunately they passed away a few years ago. But I will say they made my life as happy as they could under the circumstances." Lexi found it easy to talk to Shayla and Clint's mom.

"Shayla, I know this may seem strange to ask, since we've only known each other a few days, but would you consider being my matron of honor?"

"I would be honored to be your matron of honor. I can't think of a bigger honor than that honor."

They all laughed.

Lexi felt like her heart might explode with joy. Not only was she going to marry the man of her dreams, but his family had also become hers.

29

With Liz and Shayla standing behind on either side of her, Lexi sat at the vanity and gazed at her reflection in the mirror.

"You are a stunning bride," Liz said. "So beautiful."

Shayla nodded. "I can't wait to see my brother's face when you walk down the aisle in that gorgeous dress."

"You and Nick are so great for allowing us to get married here. This ranch is just perfect. And every time we come to visit you, Nick and the twins we can reminisce about this day."

"I'm so glad you're here and the weather has cooperated for the outdoor setting. I've never seen Clint happier."

Lexi stood and walked to the full-length mirror to take one last look. She felt like a princess in the tulle white gown with a sweetheart neckline and ruched back. She loved the light-as-air skirt, which was full and layered. In lieu of a veil, she'd chosen pink tea roses in her hair, which matched her bouquet and the color of Liz and Shayla's dresses.

"I brought you Grammy's silver bracelet for something old," Liz said.

"I love it." She put the bracelet on.

"This is for the blue part." Shayla handed her a blue, lacy garter.

"Thank you, Shayla. These traditions are so fun." She sat back down and slipped the garter on her leg.

Shayla laughed. "Clint will have fun taking it off and tossing it to his buddies."

The door opened and Clint's mom walked in. "Oh my God, Lexi. You look absolutely gorgeous." She handed Lexi a jewelry box. "This is for something new from Sam and me."

Lexi opened the box and saw two pearl earrings. "They're beautiful." She put them on and then looked at her reflection again. "I love them. Thank you, Mom. What else do I need? I have Grammy's bracelet for the old. I have the garter for the blue. These earrings for new."

"So we still need borrowed," Liz said. "How about the friendship ring you gave me?" She pulled the ring off her finger. "Of course I want it back, so you can only borrow it."

Lexi smiled. "Perfect."

After a single knock on the door, Steve's voice came through. "May I come in?"

"Of course," Lexi said, standing to face the door.

Wearing a tux, Steve walked in and his eyes began to tear. "My God, Lexi. You're the most beautiful bride I've ever seen."

She gave him a hug and a kiss on the cheek. "Thank you, Steve."

"I have something for you." He reached in his pocket and handed her a silver Mercury dime. "This goes into your shoe."

"Like this?" Lexi placed the coin in her shoe.

"Perfect. My mother gave me this on my wedding day, God rest her soul. This coin symbolizes my wish for you and Clint to have everything you desire." His voice shook with emotion. "When your child marries, I hope you will pass it on to them."

"I love you, Steve. I will treasure it always until I pass it on to my child, who will know you as their grandfather."

He wiped his eyes and looked at his watch. "We better go. You know how much Fran stressed punctuality at the rehearsal."

Had there been signs of attraction between him and Fran? She wasn't sure, but felt like there might be something happening.

"I don't want to deliver you a second too late." He held out his arm for her, as Clint's mom, Liz and Shayla walked out ahead of them.

THE BRIGHT BLUE expanse above everyone's head made it clear to Clint they were in the aptly named, "Big Sky Country."

The photos he'd seen of his sister's ranch paled in comparison to the beauty that surrounded him. He couldn't ask for a more romantic place for his new bride.

He looked at the majestic, snow-capped mountains off in the distance. He could feel the warm breeze on his skin. The smell of fresh air invigorated him. Listening to Max strum a ballad on his guitar seemed to set the perfect tone for this incredible day—the day he would marry the love of his life.

Anxious to see his bride, he looked at the people who had come to celebrate with them.

Wearing a blue cashmere suit, Fran stood next to him. With Max's help, the state of Montana had approved Fran's credentials to conduct the ceremony.

Clint stood with her under the arch of pink and white roses that he and all the men had built together. Beside him were Nick and Madd, his two best men.

On the groom's side and in the rows behind his father sat Blake, Doc, Andre, and Geoff and the rest of the team.

On the bride's side sat Steve's kids, Sara and Brad, with their families, as well as some of Lexi's friends from college.

As Ahmed escorted his mother to the seat next to his father, Clint realized Lexi was about to walk down the aisle, which caused his pulse to race.

A fleeting, crazy thought shot through his mind. *She is going to walk down the aisle, isn't she? Of course she is, you idiot.*

This was more nerve-racking than any mission he'd ever been on.

As Max began playing the processional music, everything inside Clint seemed to vibrate.

First came his sister, Shayla, followed by Liz. When the twins, Brian as the ring bearer and Brianna as the flower girl, came down the aisle all the adults smiled and Nick and Shayla beamed with pride.

Once the two kids got in their places next to their parents under the arch, Max switched to the song "*Here Comes the Bride*" and everyone stood.

When Clint saw Lexi walk out of the house with Steve, he couldn't breathe. She looked like an angel from heaven.

"So beautiful," he whispered. "She is going to marry me."

Nick touched his arm. "You better breathe, Clint, or you're going to pass out."

Catching his breath, he nodded, as Lexi and Steve stopped in front of the arch.

"Who are the parents of this beautiful bride?" Fran asked.

Steve pulled out a photo of Lexi's parents, placing it on a stand. "Thomas and Sherry Bly, who are with us in spirit. I stand here in their stead to give my blessing and theirs to this union."

Lexi kissed him on the cheek and then stepped next to Clint. They took each other's hand as Steve sat down on the bride's side with several of Lexi's friends and sorority sisters behind.

As they'd done in rehearsal, Clint and Lexi continued looking at each other as Fran began.

"We are gathered here today to celebrate one of life's greatest moments," Fran said. "The joining of two hearts and to give recognition to the worth and beauty of love, and to add our best wishes to the words which shall unite this couple in marriage. Should there be anyone who has cause why this couple should not be united in marriage, then you shouldn't have been invited here so please leave now and forever hold your peace."

Everyone laughed, including Lexi and him.

"Today we have come together to witness the joining of these two lives. For them, something extraordinary has happened. They met each other, fell in love and are finalizing it with their wedding. A good marriage must be created. It is never being too old to hold hands. It's remembering to say I love you every day. And it is not just marrying the right person, it's being the right partner. Lexi and Clint have written their own vows. Who would like to begin?"

"Me," Lexi said, which was no surprise to him. "I know it's not traditional, but Clint and I are far from the norm."

"Very true." Fran smiled. "Go ahead."

Lexi transfixed him with her loving gaze. "Clint, though we met under difficult and strange circumstances I'll never forget our first few days in Paris together. Remember the train when we met that sweet older couple, George and Gayle, who thought we were already married. At the time, I thought if it were true I had the most handsome husband in all of Europe. What I've come to learn is that not only are you handsome, but you are the most kind, generous, and caring man I've ever known. When I learned you hated cilantro, I thought we could never be together, because I adore Mexican food."

Everyone laughed.

"I didn't give it much of a thought when you vowed never to eat coconut again after I told you how much I detested it since eating it was like chewing on strings. But when your mother told me that coconut cream pie was your favorite dessert, I realized what a sacrifice you were willing to make for me. I vow today before God and these witnesses that you can have as much coconut cream pie as you desire, and I will even make it for you. That's how much I love you, now and forever. In fact, with the help of your mother in lieu of a groom's cake we have coconut cream pie."

He laughed and everyone else cheered.

"No matter what happens from here on, sweetheart, I promise to stay by your side to build a future together." She squeezed his hands. "Top that if you think you can."

"Just watch and listen, sweetheart. Watch and listen."

She grinned, which thrilled him.

"First off, about the cilantro. I love Mexican food, too, just without that soapy tasting weed. But if you want cilantro, I'll load up a truck with it and you can have it every night. Because, sweetheart, I promise to do my best to give you anything you desire. As long as I can take a breath, I promise to love you each and every day. I love your sassiness and determination. I can't get enough of your wit. You always make me smile. I've never enjoyed life so much as I have since I met you. You are my everything, now and forever." He squeezed her hand. "How's that, missy?"

"Perfect."

They both turned to Fran.

"May I please have the rings?" Fran took them from Shayla and Nick and held them up for everyone to see. "Wedding rings are an unbroken circle of love, signifying to all the union of this couple in marriage." She looked at them. "Who's going first?"

"This time I am," Clint said, taking the ring from her.

Lexi smiled and held out her left hand.

"This ring is my gift to you, a promise that I will always love, honor, cherish and protect you all the days of my life. With this ring, I thee wed." He slipped the band on her ring finger.

"Lexi?" Fran handed the other band to her.

"This ring is my gift to you, a promise that I will always love, honor, cherish and protect you all the days of my life. With this ring, I thee wed." She slipped the band on his ring finger.

"Lexi and Clint, together as you light the candle of unity, you symbolize the flame of your own individual selves joining to ignite the partnership of marriage. You bring the warmth, strength and wisdom of your family and friend's fire as kindling for your own."

As he and Lexi lit the center candle, Max sang the song about how love is a fire that cannot be quenched.

"By the power vested in me by the state of Montana, I now pronounce you husband and wife. You may now kiss each other."

Clint pulled Lexi in for their first kiss as husband and wife.

"It's my honor to present to you, Mr. and Mrs. Knight."

Everyone cheered, as he and Lexi walked up the aisle and into their life together.

30

L exi stood on the balcony, sipping her coffee and watching the waves of the ocean crash on the beach.

Clint came up behind her, wearing swim trunks. "I could call Blake and extend our honeymoon a few more days."

"That would be marvelous, but you know we have to get back to work. Drake and Camille are at large and Lila Cross is still in danger."

"Blake has Max and Doc keeping a close eye on Ms. Cross, and the rest of the team is working day and night on locating Drake and Camille." He kissed the back of her neck. "Just another day is all I'm asking for."

She turned around to face him. "Honey, I promise we'll come back again."

"I'll hold you to it, Mabel."

"I wouldn't expect anything less from you, Harold." She kissed him. "And since our flight doesn't leave until tomorrow, we have the rest of this day to enjoy."

"How about a swim to start out with?"

"Perfect. Let me put on my bathing suit." As she walked into their room, her phone buzzed.

The caller ID showed the call was coming from Liz.

"Hey, Liz."

"I'm so sorry to call you on your honeymoon." Liz's anxious tone alarmed her. "But I'm scared, Lexi. I haven't been able to get ahold of Fran."

"I'm here. Tell me what's going on?"

Liz screamed and the line went dead.

The End

Next up:

Liz's Guardian - book 2

ABOUT THE AUTHOR

Lana McLemore was first recognized for her writing talent in the sixth grade for the satirical play "Magic Mirror." The play was performed for the entire school and received rave reviews from teachers, parents and fellow students.

Being the mother of three, Lana moved her pursuit of a writing career to the backburner. Later, Lana wrote with her son as a ghostwriter for several years. And then...
...along came the pandemic of 2020.

During the shelter-in-place orders, Lana took her idea about a romantic suspense series "Men Without A Cause" and wrote her first book, Lexi's Protector. She's thrilled to shed her ghostly garb and come out into the light, because happily-ever-after is in her DNA!

f

AUTHOR FRIENDS

Lexi Blake

Shayla Black

Sidney Bristol

Lila Dubois